Praise for #1 *New York Times* bestselling author

NORA ROBERTS

"America's favorite writer."

—*The New Yorker*

"When Roberts puts her expert fingers on the pulse of romance, legions of fans feel the heartbeat."

—*Publishers Weekly*

"Nora Roberts is among the best."

—*The Washington Post*

"Roberts' bestselling novels are some of the best in the romance genre."

—*USA TODAY*

"Roberts' style has a fresh, contemporary snap."

—*Kirkus Reviews*

"You can't bottle wish fulfillment, but Nora Roberts certainly knows how to put it on the page."

—*New York Times*

NORA ROBERTS

A MOTHER'S LOVE

Published by Silhouette Books

America's Publisher of Contemporary Romance

SILHOUETTE BOOKS

A Mother's Love

ISBN-13: 978-1-335-00569-4

Copyright © 2018 by Harlequin Books S.A.

The publisher acknowledges the copyright holder of the individual works as follows:

Dual Image
Copyright © 1985 by Nora Roberts

The Best Mistake
Copyright © 1994 by Nora Roberts

Recycling programs for this product may not exist in your area.

CONTENTS

DUAL IMAGE

Chapter 1

Balancing a bag of groceries in one arm, Amanda let herself into the house. She radiated happiness. From outside came the sound of birds singing in the spring sunshine. The gold of her wedding ring caught the light. As a newlywed of three months, she was anxious to prepare a special, intimate dinner as a surprise for Cameron. Her demanding hours at the hospital and clinic often made it impossible for her to cook, and as a new bride she found pleasure in it. This afternoon, with two appointments unexpectedly canceled, she intended to fix something fancy, time-consuming and memorable. Something that went well with candlelight and wine.

As she entered the kitchen she was humming, a rare outward show of emotion for she was a reserved woman. With a satisfied smile, she drew a bottle of

Cameron's favorite Bordeaux from the bag. As she studied the label, a smile lingered on her face while she remembered the first time they'd shared a bottle. He'd been so romantic, so attentive, so much what she'd needed at that point in her life.

A glance at her watch told her she had four full hours before her husband was expected home. Time enough to prepare an elaborate meal, light the candles and set out the crystal.

First, she decided, she was going upstairs to get out of her practical suit and shoes. There was a silk caftan upstairs, sheer, in misty shades of blue. Tonight, she wouldn't be a psychiatrist, but a woman, a woman very much in love.

The house was scrupulously neat and tastefully decorated. Such things came naturally to Amanda. As she walked toward the stairs, she glanced at a vase of Baccarat crystal and wished fleetingly she'd remembered fresh flowers. Perhaps she'd call the florist and have something extravagant delivered. Her hand trailed lightly over the polished banister as she started up. Her eyes, usually serious or intent, were dreamy. Carelessly, she pushed open the bedroom door.

Her smile froze. Utter shock replaced it. As she stood in the doorway, all color seemed to drain out of her cheeks. Her eyes grew huge before pain filled them. Out of her mouth came one anguished word.

"Cameron."

The couple in bed, locked in a passionate embrace, sprang apart. The man, smoothly handsome, his sleek hair disheveled, stared up in disbelief. The woman—

feline, sultry, stunning—smiled very, very slowly. You could almost hear her purr.

"Vikki." Amanda looked at her sister with anguished eyes.

"You're home early." There was a hint, only a suspicion of a laugh in her sister's voice.

Cameron put a few more inches between himself and his sister-in-law. "Amanda, I…"

In one split second, Amanda's face contorted. With her eyes locked on the couple in bed, she reached in her jacket pocket and drew out a small, lethal revolver. The lovers stared at it in astonishment, and in silence. Coolly, she aimed and fired. A puff of confetti burst out.

"Ariel!"

Dr. Amanda Lane Jamison, better known as Ariel Kirkwood, turned to her harassed director as the couple in bed and members of the television crew dissolved into laughter.

"Sorry, Neal, I couldn't help myself. Amanda's *always* the victim," she said dramatically while her eyes danced. "Just think what it might do for the ratings if she lost her cool just once and murdered someone."

"Look, Ariel—"

"Or even just seriously injured them," she went on rapidly. "And who," she continued, flinging her hand toward the bed, "deserves it more than her spineless husband and scheming sister?"

At the hoots and applause of the crew, Ariel took a bow, then reluctantly turned over her weapon to her director when he held out his hand.

"You," he said with a long-suffering sigh, "are a certified loony, and have been since I've known you."

"I appreciate that, Neal."

"This time the tape's going to be running," he warned and tried not to grin. "Let's see if we can shoot this scene before lunch."

Agreeably, Ariel went down to the first floor of the set. She stood patiently while her hair and makeup were touched up. Amanda was always perfection. Organized, meticulous, calm—all the things Ariel herself wasn't. She'd played the character for just over five years on the popular daytime soap opera *Our Lives, Our Loves*.

In those five years, Amanda had graduated with honors from college, had earned her degree in psychiatric medicine and had gone on to become a respected therapist. Her recent marriage to Cameron Jamison appeared to be made in heaven. But, of course, he was a weak opportunist who'd married her for her money and social position, while lusting after her sister—and half the female population of the fictional town of Trader's Bend.

Amanda was about to be confronted with the truth. The story line had been leading up to this revelation for six weeks, and the letters from viewers had poured in. Both they and Ariel thought it was about time Amanda found out about her louse of a husband.

Ariel liked Amanda, respected her integrity and poise. When the cameras rolled, Ariel *was* Amanda. While in her personal life she would much prefer a day at an amusement park to an evening at the ballet, she understood all the nuances of the woman she portrayed.

When this scene was aired, viewers would see a neat, slender woman with pale blond hair sleeked back into a sophisticated knot. The face was porcelain, stunning, with an icy kind of beauty that sent out signals of restrained sexuality. Class. Style.

Lake-blue eyes, high curved cheekbones added to the look of polished elegance. A perfectly shaped mouth tended toward serious smiles. Finely arched brows that were shades darker than the delicate blond of her hair accented luxurious lashes. A flawless beauty, perfectly composed—that was Amanda.

Ariel waited for her cue and wondered vaguely if she'd turned off her coffeepot that morning.

They ran through the scene again, from cue to cut, then a second time when it was discovered that Vikki's strapless bathing suit could be seen when she shifted in bed. Then came reaction shots—the camera zoomed in close on Amanda's pale, shocked face and held for several long, dramatic seconds.

"Lunch."

Response was immediate. The lovers bounded out of either side of the bed. In his bathing trunks, J. T. Brown, Ariel's on-screen husband, took her by the shoulders and gave her a long hard kiss. "Look, sweetie," he began, staying in character, "I'll explain about all this later. Trust me. I gotta call my agent."

"Wimp," Ariel called after him with a very un-Amandalike grin before she hooked her arm through that of Stella Powell, her series sister. "Pull something over that suit, Stella. I can't face the commissary food today."

Stella tossed back her tousled mass of auburn hair. "You buying?"

"Always sponging off your sister," Ariel mumbled. "Okay, I'll spring, but hurry up. I'm starving."

On her way to her dressing room, Ariel walked off the set, then through two more—the fifth floor of Doctors Hospital and the living room of the Lanes, Trader

Bend's leading family. It was tempting to shed her costume and take down her hair, but it would only mean fooling with wardrobe and makeup after lunch. Instead, she just grabbed her purse, an outsize hobo bag that looked a bit incongruous with Amanda's elegant business suit. She was already thinking about a thick slice of baklava soaked in honey.

"Come on, Stella." Ariel stuck her head in the adjoining dressing room as Stella zipped up a pair of snug jeans. "My stomach's on overtime."

"It always is," her coworker returned as she pulled on a bulky sweatshirt. "Where to?"

"The Greek deli around the corner." More than ready, Ariel started down the hall in her characteristically long, swinging gait while Stella hurried to keep up. It wasn't that Ariel rushed from place to place, but simply that she wanted to see what was next.

"My diet," Stella began.

"Have a salad," Ariel told her without mercy. She turned her head to give Stella a quick up-and-down glance. "You know, if you weren't always wearing those skimpy outfits on camera, you wouldn't have to starve yourself."

Stella grinned as they came to the street door. "Jealous."

"Yeah. I'm always elegant and *always* proper. You have all the fun." Stepping outside, Ariel took a deep breath of New York. She loved it—had always loved it in a way usually reserved for tourists. Ariel had lived on the long thin island of Manhattan all of her life, and yet it remained an adventure to her. The sights, the smells, the sounds.

It was brisk for mid-April, and threatening to rain.

The air was damp and smelled of exhaust. The streets and sidewalks were clogged with lunchtime traffic—everyone hurrying, everyone with important business to attend to. A pedestrian swore and banged a fist on the hood of a cab that had clipped too close to the curb. A woman with spiked orange hair hustled by in black leather boots. Somone had written something uncomplimentary on a poster for a hot Broadway play. But Ariel saw a street vendor selling daffodils.

She bought two bunches and handed one to Stella.

"You can never pass up anything, can you?" Stella mumbled, but buried her face in the yellow blooms.

"Think of all I'd miss," Ariel countered. "Besides, it's spring."

Stella shivered and looked up at the leaden sky. "Sure."

"Eat." Ariel grabbed her arm and pulled her along. "You always get cranky when you miss meals."

The deli was packed with people and aromas. Spices and honey. Beer and oil. Always a creature of the senses, Ariel drew in the mingled scents before she worked her way to the counter. She had an uncanny way of getting where she was going through a throng without using her elbows or stepping on toes. While she moved, she watched and listened. She wouldn't want to miss a scent, or the texture of a voice, or the clashing colors of food. As she looked behind the glass-fronted counter, she could already taste the things there.

"Cottage cheese, a slice of pineapple and coffee—black," Stella said with a sigh. Ariel sent her a brief, pitying look.

"Greek salad, a hunk of that lamb on a hard roll and a slice of baklava. Coffee, cream and sugar."

"You're disgusting," Stella told her. "You never gain an ounce."

"I know." Ariel moved down the counter to the cashier. "It's a matter of mental control and clean living." Ignoring Stella's rude snort she paid the bill then made her way through the crowded deli toward an empty table. She and a bull of a man reached it simultaneously. Ariel simply held her tray and sent him a stunning smile. The man straightened his shoulders, sucked in his stomach and gave way.

"Thanks," Stella acknowledged and dismissed him at the same time, knowing if she didn't Ariel would invite him to join them and upset any chance of a private conversation. The woman, Stella thought, needed a keeper.

Ariel did all the things a woman alone should know better than to do. She talked to strangers, walked alone at night and answered her door without the security chain attached. It wasn't that she was daring or careless, but simply that she believed in the best of people. And somehow, in a bit more than twenty-five years of living, she'd never been disillusioned. Stella marveled at her, even while she worried about her.

"The gun was one of your best stunts all season," Stella remarked as she poked at her cottage cheese. "I thought Neal was going to scream."

"He needs to relax," Ariel said with her mouth full. "He's been on edge ever since he broke up with that dancer. How about you? Are you still seeing Cliff?"

"Yeah." Stella lifted her shoulder. "I don't know why, it's not going anywhere."

"Where do you want it to go?" Ariel countered. "If you have a goal in mind, just go for it."

With a half laugh, Stella began to eat. "Not everyone

plunges through life like you, Ariel. It always amazes me that you've never been seriously involved."

"Simple." Ariel speared a fork into her salad then chewed slowly. "I've never met anyone who made my knees tremble. As soon as I do, that'll be it."

"Just like that?"

"Why not? Life isn't as complicated as most people make it." She added a dash of pepper to the lamb. "Are you in love with Cliff?"

Stell frowned—not because of the question, she was used to Ariel's directness. But because of the answer. "I don't know. Maybe."

"Then you're not," Ariel said easily. "Love's a very definite emotion. Sure you don't want any of this lamb?"

Stella didn't bother to answer the question. "If you've never been in love, how do you know?"

"I've never been to Turkey, but I'm sure it's there."

With a laugh, Stella picked up her coffee. "Damn, Ariel, you've always got an answer. Tell me about the script."

"Oh, God." Ariel put down her fork, and leaning her elbows on the table, folded her hands. "It's the best thing I've ever read. I want that part. I'm going to get that part," she added with something that was apart from confidence. It was simple fact. "I swear, I've been waiting for the character of Rae to come along. She's heartless," Ariel continued, resting her chin on her folded hands. "Complex, selfish, cold, insecure. A part like that…" She trailed off with a shake of her head. "And the story," she added on a long breath as her mind jumped from one aspect to the next. "It's nearly as cold and heartless as she is, but it gets to you."

"Booth DeWitt," Stella mused. "It's rumored that he based the character of Rae on his ex-wife."

"He didn't gloss it over either. If he's telling it straight, she put him through hell. In any case," she said, as she began to eat again, "it's the best piece of work that's come my way. I'm going to read for it in a couple of days."

"TV movie," Stella said thoughtfully. "Quality television with DeWitt writing and Marshell producing. You'd have our own producer at your feet if you got it. Boy, what a boost for the ratings."

"He's already playing politics." With a small frown, Ariel broke off a chunk of baklava. "He got me an invitation to a party tonight at Marshell's condo. DeWitt's supposed to be there. From what I hear, he's got the last say on casting."

"He's got a reputation for wanting to push his own buttons," Stella agreed. "So why the frown?"

"Politics're like rain in April—you know it's got to happen, but it's messy and annoying." Then she shrugged the thought away as she did anything unavoidable. In the end, from what she knew of Booth DeWitt, she'd earn the part on her own merit. If there was one thing Ariel had an abundance of, it was confidence. She'd always needed it.

Unlike Amanda, the character she played on the soap, Ariel hadn't grown up financially secure. There'd been a great deal more love than money in her home. She'd never regretted it, or the struggle to make ends meet. She'd been sixteen when her mother had died and her father had gone into a state of shock that had lasted nearly a year. It had never occurred to her that she was too young to take on the responsibilities of running a home and raising two younger siblings. There'd been no one else to do it. She'd sold powder and perfume in a department store to pay her way through college, while managing the family home and taking any bit part that came her way.

They'd been busy, difficult years, and perhaps that in itself had given her the surplus of energy and drive she had today. And the sense that whatever had to be done, could be done.

"Amanda."

Ariel glanced up to see a small, middle-aged woman carrying a take-out bag that smelled strongly of garlic. Because she was called by her character's name almost as often as she was by her own, she smiled and held out her hand. "Hello."

"I'm Dorra Wineberger and I wanted to tell you you're just as beautiful as you are on TV."

"Thank you, Dorra. You enjoy the show?"

"I wouldn't miss it, not one single episode." She beamed at Ariel then leaned closer. "You're wonderful, dear, and so kind and patient. I just feel someone ought to tell you that Cameron— He's not good for you. The best thing for you to do is send him packing before he gets his hands on your money. He's already pawned your diamond earrings. And this one…" Dorra folded her lips and glared at Stella. "Why you bother with this one, after all the trouble she's caused you… If it hadn't been for her, you and Griff would be married like you should be." She sent Stella an affronted glare. "I know you've got your eyes on your sister's husband, Vikki."

Stella struggled with a grin and, playing the role, tossed her head and slanted her eyes. "Men are interested in me," she drawled. "And why not?"

Dorra shook her head and turned back to Ariel. "Go back to Griff," she advised kindly. "He loves you, he always has."

Ariel returned the quick squeeze of her hand. "Thanks for caring."

Both women watched Dorra walk away before they turned back to each other. "Everyone loves Dr. Amanda," Vikki said with a grin. "She's practically sacred."

"And everyone loves to hate Vikki." With a chuckle, Ariel finished off her coffee. "You're so rotten."

"Yeah." Stella gave a contented sigh. "I know." She chewed her pineapple slowly, with a wistful look at Ariel's plate. "Anyway, it always strikes me as kind of weird when people get me confused with Vikki."

"It just means you're doing your job," Ariel corrected. "If you go into people's homes every day and don't draw emotion out of them, you better look for another line of work. Nuclear physics, log rolling. Speaking of work," she added with a glance at her watch.

"I know... Hey, are you going to eat the rest of that?"

Laughing, Ariel handed her the baklava as they rose.

It was well after nine when Ariel paid off the cab in front of P. B. Marshell's building on Madison Avenue. She wasn't concerned with being late because she wasn't aware of the time. She'd never missed a cue or a call in her life, but when it wasn't directly concerned with work, time was something to be enjoyed or ignored.

She overtipped the cabbie, stuffed her change in her bag without counting it, then walked through the light drizzle into the lobby. She decided it smelled like a funeral parlor. Too many flowers, too much polish. After giving her name at the security desk, she slipped into an elevator and pushed the penthouse button. It didn't occur to her to be nervous at the prospect of entering P. B. Marshell's domain. A party to Ariel was a party. She hoped he served champagne. She had a hankering for it.

The door was opened by a stiff-backed, stone-faced man in a dark suit who asked Ariel's name in a discreet British accent. When she smiled, he accepted her offered hand before he realized it. Ariel walked past the butler, leaving him with the impression of vitality and sex—a combination that left him disconcerted for several minutes. She lifted a glass of champagne from a tray, and spotting her agent, crossed the room to her.

Booth saw Ariel's entrance. For an instant, he was reminded of his ex-wife. The coloring, the bone structure. Then the impression was gone, and he was looking at a young woman with casually curling hair that flowed past her shoulders. It seemed misted with fine drops of rain. A stunning face, he decided. But the look of an ice goddess vanished the moment she laughed. Then there was energy and verve.

Unusual, he thought, as vaguely interested in her as he was in the drink he held. He let his eyes skim down her and decided she'd be slim under the casual pleated pants and boxy blouse. Then again, if she was, she would have exploited her figure rather than underplaying it. From what Booth knew of women, they accented whatever charms at their disposal and concealed the flaws. He'd come to accept this as a part of their innate dishonesty.

He gave Ariel one last glance as she rose on her toes

to kiss the latest rage in an off-Broadway production. God, he hated these long, crowded pseudoparties.

"...If we cast the female lead."

Booth turned back to P. B. Marshell and lifted his glass. "Hmm?"

Too used to Booth's lapses of attention to be annoyed, Marshell backtracked. "We can get this into production and wrapped in time for the fall sweeps if we cast the female lead. That's virtually all that's holding us back now."

"I'm not worried about the fall sweeps," Booth returned dryly.

"The network is."

"Pat, we'll cast Rae when we find Rae."

Marshell frowned into his Scotch, then drank it. At two hundred and fifty pounds, he needed several glasses to feel any effect. "You've already turned down three top names."

"I turned down three actresses who weren't suitable," Booth corrected. He drank from his own glass as a man who knew liquor and maintained a cautious relationship with it. "I'll know Rae when I see her." His lips moved into a cool smile. "Who'd know better?"

A free, easy laugh had Marshell glancing across the room. For a moment his eyes narrowed in concentration. "Ariel Kirkwood," he told Booth, gesturing with his empty glass. "The network execs would like to push her your way."

"An actress." Booth studied Ariel again. He wouldn't have pegged her as such. Her entrance had caught his attention simply because it hadn't been an *entrance*. There was something completely unselfconscious about her that was rare in the profession. She'd been at the party long enough to have wangled an introduction to him and Marshell, yet she seemed content to stay across the room sipping champagne and flirting with an up-and-coming actor.

She stood easily, in a relaxed manner that wasn't a pose but would photograph beautifully. She made an unattractive face at the actor. The contrast of the ice-goddess looks and the freewheeling manner piqued his curiosity.

"Introduce me," Booth said simply and started across the room.

Ariel couldn't fault Marshell's taste. The condo was stylishly decorated in elegant golds and creams. The carpet was thick, the walls lacquered. She recognized the signed lithograph behind her. It was a room she knew Amanda would understand and appreciate. Ariel enjoyed visiting it. She'd never have lived there. She laughed up at Tony as he reminisced about the improvisation class they'd taken together a few years before.

"And you started using gutter language to make sure everyone was awake," she reminded him and tugged on the goatee he wore for his current part.

"It worked. What cause is it this week, Ariel?"

Her brows lifted as she sipped her champagne. "I don't have weekly causes."

"Biweekly," he corrected. "Friends of Seals, Save the Mongoose. Come on, what are you into now?"

She shook her head. "There's something that's taking up a lot of my time right now. I can't really talk about it."

Tony's grin faded. He knew that tone. "Important?"

"Vital."

"Well, Tony." Marshell clapped the young actor on the back. "Glad to see you could make it."

Though it was very subtly done, Tony came to attention. "It was nice that you were having this on a night when the theater's dark, Mr. Marshell. Do you know Ariel Kirkwood?" He laid a hand on her shoulder. "We go back a long way."

"I've heard good things about you." Marshell extended his hand.

"Thank you." Ariel left her hand in his a moment as she sorted her impressions. Successful—fond of food from the bulk of him—amiable when he chose to be. Shrewd. She liked the combination. "You make excellent films, Mr. Marshell."

"Thank you," he returned and paused, expecting her to do some campaigning. When she left it at that, he turned to Booth. "Booth DeWitt, Ariel Kirkwood and Tony Lazarus."

"I've seen your play," Booth told Tony. "You know your character very well." He shifted his gaze to Ariel. "Ms. Kirkwood."

Disconcerting eyes, she thought, so clear and direct a green in such a remote face. He gave off signals of aloofness, traces of bitterness, waves of intelligence. Obviously he didn't concern himself overmuch with trends or fashion. His hair was thick and dark and a bit long for the current style. Yet she thought it suited his face. She thought the face belonged to the nineteenth century. Lean and scholarly with a touch of ruggedness and a harshness in the mouth that kept it from being smooth.

His voice was deep and appealing, but he spoke with a clipped quality that indicated impatience. He had the eyes of an observer, she thought. And the air of a man who wouldn't tolerate interference or intimacies. She wasn't certain she'd like him, but she did know she admired his work.

"Mr. DeWitt." Her palm touched his. Strength—she'd expected that. It was in his build, long, rangy—and in his face. Distance—she'd expected that as well. "I enjoyed *The Final Bell*. It was my favorite film of last year."

He passed this off as he studied her face. She exuded sex, in her scent, in her looks—not flagrant or elusive, but light and free. "I don't believe I'm familiar with your work."

"Ariel plays Dr. Amanda Lane Jamison on *Our Lives, Our Loves*," Tony put in.

Good God, a soap opera, Booth thought. Ariel caught the faint disdain on his face. It was something else she'd expected. "Do you have a moral objection to entertainment, Mr. DeWitt?" she said easily as she sipped champagne. "Or are you just an artistic snob?" She smiled as she spoke, the quick, dashing smile that took any sting from the words.

Beside her, Tony cleared his throat. "Excuse me a minute," he said and exited stage left. Marshell mumbled something about freshening his drink.

When they were alone, Booth continued to study her face. She was laughing at him. He couldn't remember the last time anyone had had the courage, or the occasion, to do so. He wasn't certain if he was annoyed or intrigued. But at the moment he wasn't what he'd been for the past hour. Bored.

"I haven't any moral objections to soap operas, Ms. Kirkwood."

"Oh." She sipped her champagne. A sliver of sapphire on her finger winked in the light and seemed to reflect in her eyes. "A snob then. Well, everyone's en-titled. Perhaps there's something else we can talk about. How do you feel about the current administration's for-eign policy?"

"Ambivalent," he murmured. "What sort of charac-ter do you play?"

"A sterling one." Her eyes continued to dance. "How do you feel about the space program?"

"I'm more concerned about the planet I'm on. How long have you been on the show?"

"Five years." She beamed a smile at someone across the room and raised her hand.

He looked at her again, carefully, and for the first time since he'd come into the party, he smiled. It did something attractive to his face, though it didn't make him quite as approachable as it indicated. "You don't want to talk about your work, do you?"

"Not particularly." Ariel returned his smile with her own open one. Something stirred faintly in him that he'd thought safely dormant. "Not with someone who con-siders it garbage. In a moment, you'd ask me if I'd ever considered doing any serious work, then I'd probably get nasty. My agent tells me I'm supposed to charm you."

Booth could feel the friendliness radiating from her and distrusted it. "Is that what you're doing?"

"I'm on my own time," Ariel returned. "Besides—" she finished off her champagne "—you aren't the type to be charmed."

"You're perceptive," Booth acknowledged. "Are you a good actress?"

"Yes, I am. It would hardly be worth doing some-thing if you weren't good at it. What about sports?" She twirled her empty glass. "Do you think the Yankees stand a chance this year?"

"If they tighten up the infield." Not your usual type, he decided. Any other actress up for a prime part in one of his scripts would've been flooding him with compliments and mentioning every job she'd ever had in front of the camera. "Ariel..." Booth plucked a fresh glass of champagne from a passing waiter and handed it to her. "The name suits you. A wise choice."

She felt a pull, a quick, definite pull, that seemed to come simply from the way he'd said her name. "I'll tell my mother you said so."

"It's not a stage name?"

"No. My mother was reading *The Tempest* when she went into labor. She was very superstitious. I could have been Prospero if I'd been a boy." With a little shudder, she sipped. "Well, Booth," she began, deciding she'd been formal long enough. "Shouldn't we just come out with the fact that we both know I'll be reading for the part of Rae in a couple of days? I intend to have it."

He nodded in acknowledgment. Though she was refreshingly direct, this was more what he'd expected. "Then I'll be frank enough to tell you that you're not the type I'm looking for."

She lifted a brow without any show of discomfort. "Oh? Why?"

"For one thing, you're too young."

She laughed—a free, breezy sound that seemed completely unaffected. He didn't trust that either. "I think my line is I can be older."

"Maybe. But Rae's a tough lady. Hard as a rock." He lifted his own drink but never took his eyes off her. "You've got too many soft points. They show in your face."

"Because this is me. And I've yet to play myself in front of a camera." She paused a moment as the idea worked around in her head. "I don't think I'd care to."

"Is any actress ever herself?"

Her eyes came back to his. He was watching her again with that steady intenseness most would have found unnerving. Though the pull came again, Ariel accepted the look because it was part of him. "You don't care for us much as a breed, do you?"

"No." For some reason he didn't question, Booth felt compelled to test her. He lifted a strand of her hair. Soft—surprisingly soft. "You're a beautiful woman," he murmured.

Ariel tilted her head as she studied him. His eyes had lost nothing of their directness. She might have felt pleasure in the compliment if she hadn't recognized it as calculated. Instead she felt disappointment. "And?"

His brows drew together. "And?"

"That line usually leads to another. As a writer I'm sure you have several tucked away."

He let his fingers brush over her neck. She felt the strength in them, and the carelessness of the gesture. "Which one would you like?"

"I'd prefer one you meant," Ariel told him evenly. "But since I wouldn't get it, why don't we skip the whole thing? You know, your character, Phil, is narrow-minded, cool blooded and rude. I believe you portrayed yourself very well." She lifted her glass one last time and decided it was a shame that he thought so little of women, or perhaps of people in general. "Good night, Booth."

When she walked away, Booth stood looking after her for several moments before he started to laugh. At the time, it didn't occur to him that it was the first easy laugh he'd had in almost two years. It didn't even occur to him that he was laughing at himself.

No, she wasn't his Rae, he mused, but she was good. She was very, very good. He was going to remember Ariel Kirkwood.

Chapter 2

Booth stood by the wide expanse of window in Marshell's office and watched New York hustle by. From that height, he felt removed from it, and the rush and energy radiating up from the streets and sidewalks. He was satisfied to be separate. Connections equaled involvement.

None of the actresses they'd auditioned in the past two weeks came close to what he was after. He knew what he wanted for the part of Rae—who better?

When he'd first started the script it had been an impulse—therapy, he mused with a grim smile. Cheaper than a psychiatrist and a lot more satisfying. He'd never expected to do any more than finish it, purge his system and toss it in a drawer. That was before he'd realized it was the best work he'd ever done. Perhaps anger was the tenth Muse. In any case, he was first and foremost a writer. However painful it was to expose himself and his mistakes to the public, there was no tossing his finest work in a drawer. And since he was going to have it performed, he was going to have it performed well.

He'd thought it would be difficult to cast the part of Phil, the character who was essentially himself. And yet that had been surprisingly simple. The core of the story wasn't Phil, but Rae, a devastatingly accurate mirror of his ex-wife, Elizabeth Hunter. A superb actress, a gracious celebrity—a woman without a single genuine emotion.

Their marriage had started with a whirlwind and ended in disaster. Booth didn't consider himself blameless, though he placed most of the blame on his own gullibility. He'd believed in her image, fallen hard for the perfection of face and body. He could have forgiven the faults, the flaws soon discovered. But he could never, would never, forgive being used. And yet, Booth was still far from sure whether he blamed Liz for using him, or himself for allowing it to happen.

Either way, the tempestuous five-year marriage had given him grist for a clean, hard story that was going to be an elaborate television movie. And more, it had given him a firm distrust of women, particularly actresses. Two years before, when the break had finally come, he'd promised himself that he'd never become involved with another woman who could play roles that well. Honesty, if it truly existed, was what he'd look for when he was ready.

His thoughts came back to Ariel. Perhaps she was centered in his mind because of her surface resemblance to Liz, but he wasn't certain. There was no similarity in mannerisms, voice cadence or style of dress. And the biggest contrast seemed to be in personality. She hadn't put herself out to charm him or to hold his attention. And she'd done both. Perhaps she'd simply used a different angle on an old game.

While he hadn't trusted it, he'd enjoyed her lack of artifice. The breezy laugh, the unaffected gestures, the candid looks. It had been a long time since a woman had lingered in his mind. A pity, Booth mused, that she was unsuitable for the part. He could have used the distraction. Instinct told him that Ariel Kirkwood would be nothing if she wasn't a distraction.

"I'm still leaning toward this Julie Newman." Chuck Tyler, the director, tossed an eight-by-ten glossy on Marshell's desk. "A lot of camera presence and her first reading was very good."

With the photo in one hand, Marshell tipped back in his deep leather chair. The sun at his back streamed over both the glossy and the gold he wore on either hand. "An impressive list of credits, too."

"No." Booth didn't bother to turn around, but stood watching the traffic stream. For some odd reason he visualized himself on his boat in Long Island Sound, sailing out to sea. "She lacks the elegance. Too much vulnerability."

"She can act, Booth," Marshell said with a now familiar show of impatience.

"She's not the one."

Marshell automatically reached in his pocket for the cigars he'd given up a month before. He swore lightly under his breath. "And we're running out of time and options."

Booth gave an unconcerned shrug. Yes, he'd like to be sailing, stripped to the waist with the sun on his back and the water so blue it hurt the eyes. He'd like to be alone.

When the buzzer on his desk rang, Marshell heaved a sigh and leaned forward to answer. "Ms. Kirkwood's here for her reading, Mr. Marshell."

With a grunt, Marshell flipped open the portfolio Ariel's agent had sent him, then passed it to Chuck. "Send her in."

"Kirkwood," Chuck mused, frowning over Ariel's publicity shot. "Kirkwood... Oh, yeah, I saw her last summer in an off-Broadway production of *Streetcar*."

Vaguely interested, Booth looked over his shoulder. "Stella?"

"Blanche," Chuck corrected, skimming over her list of credits.

"Blanche DuBois?" Booth gave a short laugh as he turned completely around. "She's fifteen to twenty years too young for that part."

Chuck merely lifted his eyes. "She was good," he said simply. "Very good. And from what I'm told, she's very good on the soap. I don't have to tell you how many of our top stars started that way."

"No, you don't." Booth sat negligently on the arm of a chair. "But if she's stuck with the same part for five years, she's either not good enough for a major film or major theater, or she's completely without ambition. Because she's an actress, I'd have to go with the former."

"Keep sharpening your cynicism," Marshell said dryly. "It's good for you."

Booth's grin flashed—that rare one that came and went so quickly it left the onlooker dazzled and unsure why. Ariel caught a glimpse of it as she entered the room. It went a long way toward convincing her to change her initial opinion of him. It passed through her mind, almost as quickly as Booth's grin, that perhaps he had some redeeming personal qualities after all. She was always ready to believe it.

"Ms. Kirkwood." Marshell heaved his bulk from the chair and extended his hand.

"Mr. Marshell, nice to see you again." She took a brief scan of the room, her gaze lingering only fleetingly on Booth as he remained seated on the arm of the chair. "Your office is just as impressive as your home."

Booth waited while she was introduced to Chuck. She'd dressed very simply, he noticed. Deceptively so if you considered the bold scarves she'd twisted at the waist of the demure blue dress. Violets and emeralds and wild pinks. A daring combination, and stunningly effective. Her hair was loose again, giving her an air of youth and freedom he would never equate with the character she wanted to portray. Absently, he took out a cigarette and lit it.

"Booth." Ariel gave him an easy smile before her gaze flicked over the cigarette. "They'll kill you."

He took a drag and let out a lazy stream of smoke. "Eventually." She wore the same carelessly sexy scent he'd noticed the night of the party. Booth wondered why it was that it suited her while contrasting at the same time. She fascinated. It seemed to be something she did effortlessly. "I'm going to cue you," he continued and reached for a copy of the script. "We'll use the confrontation scene in the third act. You're familiar with it?"

All business, Ariel noted curiously. Does he ever relax? Does he ever choose to? Though she was rarely tense herself, she recognized tension in him and wondered why he was nervous. What nerves she felt herself were confined to a tiny roiling knot in the center of her stomach. She always acknowledged it and knew, if anything, it would help to push her through the reading.

"I'm familiar with it," she told him, accepting another copy of the script.

Booth took a last drag on his cigarette then put it out. "Do you want a lead-in?"

"No." Now her palms were damp. Good. Ariel knew better than to want to be relaxed when twinges of emotions would sharpen her skills. Taking deep, quiet breaths she flipped through the bound script until she found the right scene. It wasn't a simple one. It stabbed at the core of the character—selfish ambition and icy sex. She took a minute.

Booth watched her. She looked more like the guileless ingenue than the calculating leading lady, he mused and was almost sorry there wasn't a part for her in the film. Then she looked up and pinned him with a cold, bloodless smile that completely stunned him.

"You always were a fool, Phil, but a successful one and so rarely boring, it's hardly worth mentioning."

The tone, the mannerisms, even the expression was so accurate, he couldn't respond. For a moment, he completely lost Ariel in the character and the woman he'd fashioned her after. He felt a twist in his stomach, not of attraction or even admiration, but of anger—totally unexpected and vilely real. Booth didn't have to look at the script to remember the line.

"You're so transparent, Rae. It amazes me that you could deceive anyone into believing in you."

Ariel laughed, rather beautifully, so that all three men felt a chill race up their spine. "I make my living

at deception. Everyone wants illusions, so did you. And
that's what you got."

With a long, lazy stretch, she ran a hand through her
hair, then let it fall, pale gold in the late-morning sunlight. It was one of Liz Hunter's patented gestures. "I
acted my way out of that miserable backwater town in
Missouri where I had the misfortune to be born, and
I've acted my way right up to the top. You were a great
help." She walked over to him with the small, cool smile
still on her lips, in her eyes. With an eloquent gesture,
she brushed her hand down his cheek. "And you were
compensated. Very, very well."

Phil grabbed her wrist and tossed it aside. Ariel
merely lifted a brow at the violence of the movement.
"Sooner or later you're going to slip," he threatened.

She tilted her head and spoke very softly. "Darling,
I never slip."

Slowly, Booth rose. The expression on his face might
have had any woman trembling, would have had any
woman making some defensive move. Ariel merely
looked up at him with the same coldly amused expression. It was he who had to force himself to calm.

"Very good, Ariel Kirkwood." Booth tossed the
script aside.

She grinned, because every instinct told her she'd
won. With the long expelled breath, she could almost
feel Rae drain out of her. "Thanks. It's a tremendous
part," she added as her stomach unknotted. "Really a
tremendous part."

"You've done your research," Marshell murmured
from behind his desk. Because he knew Elizabeth
Hunter, Ariel's five-minute read had left him uncomfortable and impressed. And he knew Booth. There was

little doubt in his mind as to what Rae's creator was feeling. "You'll be available for a callback?"

"Of course."

"I saw your Blanche DuBois, Ms. Kirkwood," Chuck put in. "I was very impressed then, and now."

She flashed him an unaffected smile though she was aware Booth was still staring at her. If he was moved, she thought, then the reading had gone better than she could have hoped. "It was my biggest challenge, up until now." She wanted to get out, walk, breathe the air, savor the almost-victory while she could. "Well, thank you." She pushed her hair from shoulder as she scanned the three men again. "I'll look forward to hearing from you."

Ariel walked toward the elevator too frightened to believe she was right, too terrified to believe she was wrong. Up until that moment, she hadn't let herself dwell on just how much she wanted the part, and just what it could mean in her life.

She wasn't without ambition, but she had chosen acting and had continued with it for the love of it. And the challenge. Playing the part of Rae would hand her all three needs on a silver platter. As she stepped into the elevator, her palms were dry and her heart was pounding. She didn't hear Booth approach.

"I'd like to talk to you." He stepped in with her and punched the button for the lobby.

"Okay." A long sigh escaped as she leaned back against the side of the car. "God, I'm glad that's over. I'm starving. Nothing makes me hungrier than a reading."

He tried to relate the woman who was smiling at him with eyes warm and alive with the woman who had just exchanged lines with him. He couldn't. She was a better actress than he'd given her credit for, and therefore, more dangerous. "It was an excellent reading."

She eyed him curiously. "Why do I feel I've just been insulted?"

After the doors slid open Booth stood for a moment, then nodded. "I think I said before that you were perceptive."

Her slim heels clicked over the tile as she crossed the lobby with him. Booth noticed a few heads turn, both male and female, to look after her. She was either unaware or unconcerned. "Why are you on daytime TV?"

Ariel slanted him a look before she began to walk north. "Because it's a good part on a well-written, entertaining show. That's number one. Number two is that it's steady work. When actors are between jobs, they wait tables, wash cars, sell toasters and generally get depressed. While I might not mind the first three too much, I hate the fourth. Have you ever seen the show?"

"No."

"Then you shouldn't turn your nose up." She stopped by a sidewalk vendor and drew in the scent of hot pretzels. "Want one?"

"No," Booth said again and tucked his hands in his pockets. Sexuality, sensuality—both seemed to pour out of her as she stood next to a portable pretzel stand on a crowded sidewalk. He continued to watch her as she took the first generous bite.

"I could live off them," she told him with her mouth full and her eyes laughing. "Good nutrition's so admirable and so hard to live with. I like to ignore it for long stretches of time. Let's walk," she suggested. "I have to when I'm keyed up. What do you do?"

"When?"

"When you're keyed up," Ariel explained.

"Write." He matched her casually swinging pace while the bulk of pedestrian traffic bustled by them.

"And when you're not keyed up you write," Ariel added as she took another bite of her pretzel. "Have you always been so serious?"

"It's steady work," he countered and she laughed.

"Very quick. I didn't think I'd like you, but you've got a nice sense of cautious humor." Ariel stopped at another vendor and bought a bunch of spring violets. She closed her eyes and breathed deep. "Wonderful," she murmured. "I always think spring's the best until summer. Then I'm in love with the heat until fall. Then fall's the best until winter." Laughing, she looked over the blooms into his eyes. "And I also tend to ramble when I'm keyed up."

When she lowered the flowers, Booth took her wrist, not with the same violence as he had during the reading, but with the same intensity. "Who are you?" he demanded. "Who the hell are you?"

Her smile faded but she didn't draw away. "Ariel Kirkwood. I can be a lot of other people when there's a stage or a camera, but when it's over, that's who I am. That's all I am. Are you looking for complications?"

"I don't have to look for them—they're always there."

"Strange, I rarely run into any." She studied him, all frank eyes and creamy beauty. Booth didn't care for the stir it brought him. "Come with me," she invited, then took his hand before he'd thought to object.

"Where?"

She threw back her head and pointed up the magnificently sheer surface of the Empire State Building.

"To the top." Laughing, she pulled him inside. "All the way to the top."

Booth looked around impatiently as she bought tickets for the observation deck. "Why?"

"Does there always have to be a reason?" She slipped the violets into the twisted scarves at her waist, then tucked her arm through his. "I love things like this. Ellis Island, the Staten Island ferry, Central Park. What's the use of living in New York if you don't enjoy it? When's the last time you did this?" Her shoulder rested against his upper arm as they crowded into an elevator.

"I think I was ten." Even with the press of bodies and mingling scents he could smell her, wild and sweet.

"Oh." Ariel laughed up at him. "You grew up. Too bad."

Booth said nothing for a moment as he studied her. She seemed to always be laughing—at him or at some private joke she was content to keep to herself. Was she really that easy with herself and her life? Was anyone? Then he asked, "Don't we all?"

"Of course not. We all get older, but the rest is a personal choice." They herded off one elevator and onto another that would take them to the top.

This was a man she could enjoy, Ariel mused as she stood beside Booth. She could enjoy that serious, high-minded streak and the dry, almost reluctant humor. Still, there was the part in the film to think of. Ariel would have to be very careful to keep her feelings for one separate from her feelings for the other. But then, she'd never been a person who'd had any trouble separating the woman and the actress.

For now, the reading was over and the afternoon was free. Her mood was light, and there was a man with her who'd be fascinating to explore. The day could hardly offer anything more.

The souvenir stands were crowded with people—different countries, different voices. Ariel decided she'd buy something foolish on her way out. She caught Booth looking around him with his eyes slightly narrowed. An observer, she thought with a slight nod of approval. She was one herself, though perhaps on a different level. He'd dissect, analyze and file. She just enjoyed the show.

"Come on outside," she invited and took his hand in a characteristic gesture. "It's wonderful." Pushing open the heavy door, Ariel welcomed the first slap of wind with a laugh. With her hand still firmly gripping Booth's, she hurried to the wall to take in New York.

She never saw it as a toy board as many did from that height, but as something real enough to touch and smell from any distance. It never failed to excite and fascinate her. Ariel rarely asked more of anything or anyone. When she was here, she always believed she could accomplish whatever she needed to.

"I love heights." She leaned out as far as she could and felt the frantic current of air swirl around her. "Staggering heights. And wind. If I could, I'd come here every day. I'd never get tired of it."

Though it was normally an intimacy he would have shunned, Booth allowed his hand to stay in hers. Her skin was smooth and elegant; her face was flushed in the brisk air while her hair blew wildly. The eyes, he thought, the eyes were too alive, too full of everything. A woman like this would demand spectacular emotions from everyone she touched. The stir he felt wasn't as easily suppressed this time. Deliberately, he looked away from her and down.

"Why not the World Trade Center?" he asked and let his gaze skim over the island he lived on.

Ariel shook her head. "It doesn't have the same feeling as this, nothing does. Just like there's only one Eiffel Tower, one Grand Canyon and one Olivier." She didn't bother to brush her hair back from her face as she tilted toward him. "They're all spectacular and unique. What do you like, Booth?"

A family walked by laughing, the mother holding her skirts, the father carrying a toddler. He watched them pause nearby and look over the wall. "In what way?"

"In any way," Ariel told him. "If you could've spent today doing anything you wanted, what would you have done?"

"Gone sailing," he said, remembering that moment in Marshell's office. "I'd've been sailing on the sound."

Interest flickered in her eyes as it seemed every emotion or thought she had did. "You have a boat?"

"Yes. I don't have much time for it."

Don't take much time for it, she corrected silently. "A solitary pursuit. That's admirable." She turned, leaning back against the wall so that she could watch the people circle the deck. The wind plastered her dress against her, revealing the slenderness, the elegance of the woman. "I don't often like to be solitary," she murmured. "I need people, the contacts, the contrasts. I don't have to know them. I just like knowing they're there."

"Is that why you act?" They were face-to-face now, their bodies casually close—as if they were friends. It struck Booth as odd, but he had no desire to back away. "So you can have an audience?"

Her expression become thoughtful, but when she smiled, it was easy. "You're a very cynical man."

"That's the second time today that's been mentioned."

"It's all right. It probably comes in handy with your writing. Yes, I act for an audience," she continued. "I won't deny my own ego, but I think I act for myself first." She lifted her face so that the air could race over it. "It's a marvelous profession. How else can you be so many people? A princess, a tramp, a victim, a loser. You write to be read, but don't you first write to express yourself?"

"Yes." He felt something odd, almost unfamiliar—a loosening of muscles, an easing of thought. It took him a moment to realize he was relaxing, and only a moment longer to draw back. When you relaxed, you got burned. That much he was certain of. "But then writers have egos that nearly rival actors'."

Ariel made a sound that was somewhere between a sigh and an expulsion of air. "She really put you through the mill, didn't she?"

His eyes frosted, his voice chilled. "That's none of your business."

"You're wrong." Though she felt a twinge of regret when she sensed his withdrawal, Ariel went on. "If I'm going to play Rae, it's very much my business. Booth..." She laid a hand on his arm, wishing she understood him well enough to get past the wall of reserve, the waves of bitterness. "If you'd wanted to keep this part of your life private, you wouldn't have written it out."

"It's a story," he said flatly. "I don't put myself on display."

"In most cases, no," she agreed. "I've always felt a

certain sense of distance in your work, though it's always excellent. And for someone so successful, you kept a fairly low profile, even when you were married to Liz Hunter. But you've let something out in this script. It's too late to pull it back now."

"I've written a story about two people who are totally unsuited to each other, who used each other. The man is a bit of an idealist, and just gullible enough to fall for an exquisite face. Before the story ends, he learns that appearances mean little and that trust and loyalty are illusions. The woman is cold, ambitious and gifted, but she'll never be satisfied with her own talents. She's a vampire in the pure sense of the word, and she sucks him dry. There may be similarities between the story and actuality, but my life is still my life."

"No trespassing." Ariel turned to look back down into the city, the world she understood. "All right, the signs are posted." She listened to the sound of the wind, the sound of voices. Someone reeked of a drugstore cologne. An empty bag of potato chips skimmed and rustled along the concrete. "I'm not a very good businesswoman. I won't apologize for my lifestyle or my personality, but I will do my best to keep our conversations very professional."

She took a deep breath and turned back to him. Some of the warmth had left her eyes, and he felt a momentary regret. "I'm a good actress, an excellent craftsman. I've known since the first moment I picked up the script that I could play Rae. And I'm astute enough to know how well my reading went."

"No, you're not a fool." Even with the regret, Booth felt more comfortable on this level. He understood her now—an actress in search of that prime part. "I wouldn't have said you were what I was looking for—until this afternoon. No one's come even close to the core of that character before you."

She felt the tickling dryness down in her throat, the sudden lurch of her heart rate. "And?" she managed.

"And I want you to come back and read with Jack Rohrer. He's cast as Phil. If the chemistry's there, you've got the part."

Ariel took a deep breath. She leaned against the sturdy observation glass and tried to take it calmly. She'd told him she'd be professional. No good, she realized as the pleasure bubbled up inside her. It simply wasn't any use. With a shout of laughter, she threw her arms around his neck and clung. The touching was vital, the sharing essential.

Ariel Kirkwood—the skinny dreamer from West 185th Street—was going to star in a DeWitt script, a P. B. Marshell production opposite Jack Rohrer. Would life never stop amazing her? As she clung to Booth, Ariel dearly hoped it wouldn't.

His hands had come to her waist in reflex, but he left them there as her laughter warmed his ear. He found it odd that he was sharply reminded of two things—his young niece's boundless pleasure when he'd given her an elaborate dollhouse one Christmas, and the first time, as a man, he'd ever held a woman. The softness was there—that unique strength and give only a woman's body has. The childlike pleasure was there—with the innocence only the young possess.

He could have held her. It moved in him to do so, just to hold something soft and sweet and without shadows. She fit so well against him. The curve of cheek against his, the alignment of bodies. She fit too well, so that he stood perfectly still and drew her no closer.

Something drifted through her pleasure and excitement. He smelt of soap—solid—as his body felt. There was nothing casual about him, nothing easy. He was all intensity and intellect. The strength drew her; his reserve drew her. He was a man who would be there to pick you up, however reluctantly, if you stumbled. Who would demand that you keep pace with him, and who would expect you to give him exactly the amount of room he wanted when he wanted it. He was a man whom a woman who ran on her emotions and her senses would do well to avoid. She wished almost painfully that his arms would come around her, even while she knew they wouldn't.

Ariel drew away but kept their faces close so that she might have a hint of what it would be like to have that serious, unsmiling mouth lowered to hers. She was breathless, and her eyes made no secret of her attraction or her surprise in feeling it.

"I'm sorry," she said quietly. "Physical displays come naturally to me. I have a feeling you don't care for them."

Had there ever been a woman he'd wanted to kiss more than this one? Almost, almost, he could taste the mouth inches from his own. Nearly, very nearly, he could feel its texture against his own. When he spoke, his voice was indifferent, his eyes remote. "There's a time and a place."

Ariel let out a long breath and decided she'd set herself up for a backhanded slap. "You're a tough man, Booth DeWitt," she murmured.

"I'm a realist, Ariel." He took out a cigarette, cupping his lighter against the wind with hands that amazed him because they weren't steady.

"What a hard thing to be." Consciously, she relaxed—shoulder muscles, stomach muscles, hands. A moment's awareness didn't equal trouble. She'd felt it before; it was a blessing and a curse in a woman like herself. Ariel didn't understand indifference to people or to things. Everything you saw, touched, heard, triggered some emotion. "But then, you're stuck with it." More at ease, she smiled at him. "I'm going to enjoy working with you, Booth, though I know it's not going to be a picnic. I'm going to give your script my very best shot, and we'll both benefit."

He nodded as the smoke whipped up and away. "I don't accept anything less than the best."

"Fine, you won't be disappointed." It was in her nature to reach out and touch, to add something personal. But one slap was enough for one day.

"Good."

With a laugh, she shook her head. "You're attractive, Booth. I haven't the least idea why because I don't think you're a very nice person."

He blew out another stream of smoke and watched her lazily. "I'm not," he agreed.

"In any case, we'll give each other what's needed professionally."

Then because she rarely resisted impulses of any kind, she kissed his cheek before thrusting the violets at him and walking away. Booth stood in the wind on top of New York with a handful of spring flowers and stared after her.

Chapter 3

Booth had been on and around sets most of his professional life. There were eighteenth-century drawing rooms, twentieth-century bedrooms, bars and restaurants and department stores. Spaceships and log cabins. With props and backdrops and ingenuity, anything could be created.

When you came to the bottom line, one set was the same as another—technicians, lights, cameras, booms, miles of cable. It was an industry of illusion and image. What looked glamorous outside the business was ultimately only a job, and often a tedious and exacting one. Long hours, lengthy delays, lights that made a studio into a furnace, bitter coffee.

From the outset of his career, he'd never been content to be isolated with his typewriter and ideas. He'd insisted from his very first screenplay on being involved with the production end. He understood the practicality and the creativity of the right camera angle, the proper lighting. It appealed to the realistic part of him. Still, he had the ability to see the set and the people while blocking out the crowding equipment. To watch as an outsider, to see as a viewer. This appealed to the dreamer he'd always kept under strict control.

Booth wasn't sure what had motivated him to visit the set of *Our Lives, Our Loves*. He knew that the script he was currently working on had hit a snag, and that he wanted to see Ariel again. Perhaps it was the scent of violets that continued to drift to him as he tried to work. Twice he'd started to throw them away...but he hadn't. Part of him, deep, long repressed, needed such things, however much he disliked acknowledging it.

So he had come to see Ariel, telling himself he simply wanted to watch her work before he committed himself to choosing her for the part of Rae. It was logical, practical. It was something he'd tried very hard to resist.

Ariel sat at the kitchen table with her bare feet propped in a chair while Jack Shapiro, who played Griff Martin, Amanda's college sweetheart, mulled over a hand of solitaire. On another part of the soundstage, her television parents were discussing their offspring. After they'd finished, she and Jack would tape their scene.

"Black six on the red seven," she mumbled, earning herself a glare from Jack.

"Solitaire," he reminded her. "As in alone."

"It's an antisocial game."

"You think headphones are antisocial."

"They are." Smiling sweetly, she moved the six herself.

"Why don't you go call the Committee for the Salvation of Three-legged Land Mammals? They probably want you at their next luncheon."

The timing wasn't quite right, she decided, to ask him to contribute to the Homes for Kittens fund she was currently involved with. "Don't get snotty," she said mildly. "You're supposed to adore me."

"Should've had my head examined after you threw me over for Cameron."

"It's your own fault for not explaining what you were doing alone in that hotel room with Vikki."

Jack sniffed and turned over another card. "You should've trusted me. A man has his pride."

"Now I'm stuck in a disastrous marriage *and* I might be pregnant."

Glancing up, he grinned. "Great for the ratings. Did you see them posted this week? We're up a whole point."

She leaned her elbows on the table. "Wait until things start heating up between Amanda and Griff again." She put a black ten on the jack of diamonds. "Sizzle, spark, smolder."

He smacked her hand. "You're a great smolderer." Unable to resist, he leered. "I haven't kissed you in six months."

"Then when you get your chance, big guy, make it good. Amanda's no pushover." Rising, she strolled away for a last-minute check with makeup.

The hospital set had already been prepared for the brief but intense meeting between the former lovers, Amanda and Griff. Some subtle dark smudges were added under her eyes to give the appearance of a sleepless night. The rest of her makeup gave her a slight pallor.

By the time the cameras rolled, Amanda was in her office, going through her patient files. She seemed very calm, very much in control. Her expression was totally serene. Abruptly, she slammed the drawer back in the cabinet and whirled around to pace. When the tape was edited, it would flash back to her discovery of her husband and sister. Amanda grabbed a china cup from her desk and hurled it against the wall. With the back of her hand to her mouth, she stared at the broken pieces. The knock at her office door had her balling her fists and making a visible struggle for control. Deliberately, she walked around her desk and sat down.

"Come in."

The camera focused on Jack as Dr. Griff Martin, rough-and-ready looks, rough-and-ready temper— Amanda's first and only lover before her marriage. Ariel knew what the director would edit in a reaction shot later, but now, with the tape running on Jack's entrance, she screwed up her face and stuck out her tongue. Jack gave her one of his character's patented lengthy looks designed to make the female heart flutter.

"Amanda, have you got a minute?"

When the lens was focused on her again, her face was properly composed with just a hint of strain beneath the serenity. "Of course, Griff." For a subtle sign of nerves, she gripped her hands together on the desktop.

"I've got a case of wife beating," he began in the clipped, almost surly tone of his character. Both Amanda and several million female viewers had found his diamond-in-the-rough style irresistible. "I need your help."

They went through the scene, laying the groundwork for a story line that would throw them together again and again over the next few weeks, building the sexual tension. When the camera was briefly at Jack's

back he crossed his eyes at Ariel and bared his teeth. As
she went back to her patient file, she made certain she
walked over his foot. Neither of them lost the rhythm
of the scene.

"You look tired." As Griff, Jack started to touch her
shoulder, then stopped himself. Frustration radiated
from his eyes. "Is everything all right?"

Amanda turned and gave him a soulful eye-locking
look. Her mouth trembled open, then closed again.
Slowly, she turned back to the file and shut the drawer
quietly. "Everything's fine. I have a heavy workload
right now. And I have a patient due in a few minutes."

"I'll get out of here then." He started for the door
and paused. With his hand on the knob, he stared at
her. "Mandy..."

Amanda kept her back to him. The camera came in
close as she shut her eyes and fought for control. "I'll
see your patient tomorrow, Griff." There was the faintest of tremors in her voice.

He waited five humming seconds. "Yeah, fine."

When she heard the door close, Amanda pressed her
hands to her face.

"Cut."

"I'm going to get you for that," Jack said as he pushed
the prop door open again. "I think you broke one of
my toes."

Ariel fluttered her lashes at him. "You're such a baby."

"All right, children," the director said mildly. "Let's
get the reaction shots."

Agreeably, Ariel moved behind Amanda's desk
again. It was then she saw Booth. Surprise and pleasure showed on her face, though his expression wasn't
welcoming. He was frowning at her, his arms crossed

over a casual black sweater. He didn't return her smile, nor did she expect him to. Booth DeWitt wasn't a man who smiled often or easily. It only made her more determined to nudge him into it.

She'd thought about him—surprisingly often. At the moment, she had enough on her mind, both personally and professionally, yet she'd found herself wondering about Booth DeWitt and what went on inside that aloof exterior. She'd seen flashes of something warm, something approachable. For Ariel, it was enough to make her dig for more.

And there'd been that pull—the pull she remembered with perfect clarity. She wanted to feel it again, to enjoy it, to understand it.

She finished the taping and had an hour before she and Stella would play out their confrontation scene on the Lane living-room set. "Jerry, I found a kitten for your daughter," she told one of the technicians as she rose. "It's a little calico, I can bring it in on Friday."

"Been to the pound again," Jack said with a sigh. Ignoring him, Ariel stepped over some cable and walked to Booth.

"Hi, want some coffee?"

"All right."

"I keep a Mr. Coffee in my dressing room. The stuff at the commissary's poison." She led the way, not bothering to ask why he was there. Her door was open, as she usually left it. Walking in, she went directly to the coffeemaker. "You have to make do with powdered milk."

"Black's fine."

Her dressing room was chaos. Clothes, magazines, pamphlets were tossed over all available space. Her dressing table was littered with jars and bottles and framed photographs of the cast. It smelled of fresh flowers, makeup and dust.

On the wall was a calendar that read February though it was midway through April. An electric clock was unplugged and stuck on 7:05. Booth counted three and one-half pairs of shoes on the floor.

In the midst of it, Ariel stood in a raw-silk suit the color of apricots with her hair pale and glowing in a sophisticated knot. She smelled like a woman should at sunset—soft, with a hint of anticipation. As the coffee began to drip, she turned back to him.

"I'm glad to see you again."

The simplicity of the statement made Booth almost believe it. Cautiously, he kept half the room between them as he watched her. "The taping was interesting. You're very good, Ariel. You milked that five-minute scene for everything there was."

Again she had the impression more of criticism than flattery. "It's important in a soap. You're working in little capsules. Some people only tune in a couple times a week. Then there are those who turn it on as a whim. You hope to grab them."

"Your character." He eyed the suit, approving the subdued style. "I'd say she's a very controlled professional woman who's currently going through some personal crisis. There were a lot of sexual sparks bouncing around between her and the young doctor."

"Very good." With a smile, Ariel picked up two cups, mismatched. "That's neatly tied up. Want some M&M's? I keep a stash in my drawer."

"No. Do you always play around on set when you're not on camera?"

She stirred powdered milk into her coffee, added a

generous spoon of sugar, then handed Booth his. "Jack and I have a running contest on who can make who blow their lines. Actually, it makes us sharper and lowers the tension level." Carelessly, she took magazines from a chair and left them stacked on the floor. "Sit down."

"How many pages of dialogue do you have to learn a week?"

"Varies," she said and sipped. "We run about eighty-five pages of script a day now that we've gone to an hour. Some days I might have twenty or thirty where my character's involved. But for the most part, I tape about three days a week—we don't do a lot of takes." Opening the drawer on her dressing table, she took a handful of candies and began to eat them one at a time. "I'm told it's the closest thing to live TV you can get."

Watching her, he drank. "You really enjoy it."

"Yes, I've been very comfortable with Amanda. Which is why I want to do other things as well. Ruts are monotonous places, but so easy to stay in."

He glanced around the room. "I can't imagine you in one."

Ariel laughed and sat on the edge of her dressing table. "A great compliment. You're frugal with them." Something in his aloof, cool expression made her smile. "Would you like to have dinner?" she asked on impulse.

For an instant surprise flickered over his face—the first time she'd seen it. "It's a bit early for dinner," he said mildly.

"I like the way you do that," she said with a nod. "Conversations with you are never boring. If you're free tonight, I could pick you up at seven."

She was asking him for a date, he thought, very simply, very smoothly, in a manner more friendly than flir-

tatious. As he had often since the first time he'd met her,
Booth wondered what made her tick. "All right, seven."
Reaching in his pocket, he pulled out a note pad and
scrawled on it. "Here's the address."

Taking it, Ariel scanned the words with a small
sound of approval. "Mmm, you've got a great view of
the park." She looked up and grinned in the way that
always made him think she'd just enjoyed a little private joke. "I'm a sucker for views."

"I've gathered that already."

Booth walked over to set down his mug and stood
close enough so that his legs brushed hers. She didn't
back away but watched him with clear, curious eyes.
There was something deadly in that face, she thought.
Something any woman would recognize and a wary one
would retreat from. Fascinated, she counted the beat of
her own rapid pulse.

"I'll let you get back to work."

With the slightest move on his part, the contact was
broken. Ariel stayed exactly where she was. "I'm glad
you stopped by," she said, though she was no longer
sure it was precisely the truth.

With a nod, he was gone. Ariel sat on the edge of
her cluttered dressing table and wondered if for the first
time in her life she'd bitten off more than she could
chew.

Because the sun was setting and it was a huge red
ball, Ariel paid off the cab two blocks from Booth's
apartment building. She wanted some time to think
about a phone call she'd received about Scott, her brother's child.

Poor little guy, she thought. So vulnerable, so grown-up. She wondered how much longer it would be before the courts decided his fate. Because she wanted him with her so badly, Ariel refused to believe anything else would happen. Her brother's son, so suddenly orphaned, so miserably unhappy with his maternal grandparents.

They didn't want him, she reflected. Not really. There was such a world of difference between love and duty. Once everything was arranged, she'd be able to give him the kind of easy, unfettered childhood she'd had—with the financial advantages she hadn't known.

She wouldn't think of the complications now. To think of them would make her start doubting the outcome, and she couldn't bear it. She and her lawyers were taking all the possible steps.

Because she wanted no publicity to touch her nephew, Ariel had kept the entire matter to herself—something she rarely did. Perhaps because she had no one to speak to about it, she worried. Every day she told herself Scott would be with her permanently before the end of summer. As long as she kept telling herself, she was able to believe it. Now it was evening, and there was no more she could do.

It was only a little past seven o'clock when she pushed the button of the elevator for Booth's floor in the sleek building on Park Avenue. She'd already set aside that one flash of nerves she felt about him and had decided to enjoy the evening. The idea that he'd been able to make her nervous at all was intriguing enough.

She liked men, the basic personality differences between them and women. Of her closest friends, many were men, in and out of the business. The key word remained *friends*—she was very cautious about lovers.

She ran on emotion, and knowing it, had always been careful of physical relationships.

She was a romantic, unashamedly. Ariel had never doubted that there was one great love waiting for everyone. She had no intention of settling for less—with hearts and flowers and skyrockets included. When she found the right man, she'd know. Whether it was tomorrow or twenty years from tomorrow didn't matter, as long as she found him. In the meantime, she filled her life with work, her friends and her causes. Ariel Kirkwood simply didn't believe in boredom.

She approved of the quiet, carpeted hallway as she strolled down to Booth's apartment. It was wainscoted and elegant. But as she lifted her hand to press the button on his door, she felt that odd flutter of nerves again.

Inside, Booth was standing by the high wide window that looked out over Central Park. He was thinking of her, had been thinking of her for most of the day. And he didn't care for it.

Twice, he'd nearly called to cancel the dinner, telling himself he had work to do. Telling himself he didn't have the time or the inclination to spend an evening with an actress he hardly knew. But he hadn't canceled because he could still see the way her eyes warmed, the way her whole face moved when she smiled.

A professional trick. Liz had had a bagful of them, and unless his perception was very, very wrong, this woman was as skilled an actress as Liz Hunter. That's what he told himself, and yet… And yet he hadn't canceled.

When the buzzer rang, Booth looked over his shoulder at the closed door. It was simply an evening, he decided. A few hours out of the day in which he could study the woman being considered for a major part in an important film. He had little doubt that she would make a pitch for the part before the night was over. With a shrug, Booth walked to the door. That was the business, and she was entitled.

Then, when he opened the door, she smiled at him. He realized he wanted her with an intensity he hadn't felt in years. "Hi. You look nice," she said.

The struggle with desire only made him more remote, made his voice more scrupulously polite. "Come in."

Ariel walked through the door then studied the room with open curiosity. Neat. Her first impression was one of meticulous order. Style. Who could fault a gleaming mix of Chippendale and Hepplewhite? The colors were muted, easy on the eyes. The furniture was arranged in such a way as to give a sense of balance. She could smell neither dust nor polish. It was as though the room was perpetually clean and rarely lived in. Somehow, she didn't think it really suited that harsh, nineteenth-century face. No, there was too much formality here for a man who looked like Booth, for a man who moved like him.

Though she felt no sense of welcome, she could appreciate the rather stationary beauty and respect the organized taste.

"A very fastidious man," she murmured, then walked over to study his view of the city.

She wore a dress with yards of skirt and whirls of color. Booth wondered if that was why he suddenly felt life jump into the room. He preferred the quiet, the settled, even the isolated. Yet somehow, for the first time, he felt the appeal of having warmth in his home.

"I was right about this," Ariel said and put her hands

into the deep pockets of her skirt. "It's lovely. Where do you work?"

"I have an office set up in another room."

"I'd probably have put my desk right here." Laughing, she turned to him so that the mix of colors in her dress seemed to vibrate. "Then again, I wouldn't get much work done." His eyes were very dark and very steady, his face so expressionless he might have been thinking of anything or nothing. "Do you stare at everyone that way?"

"I suppose I do. Would you like a drink?"

"Yes, some dry vermouth if you have it." She wandered over to a cherrywood breakfront and studied his collection of Waterford. No one chose something so lovely, or so capable of catching light and fire if they lacked warmth. Where was his, she wondered. Buried so deep that he'd forgotten it, or simply dormant from lack of use?

Booth paused beside her and offered a glass. "You like crystal?"

"I like beautiful things."

What woman didn't? he thought brittlely. A Russian lynx, a pear-shaped diamond. Yes, women liked beautiful things, particularly when someone else was providing them. He'd already done more than his share of that.

"I watched your show today," Booth began, deciding to give her the opening for her pitch and see what she did with it. "You come across very well as the competent psychiatrist."

"I like Amanda." Ariel sipped her vermouth. "She's a very stable woman with little hints of vulnerability and passion. I like seeing how subtle I can make them without hiding them completely. What did you think of the show?"

"A mass of complication and intrigue. I was surprised that the bulk of the plots didn't concern fatal diseases and bed hopping."

"You're out of step." She smiled over the rim. "Of course, every soap has some of those elements, but we've done a lot of expanding. Murder, politics, social issues, even science fiction. We do quite a bit of location shooting now in the race for ratings." She drank again. This time it was an opal, milky blue, that gleamed on her hand. "Last year we shot in Greece and Venice. I've never eaten so much in my life. Griff and Amanda had a lovers' rendezvous in Venice that was sabotaged. You must've noticed Stella—she plays my sister Vikki."

"The barracuda." Booth nodded. "I recognized the type."

"Oh, Vikki's that all right. Plotting, scheming, being generally nasty. Stella has a marvelous time with her. Vikki's had a dozen affairs, broken up three marriages, destroyed a senator's career. Just last month she pawned our mother's emerald brooch to pay off gambling debts." With a sigh, Ariel drank again. "She has all the fun."

Booth's grin flashed, lingering in his eyes as they met Ariel's. "Are you talking about Stella or Vikki?"

"Both, I suppose. I wondered if I'd be able to do that."

"What?"

"Make you smile. You don't very often, you know."

"No?"

"No." She felt the tug again, sharp and very physical. Indulging herself, she let her gaze lower briefly to his mouth and enjoyed the sensation it brought to her own. "I guess you're too busy picking up parts of people and filing them away."

Finishing off his drink, he set the glass aside. "Is that what I do?"

"Always. It's natural, I suppose, in your line of work, but I decided I was going to pull one out of you before the evening was over." He was still watching her, and though the smile was only a hint now, it was still lurking. It suited him, she thought, that trace of amusement—a cautious, even reluctant amusement. And again, she felt the tug of attraction. With her brows slightly drawn together, she stepped closer. It wasn't something she could or would walk away from.

"Aren't you curious?" she asked quietly, then went on when he didn't answer. "The thing is, I'm not certain I can go through the evening wondering what it would be like."

She put one hand on his shoulder and leaned forward just until their lips touched. There was no pressure, no demand on either side, and yet she felt that slightest of contacts through her whole system. There was a twinge deep inside her, a soft rushing sound in her ears. The mouth against hers was warmer than she'd expected and its taste more potent. Their bodies weren't touching, and the kiss remained a mere meeting of lips. Ariel felt herself open and was mildly surprised. Then, she felt her knees tremble and was stunned.

Slowly, she backed up, unaware that her eyes were wide with shock. Desire had ripped through him at the taste of her mouth, but Booth knew how to conceal his emotions. He wanted her—in the part of Rae and in his bed. To his thinking it wouldn't be long before she offered him one to ensure the other. He'd been much younger when Liz had lured him into bed for a part. He was older now and knew the game. And somehow, he felt Ariel would be more honest in her playing.

"Well…" Ariel let out a long breath while her mind raced. She wished she had five minutes alone to think this through. Somehow she'd always expected she'd fall in love in the blink of an eye, but she wasn't idealistic enough to believe it would be handed back to her. She needed to work out her next move. "And now that the pressure's off—" she set her glass aside "—why don't we go eat?"

Before she could step away, Booth took her arm. If they were going to play out the scene, he wanted to do it then and there. "What do you want?"

There was none of the quiet warmth in his voice that she'd felt in the kiss. Ariel looked into his eyes and saw nothing but a reflection of herself. An unwise man to love, she thought. And, of course, she should have expected that was what would happen to her when the time came. "To go to dinner," she told him.

"I've given you the opportunity to mention the part, you haven't. Why?"

"That's business. This isn't."

He gave a quick laugh. "In this business, it's all business," he countered. "You want to play Rae."

"I wouldn't have read for it if I didn't want it. And once I finish the next reading I'll have it." It frustrated her that she couldn't read him. "Booth, why don't you tell me what you're getting at? It'd be easier for both of us."

He inclined his head, and with his hand on her arm drew her an inch closer. "Just how much are you willing to do for it?"

His meaning was like a slap in the face. Outrage didn't come, but a piercing hurt that made her face pale and her eyes darken. "I'm willing to give the very best performance I'm capable of." Jerking out of his hold, she started for the door.

"Ariel..." He hadn't expected to call her back, but the look in her eyes had made him feel foul. When she didn't pause, he was going across the room before he could stop himself. "Ariel." Taking her arm again, he turned her around.

The hurt radiating from her was so sharp and real he couldn't convince himself not to believe it. The strength of the need to draw her against him was almost painful. "I'll apologize for that."

She stared at him, wishing it was in her to tell him to go to hell. "I'll accept it," she said instead, "since I'm sure you don't make a habit of apologizing for anything. She took a few pieces out of you, didn't she?"

His hand dropped away from her arm. "I don't discuss my private life."

"Maybe that's part of the problem. Is it women in general, or just actresses you detest?"

His eyes narrowed so that she could only see a glint of the anger. It wasn't necessary to see what you could feel. "Don't push me."

"I doubt anyone could." Though she felt the anger was a promising sign, Ariel didn't feel capable of dealing with it, or her own feelings at the moment. "It's a pity," she continued as she turned for the door again. "When whatever's frozen inside you thaws, I think you'll be a remarkable man. In the meantime, I'll stay out of your way." She opened the door, then turned back. "About the part, Booth, please deal with my agent." Quietly, she closed the door behind her.

Chapter 4

"No, Scott, if you eat any more cotton candy your teeth're going to fall right out. And then—" Ariel hauled her nephew up for one fierce hug "—you'd be stuck with stuff like smashed bananas and strained spinach."

"Popcorn," he demanded, grinning at her.

"Bottomless pit." She nuzzled into his neck and let the love flow over her.

Sunday was precious, not only because of the sunshine and balmy spring temperatures, not only because there were hours and hours of leisure time left to her, but because she had the afternoon to spend with the most important person in her life.

He even smells like his father, Ariel thought and wondered if it were possible to inherit a scent. Still holding him, with his sturdy legs wrapped around her waist, she studied his face.

Essentially, it was like looking in a mirror. There'd only been ten months between Ariel and her brother, Jeremy, and they'd often been taken for twins. Scott had pale curling hair, clear blue eyes and a face that promised to be lean and rather elegant once it had fined down from childhood. At the moment, it was sticky with pink spun sugar. Ariel kissed him firmly and tasted the sweetness.

"Yum-yum," she murmured, kissing him again when he giggled.

"What about your teeth?"

Arching a brow, she shifted his weight to a more comfortable position. "It doesn't count when it's secondhand."

He gave her a crooked smile that promised to be a heartbreaker in another decade. "How come?"

"It's scientific," Ariel claimed. "Probably the sugar evaporates after being exposed to air and skin."

"You're making that up," he told her with great approval.

Struggling with a smile, she tossed her long smooth braid behind her back. "Who me?"

"You're the best at making up."

"That's my job," she answered primly. "Let's go look at the bears."

"They better have big ones," Scott stated as he wriggled down. "*Great* big ones."

"I hear they're enormous," she told him. "Maybe even big enough to climb right out of the cages."

"Yeah?" His eyes lit up at the idea. Ariel could almost see him writing out the scenario in his mind. The escape, the panic and screams of the crowd and his ultimate heroism in driving the giant, drooling bears back behind the bars. Then, of course, his humbleness in accepting the gratitude of the zookeepers. "Let's go!"

Ariel allowed herself to be dragged along at Scott's dashing pace, winding through the stream of people who'd come to spend their day at the Bronx Zoo. This she could give him, she thought. The fun, the preciousness of childhood. It was such a short time, so concentrated. So many years were passed as an adult—with obligations, responsibilities, worries, timetables. She wanted to give him the freedom, to show him what boundaries you could leap over and the ones you had to respect. Most of all, she wanted to give him love.

She loved and wanted him, not only for the memories he brought back of her brother, but for himself—his uniqueness and odd stability. Though she was a woman who ran her life on a staggered routine that wasn't a routine at all, who enjoyed coming and going on the impulse of the moment, she'd always needed stability—someone to care for, to nurture, to give her back some portion of the emotion she spent. There was nothing like a child, with its innocence and lack of restrictions, to give and take of love. Even now, while he raced and laughed and pointed, caught up in the day and the animals, Scott was feeding her.

If Ariel had believed Scott was happy living with his grandparents, she could have accepted it. But she knew that they were smothering all the specialness that radiated from him.

They weren't unkind people, she mused, but simply set in their thinking. A child was to be formed along certain lines, and that was that. A child was a duty, a solemn one. While she understood the duty, it was joy that came first. They would raise him to be responsible, polite and well-read. And they'd forget the wonder of it.

Perhaps it would have been easier if Scott's grandparents hadn't disapproved of Ariel's brother so strongly or if Scott hadn't been conceived in youthful defiance and passion…and out of wedlock. Marriage and Scott's birth hadn't eased over the strain in the relationship, nor had the tragic and sudden accident that had taken her brother and young sister-in-law. Scott's grandparents would look at the boy and be reminded that their daughter had married against their wishes and was dead. Ariel looked at him and saw life at its best.

He needs me, she thought, and ruffled his hair as he stood staring wide-eyed at a lumbering bear. Even when her heart wasn't involved, she'd never been able to resist a need. With Scott, her heart had been lost the first time she'd seen him—red and scrawny behind a hospital glass wall.

And she understood that she needed him. To have someone receive her love was vital. She thought of Booth.

He needed her, too, she thought, as a small secret smile touched her lips. Though he didn't know it. A man like that needed the ease that love could bring to his life, and the laughter. And she wanted to give it to him.

Why? Leaning against the barrier, Ariel shook her head. She had no solid reason, and that was enough to convince her it was right. When you could dissect something and find all the answers, you could find all the wrong ones. She trusted instincts and emotions much more than she trusted the intellect. She loved—quickly, unwisely and completely. When she thought about it,

Ariel decided she should never have expected it to be otherwise.

If she told him now, he'd think she was lying or insane. She could hardly blame him. It wouldn't be easy to win the confidence of a man as wary or as cynical as Booth DeWitt. With a smile, Ariel nibbled on some of Scott's popcorn. Challenges kept the excitement in life, after all. Whether Booth realized it or not, she was about to add some excitement to his.

"Why're you laughing, Ariel?"

She grinned down at Scott, then scooped him up. He laughed as he always did at her quick, physical shows of affection. "Because I'm happy. Aren't you? It's a happy day."

"I'm always happy with you." His arms went tight around her neck. "Can't I stay with you? Can't I live at your house—all the time?"

She buried her face in the curve of his shoulder—a tender place—knowing she couldn't tell him how hard she was trying to give him that. "We have today," she said instead. "All day."

Holding him, she could smell the scent of his soap and shampoo, the scent of roasted popcorn, the hot, pungent scent of the sun. With another laugh, she set her nephew down. Today, she told herself, that was what she'd show him.

"Let's go see the snakes. I like to watch them slither."

Booth couldn't understand why she kept crowding his mind. He should have been able to push Ariel into a corner of his brain and keep her there while he worked. Instead, she kept filling it.

He could have accepted it if he'd been able to keep

her in her slot—the actress he was all but certain would play his Rae. He could have rationalized his obsession if it had remained a professional one. But Booth kept seeing her as she'd been on top of New York, with her hair blowing frantically and her eyes filled with the wonder of it. That woman had nothing in common with the character of Rae.

And he could see her as she'd looked in his apartment. Vital, fresh—with energy and integrity shimmering from her. He could remember her hurt when he'd been deliberately cruel, and his own guilt—a sensation he'd sworn he'd never feel again. He hardly knew her, and yet she was drawing things out of him he'd promised himself he wouldn't feel again. He was perceptive enough to know she was a woman who could draw out more. For that reason, he'd decided to keep a safe, professional distance between them.

Still, as Booth watched Ariel talk with Jack Rohrer before the reading, he couldn't keep the established lines firmly in place. Was it because she was beautiful and he had always been susceptible to beauty? Was it because she was just unique enough to catch the attention and hold it?

As a writer he couldn't suppress his fascination with the unusual. But he got something from her—some feeling of absolute stability despite the fact that she dressed somewhere between a Gypsy and a teenager. He'd already asked her who she was and had been far from satisfied with her answer. Perhaps, just perhaps he should find out for himself.

"They look good together," Marshell murmured.

The sound Booth made might have been agreement or disinterest, but he didn't take his eyes from Ariel.

If he hadn't remembered her first reading so well, he'd have sworn he was making a mistake even considering her for the part. Her smile was much too open, her gestures too fluid. You could look at her and feel the warmth. He found it disconcerting to realize she made him nervous.

Desire. Yes, he felt desire. Booth weighed and measured it. Strong, hard and very nearly urgent—and that with only a look. Of course, she was a woman a man had to want. He wasn't worried about the desire, or even his interest, but about the niggling sensation that something was being slipped out of him without his knowledge and against his will.

Pulling out a cigarette, he watched her through the blue-tinted smoke. It might be worth his while, both as a man and as a writer, to see how many faces she could wear, and how easily she wore them. He sat on the edge of Marshell's desk.

"Let's get started."

At the brief, quiet order, Ariel turned her head and met Booth's gaze. *He's different today,* she thought, but couldn't quite pigeonhole the reason. He still looked at her with that intrusive, serious stare that bordered on the brooding. The distance was still there; she was sensitive enough to recognize the wall he kept erected between himself and the rest of the world. But there was something…

Ariel smiled at him. When he didn't respond, she picked up her copy of the script. She was going to give the best damn reading of her career. For herself and— for some odd reason—for Booth.

"All right, I'd like you to start at the top of the scene where they've come home from the party." Absently

Booth tapped his cigarette in a gold-etched ashtray. Behind him, Marshell nibbled on a stomach mint. "Do you want to read it over first?"

Ariel glanced up from the script. *He still thinks I'm going to blow it,* she realized, and was grateful for the hard knot in her stomach. "It isn't necessary," she told him, then turned to Jack.

For the second time, Booth witnessed the transformation. How was it that even her eyes seemed to go paler, icier when she spoke as Rae? He could feel the old sexual pull and intellecutal abhorrence his ex-wife had always brought to him. With the cigarette smoldering between his fingertips, Booth listened to Rae's scorn and Phil's anger—and remembered all too clearly.

A vampire. He'd called her that and accurately. Bloodless, heartless, alluring. Ariel slipped into the character as if it were a second skin. Booth knew he should admire her for it, even be grateful that she'd made his search for the right actress end. But her chameleon skill annoyed him.

The chemistry was right. Ariel and Jack hurled their lines at each other while the anger and sexual sparks flew. There wasn't any escaping it and no logical reason to try. Without knowing why, Booth was certain that giving Ariel the part was good professional judgment and a serious personal error. He'd just have to deal with the latter as he went.

"That'll do."

The moment Booth cut the scene, Ariel threw her head back and let out breathless laughter. The release— the sudden absence of tension—was tremendous. It would always be that way, she realized, with a part as tough and as cold as this one.

"Oh God, she's so utterly hateful, so completely self-consumed." Eyes alight, face flushed, she whirled to Booth. "You despise her, and yet she pulls you in. Even when you see the knife she's going to slide under your ribs, it's hard to step away."

"Yes." Watching the scene had disturbed him more than he'd expected. Rising, Booth left his hands in his pockets. "I want you for the part. We'll contact your agent and negotiate the details."

She sighed, but the smile lingered around her mouth. "I can see I've overwhelmed you," Ariel said dryly. "But the bottom line is the part. You won't regret it. Mr. Marshell, Jack, it'll be a pleasure working with you."

"Ariel…" Marshell rose and accepted her offered hand. It had been a long time since he'd watched a scene that had left him as shaken as this one. "Unless I miss my guess—and I never do—you're going to hit it big with this."

She flashed him a grin and felt like flying. "I don't suppose I'll complain. Thank you."

Booth had her elbow before she could turn around, and before he'd realized he intended to touch her. He wanted to vent fury on something, someone, but reasoned it away. "I'll walk you out."

Feeling the tension in his fingers, she had to resist the urge to soothe it. This wasn't a man who'd appreciate stroking. "All right."

They followed the same route they'd taken the week before, but this time in silence. Ariel sensed he needed it. When they came to the street door, she waited for him to say whatever he intended to say.

"Are you free?" he asked her.

A bit puzzled, she tilted her head.

"For an early dinner," he elaborated. "I feel I owe you a meal."

"Well." She brushed the hair back from her face. His invitation, such as it was, pleased her—something she took no trouble to hide. "Technically that's the other way around. Why do you want to have dinner with me?"

Just looking at her—the laughing eyes, the generous mouth—pulled him in two directions. Get closer before you lose it. Back off before it's too late. "I'm not completely sure."

"Good enough." She took his hand and lifted her free one for a cab. "Do you like grilled pork chops?"

"Yes."

She laughed over her shoulder before pulling him into the cab. "An excellent start." After giving the driver an address in Greenwich Village, she settled back. "I think the next move is to have a conversation without a word, one single word, that has to do with business. We might just make it in each other's company for more than an hour."

"All right." Booth nodded. He'd made the decision to get to know her and get to know her he would. "But we'll steer away from politics, too."

"Deal."

"How long have you lived in New York?"

"I was born here. A native." She grinned and crossed her legs. "You're not. I read somewhere that you're from Philadelphia and very top-drawer. Lots of influential relatives." She didn't even glance around when the cab skidded and swerved. "Are you happy in New York?"

He'd never thought about equating it with happiness, but now that he did, the answer came easily. "Yes.

I need the demands and the movement for long periods of time."

"And then you need to go away," she finished. "And be alone—on your boat."

Before he could be uncomfortable with her accuracy, he'd accepted it. "That's right. I relax when I'm sailing and I like to relax alone."

"I paint," she told him. "Terrible paintings." With a laugh, she rolled her eyes. "But it helps me work the kinks out when I get them. I keep threatening people with an original Kirkwood as a Christmas present, but I haven't the heart to do it."

"I'd like to see one," he murmured.

"The problem seems to be that I splatter my mood on the canvas. Here we are." Ariel hopped out of the cab and stood on the curb.

Booth glanced around at the tiny storefronts. "Where're we going?"

"To the market." In her easy manner, she hooked her arm through his. "I don't have any pork chops at home."

He looked down at her. "Home?"

"Most of the time I'd rather cook than eat out. And tonight I'm too wired to deal with a restaurant. I have to be busy."

"Wired?" After studying her profile, Booth shook his head. His hair was dark in the lowering sun, and the movement sent it settling carelessly around his face. A contrast, Ariel mused, to the rather formal exterior. "I'd have said you look remarkably calm."

"Uh-uh. But I'm trying to save the full explosion until after my agent calls and tells me everything's carved in granite. Don't worry—" she smiled up at him "—I'm a fair cook."

If a man judged only by that porcelain face, he'd never have believed she'd know one end of the stove from the other. But Booth knew about surfaces. Maybe, just maybe, there'd be a surprise under hers. Despite all the warnings he'd given himself, he smiled. "Only fair?"

Her eyes lit in appreciation. "I hate to brag, but actually, I'm terrific." She steered him into a small, cluttered market that smelled heavily of garlic and pepper, and began a haphazard selection for the evening meal. "How're the avocados today, Mr. Stanislowski?"

"The best." The grocer looked over her head to study Booth out of the corner of his eye. "Only the best for you, Ariel."

"I'll have two then, but you pick them out." She poked at a head of romaine. "How did Monica do on her history quiz?"

"Ninety-two percent." His chest swelled a bit under his apron, but he continued to speculate on the dark, brooding man who'd come in with Ariel.

"Terrific. I need four really nice center-cut chops." While he selected them, she studied the mushrooms, well aware that he was bursting with curiosity over Booth. "You know, Mr. Stanislowski, Monica would love a kitten."

As he started to weigh the meat, the grocer sent her an exasperated glance. "Now, Ariel…"

"She's certainly old enough to care for one on her own," Ariel continued and pinched a tomato. "It'd be company for her, and a responsibility. And she did get ninety-two on that quiz." Looking over, she sent him a dashing, irresistible smile. He flushed and shifted his feet.

"Maybe if you were to bring one by, we could think about it."

"I will." Still smiling, she reached for her wallet. "How much do I owe you?"

"That was smoothly done," Booth murmured when they stepped outside. "And it's the second time I've heard you palming off a kitten. Did your cat have a litter?"

"No, I just happen to know about a number of homeless kittens." She tilted her face toward him. "If you're interested…"

"No." The answer was firm and brief as he took the bag from her.

Ariel merely smiled and decided she could work on him later. Now, she breathed in the scent of spices and baking from the open doorways. Some children raced along the sidewalk, laughing. A few old men sat out on the stoops to gossip. After the dinner hour, Ariel knew other members of the family would come out to talk and exchange news and enjoy the spring weather. Through a screened window she heard some muted snatches of Beethoven's Ninth, and farther down the pulse of top forty rock.

Two years before, Ariel had moved to the Village for the neighborhood feel, and had never been disappointed. She could sit outside and listen to the elderly reminisce, watch the children play, hear about the latest teenage heartthrob or the newest baby. It had been exactly what she'd needed when her family had gone its separate ways.

"Hi, Mr. Miller, Mr. Zimmerman."

The two old men who sat on the steps of the converted brownstone eyed Booth before they looked at

Ariel. "Don't think you should give that Cameron another chance," Mr. Miller told her.

"Boot him out." Mr. Zimmerman gave a wheeze that might have been a chuckle. "Get yourself a man with backbone."

"Is that an offer?" She kissed his cheek before climbing the rest of the steps.

"I'll have a dance at the block party," he called after her.

Ariel winked over her shoulder. "Mr. Zimmerman, you can have as many as you want." As they started up the inside steps, Ariel began to fish in her bag for her keys. "I'm crazy about him," she told Booth. "He's a retired music instructor and still teaches a few kids on the side. He sits on the stoop so he can watch the women go by." She located the keys attached to a large, plastic, grinning sun. "He's a leg man."

Automatically, Booth glanced over his shoulder. "He told you?"

"You just have to watch the direction his eyes take when a skirt passes."

"Yours included?"

Her eyes danced. "I fit into the category of niece. He thinks I should be married and raising large quantities of babies."

She fit a single key into a single lock, something Booth thought almost unprecedented for New York, then pushed open the door. He'd been expecting the unusual. And he wasn't disappointed.

The focal point of the living room was a long oversize hammock swinging from brass ceiling hooks. One end of it was piled with pillows and beside it was a washstand holding one thick candle, three-quarters burned down. There was color—he'd known there'd be an abundance of it—and a style that was undefinable.

The sofa was a long, curved French antique upholstered with faded rose brocade, while a long wicker trunk served as a coffee table. As in Ariel's dressing room, the entire area was cluttered with books, papers and scents. He caught the fragrance of candle wax, potpourri and fresh flowers. Bunches of spring blossoms were spilling from a collection of vases that ran from dime-store pottery to Meissen.

There was an umbrella stand in the shape of a stork that was filled with ostrich and peacock feathers. A pair of boxing gloves hung in the corner behind the door.

"I guess you'd class as a featherweight," Booth mused.

Ariel followed his gaze and smiled. "They were my brother's. He boxed in high school. Want a drink?" Before he could answer, she took the bag from him, then headed down a hallway.

"A little Scotch and water." When he turned, his attention and his senses were struck by a wall of paintings. They were hers, of course. Who else would paint with that kind of kinetic energy, verve and disregard for rules? There were splotches of color, lines of it, zigzags. Moving closer, Booth decided that while he wouldn't call them terrible, he wasn't quite sure what he'd call them. Vivid, eccentric, disturbing. Certainly they weren't paintings to relax by. They showed both flair and heedlessness, and whether she'd intended them to or not they suited the room to perfection.

As he continued to study the paintings, three cats came into the room. Two were hardly more than kittens, coal black and amber eyed. They dashed around his legs once before they made a beeline for the kitchen. The other was a huge tiger who managed to walk with stiff dignity on three legs. Booth could hear Ariel laugh and say something to the two cats who had found her. The tiger watched Booth with quiet patience.

"Scotch and water." Ariel came back in, barefoot, carrying two glasses.

Booth accepted the glass, then gestured with it. "Those must be some kinks you work out."

Ariel glanced toward her paintings. "Looks like it, doesn't it? Saves money on a therapist—though I shouldn't say that since I play the role of one."

"You've quite a place here."

"I learned I thrive on confusion." Laughing up at him, she sipped. "You've met Butch, I see." She bent and slid one hand over the tiger's back. He arched, letting out a grumble of a purr. "Keats and Shelley were the rude ones. They're having their dinner."

"I see." Booth glanced down to see Butch rub against Ariel's leg before he waddled over to the sofa and leaped onto a cushion. "Don't you find it difficult tending three cats in a city apartment while dealing with a demanding profession?"

She only smiled. "No. I'm going to start the grill."

Booth lifted a brow. "Where?"

"Why, on the terrace." Ariel walked over and slid open a door. Outside was a postage-stamp balcony more along the lines of a window ledge. On it she'd crammed pots of geraniums and a tiny charcoal grill.

"The terrace," Booth murmured over her shoulder. Only an incurable optimist or a hopeless dreamer would have termed it so. He found himself grateful she had. Laughing, he leaned against the doorjamb.

After straightening from the grill, Ariel stared at him. The sound of his laughter whispered along her skin and eased her mind. "Well, well. That's very nice. Do you know that's the first time since I've met you that you've laughed and meant it?"

Booth shrugged and sipped at his Scotch. "I suppose I'm out of practice."

"We'll soon fix that," Ariel said. She smiled, holding her hand out, palm up. "Got a match?"

Booth reached in his pocket, but something—perhaps the humor in her eyes—changed his mind. Stepping forward, he took her shoulders and lowered his mouth to hers.

He'd caught her off guard. Ariel hadn't expected him to do anything on impulse, and he'd given no sign of his intention. Before she had time to prepare, the power of the kiss whipped through her, touching the emotions, the senses, then taking over.

It wasn't a mere touching of lips this time, but a hard, thorough demand that had her wrapped in his arms and trapped against the side of the door. She reached up to take his face in her hands as she gave, unquestioningly, what he sought from her.

There was no gradual smoldering, no experimentation, but a leap of flame so intense and quick it seemed they were already lovers. She felt the instant intimacy and understood it. Her heart was already his, she couldn't deny him her body.

He felt the need churn and was relieved. It had been long, too long, since he'd more than indifferently wanted a woman. There was nothing indifferent about the passion he felt now. It was hard and clear, like the wind

that buffeted him when he sailed. It spelled freedom.
Drawing her closer, Booth absorbed it.

He could smell her—that warm, teasing fragrance
that seemed to pulse out of her skin. How often had that
scent come to him when he'd only thought of her? He
remembered her taste. Alluring, giving and again warm.
And the feel of her body—slender, soft, with still more
warmth. It was that that touched every aspect of her, that
promised to fill him. He needed it, though he'd gone
for years without knowing it. Perhaps he needed her.

And it was that that had him pulling back when he
wanted more and more of what she had an abundance of.

Her eyes opened slowly when her mouth was free.
Ariel looked directly, unblinkingly at him. This time
she saw more than a reflection of self. She saw longings
and caution and a glimpse of emotion that stirred her.

"I've wanted you to do that," she murmured.

Booth forced himself to level, forced himself to think
past the senses she sent swimming. "I haven't got anything for you."

That hurt, but Ariel knew love wasn't painless. "I
think you're wrong. But then, I have a tendency to rush
into things. You don't." She took a deep breath and a
step back. "Why don't you light this and I'll go make a
salad?" Without waiting for his answer she turned and
walked into the kitchen.

Steady, she ordered herself. She knew she had to be
steady to deal with Booth and the feelings he brought
to her. He wasn't a man who would accept a flood of
emotion all at once, or the demands that went with it.
If she wanted him in her life, she'd have to tread carefully, and at his pace.

He wasn't nearly as hard and cool as he tried to be,

Ariel mused. With a half smile, she began to wash the fresh vegetables. She could tell from his laugh, and from those flickers of amusement in his eyes. And, of course, she was certain she couldn't have fallen in love with a man without a sense of humor. It pleased her to be able to draw it out of him. The more they were together, the easier it was. She wondered if he knew. Humming, she began to slice an avocado.

Booth watched her from the doorway. A smile lingered on her lips, and her eyes held that light he was growing too used to. She used the kitchen knife with the careless confidence of one who was accustomed to domestic chores. In one easy movement she tossed her hair behind her back.

Why should such a simple scene hold so much appeal for him, he wondered. Just looking at her standing at the sink, her hands full, the water running, he could feel himself relaxing. What was it about her that made him want to put his feet up and his head back? At that moment, he could see himself going to her to wrap his arms around her waist and nuzzle. He must be going mad.

She knew he was there. Her senses were keen, and sharper still where Booth was involved. Keeping her back to him, she continued preparing the salad. "Have any trouble lighting it?"

He lifted a brow. "No."

"Well, it doesn't take long to heat up. Hungry?"

"A bit." He crossed the room to her. He wouldn't touch her, but he'd get just a little closer.

Smiling, she held up a thin slice of avocado, offering him a bite. Ariel could see the wariness in his eyes as he allowed her to feed him. "I'm never a bit hungry," she told him, finishing off the slice herself. "I'm always starving."

He'd told himself he wouldn't touch her, yet he found that the back of his hand was sliding over the side of her face. "Your skin," he murmured. "It's beautiful. It looks like porcelain, feels like satin." His gaze skimmed over her face, over her mouth before it locked on hers. "I should never have touched you."

Her heart was pounding. Gentleness. That was unexpected and would undermine her completely. "Why?"

"It leads to more." His fingers ran slowly down the length of her hair before he dropped his hands. "I haven't any more. You want something from me," he murmured.

Her breath trembled out. She'd never realized what a strain it was to hold in your emotions. She'd never tried. "Yes, I do. For now, just some companionship at dinner. That should be easy."

When she started to turn back to the sink, Booth stopped her. "Nothing about this is going to be easy. If I continue to see you, like this, I'm going to take you to bed."

It would be easy, so easy, just to go into his arms. But he'd never accept the generosity, and she'd never survive the emptiness. "Booth, I'm a grown woman. If I go to bed with you, it's my choice."

He nodded. "Perhaps. I just want to make sure I have one." He turned and left her alone in the room.

Ariel took a deep breath. She wasn't going to have it, she decided. No, not any of it. He'd simply have to learn how to cope without the moodiness and tension. Lifting the platter of chops, she went back into the living room.

"Lighten up, DeWitt," she ordered and caught a

glimpse of surprise on his face as she went to the grill. "I have to deal with melodrama and misery in every episode. I don't let it into my personal life. Fix yourself another drink, sit down and relax." Ariel set the chops on the grill, added some freshly ground pepper, then walked to the stereo. She switched on jazz, bluesy and mellow.

When she turned around he was still standing, looking at her. "I mean it," she told him. "I have a firm policy about worrying about what complications might come up. They're going to happen if you think about it or if you don't. So why waste your time?"

"Is it that easy for you?"

"Not always. Sometimes I have to work at it."

Thoughtfully, he drew out a cigarette. "We won't be good together," he said after he'd lit it. "I don't want anyone in my life."

"Anyone?" She shook her head. "You're too intelligent to believe a person can live without anyone. Don't you need friendship, companionship, love?"

Blowing out a stream of smoke, he tried to ignore the twinge the question brought him. He'd spent more than two years convincing himself he didn't. Why should he just now, so suddenly, realize the fruitlessness of it? "Each one of those things requires something in return that I no longer want to give."

"Want to give." Her gaze was thoughtful, her mouth unsmiling. "At least you're honest in your phrasing. The more I'm around you, the more I realize you never lie to anyone—but yourself."

"You haven't been around me enough to know who or what I am." He crushed out his cigarette and thrust his hands in his pockets. "And you're much better off that way."

"I or you?" she countered, then shook her head when he didn't answer. "You're letting her make a victim out of you," Ariel murmured. "I'm surprised."

His eyes narrowed; the green frosted. "Don't open closets unless you know what's inside, Ariel."

"Too safe." She preferred the simple anger she felt from him now. With a half laugh, she crossed to him and put her hands on his upper arms. "There's no fun in life without risks. I can't function without fun." Her fingers squeezed, gently. "Look, I enjoy being with you. Is that all right?"

"I'm not sure." She was pulling him in again, with the lightest of touches. "I'm not sure it is for either of us."

"Do yourself a favor," she suggested. "Don't worry about it for a few days and see what happens." Rising on her toes, she brushed his mouth in a gesture that was both friendly and intimate. "Why don't you fix that drink?" she added, grinning. "Because I'm burning the chops."

Chapter 5

"No, Griff, I won't discuss my marriage." Amanda picked up a delft-blue watering can and meticulously tended the plants in her office window. The sun, a product of the sweltering stage lights, poured through the glass.

"Amanda, you can't keep secrets in small towns. It's already common knowledge that you and Cameron aren't living together any longer."

Beneath the trim, tailored jacket, her shoulders stiffened. "Common knowledge or not, it's my business." Keeping her back to him, she examined a bloom on an African violet.

"You're losing weight, there are shadows under your eyes. Damn it, Mandy, I can't stand to see you this way."

She waited a beat, then turned slowly. "I'm fine. I'm capable of handling what needs to be handled."

Griff gave a short laugh. "Who'd know that better than I do?"

Something flared in her eyes, but her voice was cool and final. "I'm busy, Griff."

"Let me help you," he said with sudden, characteristic passion. "It's all I've ever wanted to do."

"Help?" Her voice chilled as she set down the can. "I don't need any help. Do you think I should confide in you, trust you after what you did to me?" As she tilted her head, the tiny sapphires in her ears glinted. She shifted on her mark. "The only difference between you and Cameron is that I let you tear up my life. I won't make the same mistake again."

Fury burst from him as he grabbed her arm. "You never asked me what Vikki was doing in my room. Not then, and not in all these months. You bounced back quick, Mandy, and ended up with another man's ring on your finger."

"It's still there," she said quietly. "So you'd better take your hands off me."

"Do you think that's going to stop me now that I know you don't love him?" Passion, rage, desire—all emanated from his eyes, his voice, his body. "I can look at you and see it," he went on before she could deny it. "I know what's inside you like no one else does. So handle it." He dragged his hands through her hair and dislodged pins. The camera dollied closer. "And handle this."

Pulling her against him, Griff crushed her mouth with his. She nearly tore away. Nearly. For a heartbeat, she was still. Amanda lifted her hands to his shoulders to push away, but clung instead. A soft, muffled moan escaped as passion flared. For a moment, they were locked together as they'd once been. Then, he dragged her away, keeping his hands tight on her arms. Desire and anger sparked between them. His tangible, hers restrained.

"You're not going to back away from me this time," he told her. "I'll wait, but I won't wait long. You come to me, Mandy. That's where you belong."

Releasing her, Griff stormed out of the office. Amanda lifted an unsteady hand to her lips and stared at the closed door.

"Cut."

Ariel marched around the prop wall of her office. "You ate those onions on purpose."

Jack tugged on her disheveled hair. "Just for you, sweetie."

"Swine."

"God, I love it when you call me names." Dramatically, Jack gathered her in his arms and bent her backward in an exaggerated dip. "Let me take you to bed and show you the true meaning of passion."

"Not until you chew a roll of breath mints, fella." Giving him a firm push, Ariel freed herself, then turned to her director. The furnace of stage lights had already been dimmed. "Neal, if that's it for today, I've got an appointment across town."

"Take off. See you at seven on Monday."

In the dressing room, Ariel stripped Amanda's elegant facade away and replaced it with slim cotton pants and a billowy, tailored man's shirt. After slipping on flat shoes she left the studio and went outside. There was a small group of fans waiting, hoping that someone recognizable would appear. They clustered around Amanda, autograph books in hand, as they chattered about the show and tossed questions.

"Are you going to go back with Griff?"

Ariel looked over at the sparkling-eyed teenager and grinned. "I don't know…he's awfully hard to resist."

"He's super! I mean, his eyes are just so *green*." She tucked her gum into the corner of her mouth and sighed. "I'd die if he looked at me the way he looks at you."

Ariel thought of another pair of green eyes and nearly sighed herself. "We'll have to wait to see what develops, won't we? I'm glad you like the show." Easing away from the crowd, she hailed a cab. The minute she gave the address, she slumped back against the seat.

She wasn't sure why she felt so tired. She supposed it was the prospect of the meeting that made her so bone weary. True, she hadn't been sleeping as well as was her habit, but she'd gone through wakeful phases before without any strain.

Booth. If Booth were the only thing on her mind, she could have dealt with it well enough. She hoped she would. But there was Scott.

The idea of confronting his grandparents didn't frighten her, but it did weary her. Ariel had spoken with them before. There was no reason to believe this session would be any different.

She remembered the way Scott had beamed and glowed at the zoo. Such a simple thing. Such a vital thing. The way he'd clung to her—it tore at her heart. If there were just some other way…

Closing her eyes, she sighed. She didn't believe there would be another way, not even with all her natural optimism. In the end, they'd come to a complicated, painful custody suit with Scott caught in the middle.

What was best? What was right? Ariel wanted someone to tell her, to advise and comfort her. But for the first time in her life she felt it impossible to confide in anyone. The more private she kept this affair, the less chance there was of Scott being hurt by it. She would just have to follow her instincts, and hope.

With her mind on a dozen other things, Ariel paid the cabbie and walked into the sleek steel building that housed her lawyer's offices. On the way from the lobby to the thirtieth floor, she gathered all her confidence together. This would be perhaps the last time she'd have the opportunity to speak with Scott's grandparents on an informal basis. She needed to give it her best shot.

The little tremor in her stomach wasn't so different from stage fright. Comfortable with it, Ariel walked into Bigby, Liebowitz and Feirson.

"Good afternoon, Ms. Kirkwood." The receptionist beamed a smile at Ariel and wondered if she could get away with a similar outfit. Not slim enough, she decided wistfully. Instead of looking dashing, she'd just look frumpy. "Mr. Bigby's expecting you."

"Hello, Marlene. How's the puppy working out?"

"Oh, he's so smart. My husband couldn't believe that a mutt could learn so many tricks. I really want to thank you for arranging it for me."

"I'm glad he's got a good home." She caught herself lacing her fingers together—a rare outward sign of tension. Deliberately Ariel dropped her hands to her sides as the receptionist rang through.

"Ms. Kirkwood's here, Mr. Bigby. Yes, sir." She rose as she replaced the receiver. "I'll take you back. If you have time before you leave, Ms. Kirkwood, my sister'd love your autograph. She never misses your show."

"I'd be happy to." Ariel's fingers groped for each other and she restrained them. *Save the nerves for later,* she told herself, *when you can afford them.* For once, she'd apply some of Amanda's steady calm to her personal life.

"Well, Ariel." The spindly, bearded man behind the massive desk rose as she entered. The room carried a vague scent of peppermint and polish. "Right on time."

"I never miss a cue." Ariel crossed the plush carpet with both hands extended. "You look good, Charlie."

"I feel good since you talked me into giving up smoking. Six months," he said with a grin. "Three days and—" he checked his watch "—four and a half hours."

She squeezed his hands. "Keep counting."

"We've got about fifteen minutes before the Andersons are due. Want some coffee?"

"Oh, yeah." On the words, Ariel sunk into a creamy leather chair.

Bigby pushed his intercom. "Would you bring some coffee back, Marlene? So…" He set down the receiver and folded his neat, ringless hands. "How're you holding up?"

"I'm a wreck, Charlie." She stretched out her legs and ordered herself to relax. First the toes, then the ankles, then all the way up. "You're practically the only one I can talk to about this. I'm not used to holding things in."

"If things go well you won't have to much longer."

She sent him a level look. "What chance do we have?"

"A fair one."

With a small sigh, Ariel shook her head. "Not good enough."

After a brief knock, Marlene entered with the coffee tray. "Cream and sugar, Ms. Kirkwood?"

"Yes, thank you." Ariel accepted the cup then immediately rose and began to pace. Maybe if she could turn some of the nerves to energy she wouldn't burst. Maybe. "Charlie, Scott needs me."

And you need him, he thought as he watched her. "Ariel, you're a responsible member of your community with a good reputation. You have a steady job with an excellent income, though it can and will be argued that it's not necessarily stable. You put your brother through college and have some sort of an involvement with every charity known to man." He saw her smile at that and was pleased. "You're young, but not a child. The Andersons are both in their midsixties. That should have some bearing on the outcome, and you'll have the emotion on your side."

"God, I hate to think of there being sides," she murmured. "There're sides in arguments, in wars. This can't be a war, Charlie. He's just a child."

"As difficult as it is, you're going to have to think practically about this."

With a nod, she sipped uninterestedly at her coffee. Practical. "But I'm single, and I'm an actress."

"There're pros and cons. This last-ditch meeting was your idea," he continued. "I don't like to see you get churned up this way."

"I have to try just once more before we find ourselves in court. The idea that Scotty might have to testify…"

"Just an easy talk with the judge in chambers, Ariel. It's not traumatic, I promise you."

"Not to you, maybe not to him, but to me…" She whirled around, her eyes dark with passion. "I'd give it up, Charlie. I swear I'd give it up this minute if I could believe he'd be happy with them. But when he looks at me…" Breaking off, she shook her head. Both hands were clenched on the coffee cup and she concentrated on relaxing them. "I know I'm being emotional about this, but it's the only way I've ever been able to judge what was right and what was wrong. If I look at it practically, I know they'll feed him and shelter him and educate him. But nurturing…" She turned to stare out of the window. "I keep coming back to the nurturing. Am I doing the best for him, Charlie? I just want to be sure."

For a moment, he sat fondling the gold pen on his desk. She asked hard questions. In the law, it wasn't a matter of best, but of justice. The two weren't always synonymous. "Ariel, you know the boy. At the risk of sounding very unlawyerlike, I say you have to do what your heart tells you."

Smiling, she turned back. "You say the right things. That's all I've ever been able to do." For a moment, she hesitated, then plunged. Since she was here for advice, she'd go all the way with it. "Charlie, if I told you I'd fallen in love with a man who thinks relationships are to be avoided at all costs and actresses are the least trustworthy individuals on the planet, what would you say?"

"I'd say it was typical of you. How long do you figure it'll take you to change his mind?"

Laughing, she dragged a hand through her hair. "Always the right thing," she said again.

"Sit down and drink your coffee, Ariel," he advised. "You're the one who says if something's meant to happen, it happens."

"When have I ever said anything so trite?" she demanded but did as he said. "All right, Charlie." She heaved a long sigh. "Do you want to give me the lecture on what I should expect and what I shouldn't say?"

"For what good it'll do." He toyed with the edge of

Ariel's file. "You'll meet the Andersons' lawyer, Basil Ford. He's very painstaking and very conservative. I've dealt with him before."

"Did you win?"

Bigby grinned at her as he leaned back in his chair. "I'd say we're about even. Since this is a voluntary, informal meeting, there won't be that much for either Ford or me to do. But if he asks you a question you shouldn't answer, I'll take care of it." Meticulously, Bigby settled the English bone-china cup back in its saucer. "Otherwise, say what you want, but don't elaborate more than necessary. Above all, don't lose your temper or your grip. If you want to yell or cry, wait until they've gone."

"You've gotten to know me very well," she murmured. "All right, I'll be calm and lucid." When the buzzer sounded on his desk, Ariel balled her hands into fists.

"Yes, Marlene, bring them in. And we'll need more coffee." He looked across at Ariel, measuring the strain in her eyes against the strength. "It's a discussion," he reminded her. "It's doubtful anything will be decided here today."

She nodded and concentrated on relaxing her hands.

When the door opened, Bigby rose, all joviality. "Basil, good to see you." He stretched his hand out to meet that of the erect, gray-suited man with thinning hair. "Mr. and Ms. Anderson, please have a seat. We'll have coffee in a moment. Basil Ford, Ariel Kirkwood."

Ariel nearly let out a tense giggle at the cocktail introduction. "Hello, Mr. Ford." She found his handshake firm and his gaze formidable.

"Ms. Kirkwood." He sat smoothly with his briefcase by his side.

"Hello, Mr. Anderson, Ms. Anderson."

Ariel received a nod from the woman and a brief formal handshake from her husband. Attractive people. Solid people. She'd always felt that from them—along with their rigidity. Both stood straight, a product of their military training. Anderson had retired from active service as a full colonel ten years before, and in her youth, his wife had been an Army nurse.

They'd met during the war, had served together and married. You could sense their closeness—the intimacy of thoughts and values. Perhaps, Ariel mused, that was why they had trouble seeing anyone else's viewpoint.

Together, the Andersons sat on a cushy two-seater sofa. Both were conservatively dressed: her iron-gray hair was skimmed back and his snowy white was cropped close. Feeling the waves of their disapproval, Ariel bit back a sigh. Instinct and experience told her she'd never get through to them on an emotional level.

While coffee was served, Bigby steered the conversation into generalities. The Andersons answered politely and ignored Ariel as much as possible. Because they spoke around her, she took care not to ask them any direct questions. She'd antagonize them soon enough.

She recognized the signal when Bigby sat behind his desk and folded his hands on the surface.

"I believe we can all agree that we have one mutual concern," he began. "Scott's welfare."

"That's why we're here," Ford said easily.

Bigby skimmed his gaze over Ford and concentrated on the Andersons. "Since that's the case, an informal meeting like this where we can exchange points of view and options should be to everyone's benefit."

"Naturally, my clients' main concern is their grandchild's well-being." Ford spoke in his beautiful orator's voice before he sipped his coffee. "Ms. Kirkwood's interest is understood, of course. As to the matter of custody, there's no question as to the rights and capability of Mr. and Ms. Anderson."

"Nor of Ms. Kirkwood's," Bigby put in mildly. "But it isn't rights and capabilities we're discussing today. It's the child himself. I'd like to make it clear that, at this point, we're not questioning your intentions or your ability to raise the child." He spoke to the Andersons again, skillfully bypassing his colleague. "The issue is what's best for Scott as an individual."

"My grandson," Anderson began in his deep, raspy voice, "belongs where he is. He's well fed, well dressed and well disciplined. His upbringing will have a sense of order. He'll be sent to the best schools available."

"What about well loved?" Ariel blurted out before she could stop herself. "What money can't buy…" Leaning forward she focused her attention on Scott's grandmother. "Will he be well loved?"

"An abstract question, Ms. Kirkwood," Ford put in briskly. "If we could—"

"No, it isn't," Ariel interrupted, sparing him a glance before she turned back to the Andersons. "There's nothing more solid than love. Nothing more easily given or withheld. Will you hold him at night if he's frightened of shadows? Will you understand how important it is to pretend that he's protecting you? Will you always listen when he needs to talk?"

"He won't be coddled if that's what you mean." Anderson set down his coffee and rested a hand on one knee. "A child's values are molded early. These fantasies—that you encourage—aren't healthy. I have no intention of allowing my grandson to live in a dreamworld."

"A dreamworld." Ariel stared at him and saw a solid rock wall of resistance. "Mr. Anderson, Scott has a beautiful imagination. He's full of life, and visions."

"Visions." Anderson's lips thinned. "Visions will do nothing but make him look for what isn't there, expect what he can't have. The boy needs a firm basis in reality. In what *is*. You make your living from pretending, Ms. Kirkwood. My grandson won't live his life in a storybook."

"There're twenty-four hours in every day, Mr. Anderson. Isn't there enough reality in that so we can put a small portion of time aside for wishing? All children need to believe in wishes, especially Scott after so much has been taken away from him. Please…" Her gaze shifted to the stiff-backed woman on the sofa. "You've known grief. Scott lost the two people in the world who meant love and security and normality. All of those things have to be given back to him."

"By you?" Ms. Anderson sat very still, her eyes remained very level. In them Ariel saw remnants of pain. "My daughter's child will be raised by me."

"Ms. Kirkwood." Ford interrupted smoothly, then crossed his legs. "To touch on more practical matters, I'm aware that you currently have a key role in a— Daytime drama, I believe is the word. This equals a regular job with a steady income. But to be down-to-earth for a moment, it's habitual for these things to change. How would you support a child if your income was interrupted?"

"My income won't be interrupted." Bigby caught her

eye, so with an effort Ariel held on to her temper. "I'm under contract. I'm also signed to do a film with P. B. Marshell." Noticing the flicker of speculation, Ariel blessed fate for throwing the part her way.

"That's very impressive," Ford told her. "However, I'm sure you'd be the first to admit that your profession is renowned for its ups and downs."

"If we're talking financial stablity, Mr. Ford, I assure you that I'm capable of giving Scott all the material requirements necessary. If my career should take a downswing, I'd simply supplement it. I've experience in both the retail and the restaurant business." A half smile teased her mouth as she thought of her days selling perfume and powder, and waiting tables. Oh, yes, *experience* was the right word. "But I can't believe any of us would put a bank statement first when we're discussing a child." It was said calmly, with only a hint of disdain.

"I'm sure we all agree that the child's monetary well-being is of primary importance," Bigby put in. The subtle tone of his voice was his warning to Ariel. "There's no question that both the Andersons and my client are capable of providing Scott with food, shelter, education, etc."

"There's also the matter of marital status." Ford stroked a long finger down the side of his nose. "As a single woman, a single professional woman, Ms. Kirkwood, just how much time would you be able to spare for Scott?"

"Whatever he needs," Ariel said simply. "I recognize my priorities, Mr. Ford."

"Perhaps." He nodded, resting a hand on the arm of his chair. "And perhaps you haven't thought this through completely. Having never raised a child, you might not be fully aware of the time involved. You have an active social life, Ms. Kirkwood."

His words and tone were mild, his meaning clear. Any other time, in any other place, she would have been amused. "Not as active as it reads in print, Mr. Ford."

Again, he nodded. "You're also a young woman, attractive. I'm sure it's reasonable to assume that marriage is highly likely at some time in the future. Have you considered how a potential husband might feel about the responsibility of raising someone else's child?"

"No." Her fingers laced together. "If I loved a man enough to marry him, he'd accept Scott as part of me, of my life. Otherwise, he wouldn't be the kind of man I'd love."

"If you had to make a choice—"

"Basil." Bigby held up a hand, and though he smiled, his eyes were hard. "We shouldn't get bogged down in this sort of speculation. No one expects us to solve this custody issue here today. What we want is to get a clear picture of everyone's feelings. What your clients and mine want for Scott."

"His well-being," Anderson said tersely.

"His happiness," Ariel murmured. "I want to believe they're the same thing."

"You're no different from your brother." Anderson's voice was sharp and low, like the final snap of a whip. "Happiness. He preached happiness at all costs to my daughter until she tossed aside all her responsibilities, her education, her values. Pregnant at eighteen, married to a penniless student who put more effort into flying a kite than keeping a decent job."

Ariel's mouth trembled open as the pain struck. No, she wouldn't waste her breath defending her brother.

He needed no defense. "They loved each other," she said instead.

"Loved each other." Color rose in Anderson's cheeks, the first and only sign of emotion Ariel had seen from him. "Can you honestly believe that's enough?"

"Yes. They were happy together. They had a beautiful child together. They had dreams together." Ariel swallowed as the urge to weep pounded at her. "Some people never have that much."

"Barbara would still be alive if we'd kept her away from him."

Ariel looked over at the older woman and saw more than pain now. The strong, bony hands shook slightly, the voice broke. It was a combination of grief and fury that Ariel recognized and understood. "Jeremy's gone, too, Ms. Anderson," she said quietly. "But Scott's here."

"He killed my daughter." The woman's eyes glowed against a skin gone abruptly pale.

"Oh, no." Ariel reached out, shocked by the words, drawn by the pain. "Ms. Anderson, Jeremy adored Barbara. He'd never have done anything to hurt her."

"He took her up in that plane. Barbara had no business being up in one of those small planes. She wouldn't have been if he hadn't taken her."

"Ms. Anderson, I know how you feel—"

She jerked away from Ariel's offer of comfort, her breath suddenly coming fast and shallow. "Don't you tell me you know how I feel. She was my only child. My only child." Rising, she sent Ariel an icy stare that shimmered with tears. "I won't discuss Barbara with you, or Barbara's son." She walked from the office in quick, controlled steps that were silent on the carpet.

"I won't have you upsetting my wife." Mr. Anderson stood, erect and unyielding. "We've known nothing but misery since the first time we heard the name Kirkwood."

Though her knees had begun to shake, Ariel rose to face him. "Scott's name is Kirkwood, Mr. Anderson."

Without a word, he turned and strode out of the room.

"My clients are understandably emotional on this issue." Ford's voice was so calm Ariel barely heard it. With the slightest nod of agreement, she wandered to stare out the window.

She didn't register the subdued conversation the attorneys carried on behind her. Instead, she concentrated on the flow of traffic she could see but not quite hear from thirty floors below. She wanted to be down there, surrounded by cars and buses and people.

Strange how she'd nearly convinced herself she was resigned to her brother's death. Now, the helpless anger washed over her again until she could have screamed with it. Screamed just one word. *Why?*

"Ariel." Bigby put a hand on her shoulder and repeated her name before Ariel turned her head. Ford and his clients had left. "Come sit down."

She lifted a hand to his. "No, I'm all right."

"Like hell you are."

With a half laugh, she rested her forehead against the glass. "I will be in a minute. Why is it, Charlie, I never believe how hard or how ugly things can be until they happen? And even then— Even then I can't quite understand it."

"Because you look for the best. It's a beautiful talent of yours."

"Or an escape mechanism," she murmured.

"Don't start coming down on yourself, Ariel." His voice was sharper then he'd intended, but he had the satisfaction of seeing her shoulders straighten. "Another of your talents is being able to pull in other people's emotions. Don't do it with the Andersons."

Letting out a long sigh, she continued to stare down to the street. "They're hurting. I wish there was a way we could share the grief instead of hurling it at one other. But there's nothing I can do about them," she whispered and closed her eyes briefly, tightly. "Charlie, Scott doesn't belong with them. He's all I care about. Not once, not one single time did either of them call him by name. He was always the boy, or my grandchild, never Scott. It's as though they can't give him his own identity, maybe because it's too close to Jeremy's." For an extra moment she rested her palms against the window ledge. "I only want what's right for Scott—even if it's not me."

"It's going to go to court, Ariel, and it's going to be very, very hard on you."

"You've explained all that before. It doesn't matter."

"I can't give you any guarantees on the outcome."

She moistened her lips and turned to face him. "I understand that, too. I have to believe that whatever happens will be what's best for Scott. If I lose, I was meant to lose."

"At the risk of being completely unprofessional—" he touched the tips of her hair "—what about what's best for you?"

With a smile, she cupped his face in her hand and kissed his cheek. "I'm a survivor, Charlie, and a whole hell of a lot tougher than I look. Let's worry about Scott."

He was capable of worrying about more than one

thing at a time, and she was still pale, her eyes still a bit too bright. "Let me buy you a drink."

Ariel rubbed her knuckles against his beard. "I'm fine," she said definitely. "And you're busy." Turning, she picked up her purse. Her stomach was quivering. All she wanted to do was to get out in the air and clear her head. "I just need to walk for a bit," she said half to herself. "After I think it all the way through again I'll feel better."

At the door she paused and looked back. Bigby was still standing by the window, a frown of concern on his face. "Can you tell me we have a chance of winning?"

"Yes, I can tell you that. I wish I could tell you more."

Shaking her head, Ariel pulled open the door. "It's enough. It has to be enough."

Chapter 6

Booth considered taking everything he'd written that day and ditching it. That's what sensible people did with garbage. Leaning back in his chair, he scowled at the half-typed sheet staring back at him, and at the stack of completed pages beside his machine. Then again, tomorrow it might not seem quite so much like garbage and he could salvage something.

He couldn't remember the last time he'd hit a wall like this in his work. It was like carving words into granite—slow, laborious, and the finished product was never perfectly clear and sharp. You got sweaty, your muscles and eyes ached, and you barely made a dent. He'd given the script ten hours that day, and perhaps half of that with his full concentration. It was out of character. It was frustrating.

It was Ariel.

What the hell was he going to do about it? Booth ran his hands over his face with a weariness that came from lack of production rather than lack of energy. There'd never been a woman he couldn't block out of his mind for long periods of time—even Liz at the height of their disastrous marriage. But this woman… With a sound of annoyance, Booth pushed away from the typewriter. This woman was breaking all the rules. His rules—the ones he'd formed for personal survival.

The worst of it was he just wanted to be with her. Just to see her smile, hear her laugh, listen to her talk about something that didn't have to make sense.

And the hardest of it was the desire. It shifted and rippled continually under the surface of his thoughts. He had the blessing-curse of a writer's imagination. No effort was needed for Booth to feel the way her skin would heat under his hands, the way her mouth would give and take. And it took no effort to project mentally how she could foul up his life.

Because they'd be working together, he could only avoid her so much. Making love with her was inevitable—so inevitable he knew he'd have to weigh the consequences. But for now, with his rooms quiet around him and thoughts of Ariel crowding his mind, Booth couldn't think beyond having her. Prices always had to be paid… Who would know that better than he?

Glancing down at his work, Booth admitted that he was already paying. His writing was suffering because he couldn't control his concentration. His pace, usually smooth, was erratic and choppy. What he was producing lacked the polish so integral to his style.

Too often, he caught himself staring into space—something writers do habitually. But it wasn't his characters who worked in his mind. Too often, he found himself awake before dawn after a restless night. But it wasn't his plot that kept him from sleep.

It was Ariel.

He thought of her too much, too exclusively for comfort. And he was a man who hoarded his comfort. His work was always, had always been, of paramount importance to him. He intended it to continue to be. Yet he was allowing someone to interfere, intrude.

Allowing? Booth shook his head as he lit a cigarette. He was a man of words, of shades of meanings, and knew that wasn't the proper one. He hadn't allowed Ariel into his mind—she'd invaded it.

The smoke seared his throat. Too many cigarettes, he admitted as he took another drag. Too many long days and nights. He was pushing it—and there were moments, a few scattered moments when he took the time to wonder why.

Ambition wasn't the issue. Not if ambition equaled the quest for glory and money. Glory had never concerned him, and money had never been a prime motivation. Success perhaps, in that he had always sought then insisted on quality when anything was associated with his name. But it was more a matter of obsession— that was what his writing had been since he'd first put pen to paper.

When a man had one obsession, it was easy to have two. Booth stared at the half-typed page and thought of Ariel.

The doorbell rang twice before he roused himself to answer it. If his work had been flowing at all, he would have ignored it completely. Interruptions, he thought ruefully as he left the littered desk behind, sometimes had their advantages.

"Hi." Ariel smiled at him and kept her hands in her pockets. It was the only way she could keep them from lacing together. "I know I should've called, but I was walking and took the chance that you wouldn't be frantically writing some monumental scene." *You're babbling,* she warned herself and clenched both hands.

"I haven't written a monumental scene in hours." He studied her a moment, perceptive enough to know that beneath the smile and animated voice there was trouble. A week before, perhaps even days before, he'd have made an excuse and shut her out. "Come in."

"I must've caught you at a good time," Ariel commented as she crossed the threshold. "Otherwise you'd've growled at me. Were you working?"

"No, I'd stopped." She looked ready to burst, he mused. The casualness, the glib remarks didn't mask the outpouring of emotion. It showed in her eyes, in her movements. A quick glance showed him that her hands were fists in her pockets. Tension? One didn't associate the word with her. He wanted to touch her, to soothe, and had to remind himself that he didn't need anyone else's problems. "Want a drink?"

"No— Yes," she amended. Perhaps it would calm her more than the two-hour walk had done. "Whatever's handy. It's a beautiful day." Ariel paced to the window and found herself reminded too much of standing in Bigby's office. She turned her back on the view. "Warm. Flowers are everywhere. Have you been out?"

"No." He handed her a dry vermouth without offering her a chair. In this mood he knew she'd never sit still.

"Oh, you shouldn't miss it. Perfect days're rare." She drank, then waited for her muscles to loosen. "I was going to walk through the park, then found myself here."

He waited a moment as she stared down into her glass. "Why?"

Slowly, Ariel lifted her eyes to his. "I needed to be with someone—it turned out to be you. Do you mind?"

He should have. God knows he wanted to. "No." Without thinking, Booth took a step closer—physically, emotionally. "Do you want to tell me about it?"

"Yes." The word came out on a sigh. "But I can't." Turning away, she set down her glass. She wasn't going to level. Why had she been so sure she would? "Booth, it isn't often I can't handle things or find myself so scared that running away looks like the best out. When it happens, I need someone."

He was touching her hair before he could stop himself, was turning her to face him before he'd weighed the pros and cons. And he was holding her before either of them could be surprised by the simplicity of it.

Ariel clung as relief flowed over her. He was strong—strong enough to accept her strength and understand the moments of weakness. She needed that very basic human support, without question, without demands. His chest was hard and firm against her. Over her back his hands ran gently. He said nothing. For the first time in hours, Ariel felt her balance return. Kindness gave her hope; she was a woman who'd always been able to survive on that alone.

What's troubling her, Booth wondered. He could feel the panic in the way her hands gripped him. Even when he felt her begin to relax he remembered that first frantic grip. Her work, he thought. Or something more personal? Either way, it had nothing to do with him. And yet... While she was soft and vulnerable in his arms he felt it had everything to do with him.

He should step back. His lips brushed through her hair as he breathed in her fragrance. It was never safe to lower the wall. His lips skimmed along her temple.

"I want to help you." The words ran through his mind and spilled out before he was aware of them.

Ariel's arms tightened around him. That phrase meant more, infinitely more, than I love you. Without knowing it, he'd just given her everything she needed. "You have." She tilted her head back so that she could see his face. "You are."

Lifting a hand, she ran her fingers over the long firm bones in his face, over the taut skin roughened by a day's growth of beard. Love was something that moved in her too strongly to be ignored. She needed to share it, if not verbally, then by touch.

Softly, slowly, she closed the distance and brushed his lips with hers. Her lids lowered, but through her lashes she watched his eyes as he watched hers. The intensity in his never altered. Ariel knew he was absorbing her mood, and testing it.

It was he who shifted the angle, without increasing the pressure. Easily he toyed with her mouth, nipping into the softness of her bottom lip, tracing the shape with just the tip of his tongue until the flutter in her stomach spread to her chest. He needed to draw in the sensation of her as a woman, as an individual. He wanted to know her physically; he needed to understand the subtleties of her mind. As she felt her body give, her mind yield, Ariel wondered how it was he didn't hear the love shouting out of her.

He was struck by the emotion that raced from her. He'd never held a woman capable of such feeling, or one who, by possessing it, demanded it in return. It wasn't a simple matter of response. Even as his senses began to swim, Booth understood that. He wanted to give to her. And though he wanted, he knew he couldn't. Risks were for the foolish, and he couldn't afford to play the fool a second time.

Compassion, however, touched off compassion. If nothing else, he could give her a few hours' relief from whatever plagued her mind. He ran his hands up her arms for the sheer pleasure of it. "How nice a day is it?" he asked.

Ariel smiled. Her fingers were still on his face, her lips only inches from his. "It's spectacular."

"Let's go out." Booth paused only long enough to take her hand before he headed for the door.

"Thank you." Ariel touched her head briefly to his shoulder in one more simple show of affection he wasn't accustomed to. It warmed him—and cautioned him.

"What for?"

"For not asking questions." Ariel stepped into the elevator, leaned back against the wall and sighed.

"I generally stay out of other people's business."

"Do you?" She opened her eyes and the smile lingered. "I don't. I'm an inveterate meddler—most of us are. We all like to get inside other people. You just do it more subtly than most."

Booth shrugged as the elevator reached lobby level. "It's not personal."

Ariel laughed as she stepped out. Swinging her purse

over her shoulder, she moved in her habitual quick step. "Oh, yes, it is."

He stopped a moment and met the humor in her eyes. "Yes," he admitted. "It is. But then, as a writer I can observe, dissect, steal other people's thoughts and feelings without having to get involved enough to advise or comfort or even sympathize."

"You're too hard on yourself, Booth," Ariel murmured. "Much too hard."

His brow quirked in puzzlement. Of all the things he'd ever been accused of, that wasn't one of them. "I'm a realist."

"On one level. On another you're a dreamer. All writers are dreamers on some level—the same way all actors are children on one. It has nothing to do with how clever you are, how practical, how smart. It goes with the job." She stepped out into the warmth and the sun. "I like being a child, and you like being a dreamer. You just don't like to admit it."

Annoyance. He should've felt annoyance but felt pleasure instead. As long as he could remember, no one else had ever understood him. As long as he could remember, he'd never cared. "You've convinced yourself you know me very well."

"No, but I've made a few scratches in the surface." She sent him a saucy look. "And you've a very tough surface."

"And yours is very thin." Unexpectedly he cupped her face in his hand for a thorough study. His fingers were firm, as if he expected resistance and would ignore it. "Or seems to be." How could he be sure, he wondered. How could one person ever be sure of another?

Ariel was too used to being examined, and already

too used to Booth to be disconcerted. "There's little underneath that doesn't show through."

"Perhaps that's why you're a good actress," he mused. "You absorb the character easily. How much is you, and how much is the role?"

He was far from ready to trust, she realized when he dropped his hand. "I can't answer that. Maybe when the film's over, you'll be able to."

He inclined his head in acknowledgment. It was a good answer—perhaps the best answer. "You wanted to walk in the park."

Ariel tucked her arm companionably through his. "Yeah. I'll buy you an ice cream."

Booth turned his head as they walked. "What flavor?"

"Anything but vanilla," Ariel said expansively. "There's nothing remotely vanilla about today."

She was right, Booth decided. It was a spectacular day. The grass was green, the flowers vivid and pungent. He could smell the park smells. Peanuts and pigeons. Enthusiastic joggers pumped by in colorful sweatbands and running shorts, streaks of sweat down their backs.

Spring would soon give way to early summer. The trees were full, the leaves a hardy shade rather than the tender hue they'd been only weeks before. Shade spread in invitation while the sun baked the benches and paths. He knew Ariel would choose the sun. And he wondered, as he strolled along beside her, why he'd gone so long without seeking it himself.

As Ariel bit into an ice cream confection coated with chocolate and nuts, she thought of Scott. But this time, the apprehension was gone. She'd only needed to lean on someone for a moment, draw on someone else's emotional strength, to have her faith return. Her head was clear again, her nerves gone. With a laugh, she turned into Booth's arms and kissed him hard.

"Ice cream does that to me." She was still laughing as she dropped onto a swing. "And sunshine." She leaned way back and kicked her feet to give herself momentum. The tips of her hair nearly skimmed the ground. It was pale, exquisitely pale in the slanting sun. As it fell back, it left her face unframed and stunning. Her skin was flushed with color as she pushed off again and let herself glide.

"You seem to be an expert." Booth leaned against the frame of the swing as her legs flashed by him.

"Absolutely. Want to join me?"

"I'll just watch."

"It's one of your best things." Ariel threw out her legs again for more height and enjoyed the thrill that swept through her stomach. "When's the last time you were on one of these?"

A memory surged through his mind—of himself at five or six and his primly uniformed, round-faced nanny. She'd pushed him on a swing while he'd squealed and demanded to go higher. At the time he hadn't believed there was any more to life than that rushing pendulum ride. Abruptly, he appreciated Ariel's claim that she enjoyed being a child.

"A hundred years ago," he murmured.

"Too long." Skimming her feet on the ground, she slowed the swing. "Get on with me." She blew the hair out of her eyes and grinned at his blank expression. "You can stand, one foot on either side of me. It's sturdy enough—if you are," she added with just enough of a challenge in the tone to earn a scowl.

"Practicing your psychiatry?"

Her grin only widened. "Is it working?"

She was laughing at him again, and knowing it, Booth took the bait. "Apparently." He stepped behind her to grab the chain with his hands. "How high do you want to go?"

Ariel tipped back her head to give him an upside-down smile. "As high as I can."

"No crying uncle," Booth warned as he began to push her.

"Ha." Ariel tossed back her hair and shifted her grip. "Fat chance, DeWitt."

She felt him jump nimbly onto the swing as they began to fly, then threw her body into it until the rhythm steadied. The sky tilted over her, blue and dusted with clouds. The ground swayed, brown and green. She rested her head against a firm, muscled thigh and let the sensations carry her.

Grass. She could smell it, sun drenched and trampled, mixed with the dusty scent of dry earth. Children's laughter, cooing pigeons, traffic—Ariel could hear each separate sound individually and as a mixture.

The air tasted of spring—sweet, light. An image of a watermelon ran through her mind. Yes, that was what she thought of as the breeze fluttered over her cheeks. But overall, most of all, it was Booth who played with her senses. It was him she felt firmly against her back, his quiet breathing she heard beneath all the other sounds. She could smell him—salt and soap and tobacco. She had only to shift the angle of her head to see his strong, capable hands around the chain of the child's swing. Ariel closed her eyes and absorbed it all. It was like coming home. Content, she slid her hands higher on the chain so that they brushed his. The contact, warm flesh to warm flesh, was enough.

He'd forgotten what it was like to do something for no reason. And by forgetting it, Booth had forgotten the purity of pleasure. He felt it now, without the intellectual justifications he so often restricted himself with. Because he understood that freedom brought vulnerability, he'd doled it out to himself miserly. Only on those rare occasions when he was completely alone, away from responsibilities and his work, had he allowed his heart and mind to drift. Now, it happened so spontaneously he hardly realized it. Bypassing the dangers of relaxation, Booth enjoyed the ride.

"Higher!" Ariel demanded on a breathless laugh as she leaned into the arch. "Much higher!"

"Much higher and you'll land on your nose."

Her sound of pleasure rippled over the air. "Not me. I land on my feet. Higher, Booth!"

When she turned her head up to laugh into his face, he lost himself in her. Beauty—it was there, but not the cool, distant beauty he saw on camera. Looking at her now, he saw nothing of his Rae, nothing of her Amanda. There was only Ariel. For the first time in longer than he cared to remember, he felt a twinge of hope. It scared the hell out of him.

"Faster!" she shouted, not giving him any time to dwell on what was happening inside him. Her laughter was infectious, as was her enthusiasm. They soared together until his arms ached. When the swing began to slow, she leaped from it and left him wobbling.

"Oh, that was wonderful." Still laughing, Ariel

turned in a circle, arms wide. "Now I'm starving. Absolutely starving."

"You just had ice cream." Booth leaped off the swing to find himself breathless and his blood pumping.

"Not good enough." Ariel whirled around to him and linked her hands behind his head. "I need a hot dog—really need a hot dog with everything."

"A hot dog." Because it seemed so natural, he bent to kiss her. Her mouth was warm, the lips curved. "Do you know what they put in those things?"

"No. And I don't want to. I want to stuff myself with whatever nasty stuff it has in it and feel wonderful."

Booth ran his hands down her sides. "You do feel wonderful."

Her smile changed, softened. "That's about the nicest thing you've ever said to me. Kiss me again, right here, while I'm still flying."

Booth drew her closer as his lips tasted hers. Fleetingly he wondered why the gentle kiss moved him equally as much as the passion had yet somehow differently. He wanted her. And along with her body he wanted that energy, that verve, the joie de vivre. He wanted to explore and measure it, and to test it for its genuineness. Booth was still far from sure that anyone in the world he knew could be quite so real. And yet, he was beginning to want to believe it.

Drawing her away he watched her lashes flutter up, her lips curve. But he remembered that sense of panic he'd felt from her when he'd first opened his door. If her emotions were as vibrant as they seemed, she wouldn't be limited to joy and vivacity.

"A hot dog," he repeated and speculated on how

much he would learn of her and how long it would take. "It's your stomach, but I'll spring for it."

"I knew you could be a sport, Booth." She slipped her arm around his waist as they walked. "I just might have two."

"Masochistic tendencies run in your family?"

"No, just gluttony. Tell me about yours."

"I don't have masochistic tendencies."

"Your family," she corrected, chuckling. "They must be very proud of you."

His brow lifted while a ghost of a smile played around his mouth. "That depends on your point of view. I was supposed to follow family tradition and go into law. Throughout most of my twenties I was the black sheep."

"Is that so?" Tilting her head, she studied him with fresh interest. "I can't imagine it. I've always had a fondness for black sheep."

"I would've made book on it," Booth said dryly. "But one might say I've been accepted back into the fold in the past few years."

"It was the Pulitzer that did it."

"The Oscar didn't hurt," Booth admitted, seeing the humor in something he'd barely noticed before. "But the Pulitzer had more clout with the DeWitts of Philadelphia."

Ariel scented the hot dog stand and guided him toward it. "You'll be adding an Emmy to the list next year."

He pulled out his wallet as Ariel leaned over the stand and breathed deeply. "You're very confident."

"It's the best way to be. Are you having one?"

The scent was too good to resist. When had he eaten

last? What had he eaten? Booth shrugged the thoughts way. "I suppose."

Ariel grinned and held up two fingers to the concessionaire. When hers was in its bun she began to go through the condiments one at a time. "You know, Booth—" she piled on relish "—*The Rebellion* was brilliant, clean, hard-hitting, exquisite characterizations, but it wasn't as entertaining as your *Misty Tuesday*."

Booth watched her take the first hefty bite. "My purpose in writing isn't always to entertain."

"No, I understand that." Ariel chewed thoughtfully, then accepted the soda Booth offered her. "It's just my personal preference. That's why I'm in the profession. I want to be entertained, and I need to entertain."

He added a conservative line of mustard to his hot dog. "That's why you've been satisfied with daytime drama."

She shot him a look as they began to walk again. "Don't get snide. Quality entertainment's the core of it. If I was handy juggling plates and riding a unicycle, that's what I'd do."

After the first bite, Booth realized the hot dog was the best thing he'd eaten in a week, perhaps in months. "You have a tremendous talent," he told her, but didn't notice the surprised lift of her brow at the ease of the compliment. "It's difficult for me to understand why you aren't doing major films or theater. A series, even a weekly series is dragging, backbreaking work. Being a major character in a show that airs five days a week has to be exhausting, impossible and frustrating."

"Exactly why I do it." She licked mustard from her thumb. "I was raised right here in Manhattan. The pace's in my blood. Have you ever considered why L.A. and New York are on opposite ends of the continent?"

"A lucky geographical accident."

"Fate," Ariel corrected. "Both might be towns where show business is of top importance, but no two cities could have more opposing paces. I'd go crazy in California—mellow isn't my speed. I like doing the soap because it's a daily challenge, it keeps me sharp. And when there's the time and the opportunity, I like doing things like *Streetcar*. But…" She finished off her hot dog with a sigh. "Doing the same play night after night becomes too easy, and you get too comfortable."

He drank down cola—a flavor he'd nearly forgotten. "You've been playing the same character for five years."

"Not the same thing." She crunched an ice cube and enjoyed the shock of cold. "Soaps're full of surprises. You never know what kind of angle they're going to throw at you to pump up ratings or lead in a fresh story line." She scooted around a middle-aged matron walking a poodle. "Right now Amanda's facing a crumbling marriage and a personal betrayal, the possibility of an abortion and a rekindling of an old affair. Not dull stuff. And though it's top secret, I'll tell you she's going to work with the police on a profile of the Trader's Bend Ripper."

"The what?"

"As in Son of Jack the Ripper," she said mildly. "Her former lover Griff's the number-one suspect."

"Doesn't it ever bother you that so much melodrama goes on in a small town with four or five connecting families?"

She stopped to look at him. "Do you know your Coleridge?"

"Passably."

"'The willing suspension of disbelief.'" Ariel crumbled her napkin, then tossed both it and her empty cup into a trash can. "It's all that's necessary to get along in this world. Believe it might happen, it could happen. Plausibility's all that's necessary. As a writer, you should know that."

"Perhaps I should. I've always leaned more toward reality."

"If it works for you." The lift of her shoulders seemed to indicate that all was accepted. "But sometimes it's easier to believe in coincidence, or magic or simple luck. Straight reality without any detours is a very hard road."

"I've had a few detours," he murmured. It occurred to him that Ariel Kirkwood had already led him off the paved road he'd adhered to for years. Booth began to wonder just where her twisting direction would lead them. Lost in thought, he didn't notice that they were in front of his building until she stopped. His work was waiting, his privacy, his solitude. He wanted none of it.

"Come up with me."

The request was simple, the meaning clear. And her need was huge. Shaking her head, Ariel touched the hair that had fallen over his forehead. "No, it's best that I don't."

He took her hand before she could drop it back to her side. "Why? I want you, you want me."

If it were only so simple, she thought as the desire to love him grew and grew. But she knew, instinctively, that it wouldn't be simple, not for either of them once begun. For him there was too much distrust, for her too many vulnerabilities.

"Yes, I want you." Ariel saw the change in his eyes

and knew it would be much more difficult to walk away than to go with him. "And if I came upstairs, we'd make love. Neither of us is ready for that, Booth, not with each other."

"If it's a game you're playing to make me want you more, it's hardly necessary."

She drew her hand from his and stood on her own. "I like to play games," she said quietly. "And I'm very good at most of them. Not this kind."

Pulling out a cigarette, he lit it with a snap of his lighter. "I've no patience for the wine and candlelight routine, Ariel."

He saw the humor light in her eyes and could have cursed her. "How lucky that I don't have a need for them." Putting her hands on his shoulders, she leaned forward and kissed him. "Think of me," she requested and turned quickly to walk away.

As he stared after her, Booth knew he'd think of little else.

Chapter 7

It was going to be hard work, with long days, short nights and constant demands on both the body and the mind. Ariel was going to love every minute of it.

The producers of the soap were cooperating fully with Marshell; the network strategy was to everyone's advantage. The word, the big word, was always *ratings*. But it was Ariel who had to squeeze in the time for both projects, and Ariel who had to learn hundreds of pages of script as Amanda and as Rae.

Under different circumstances they might have simply written around her for a few weeks on *Our Lives, Our Loves,* but with Amanda and Griff's relationship heating up and the Ripper on the prowl, it wasn't possible. Amanda had a key role in too many vital scenes. So instead, Ariel had to shoot a backbreaking number of those scenes in a short period of time. This would give her three straight weeks to concentrate exclusively on the film. If that project ran behind schedule, she'd have to compensate by dividing her time and energies between Amanda and Rae.

The idea of eighteen-hour days and 5:00 a.m. calls couldn't dull her enthusiasm. The pace, merciless as it was, was almost natural to her in any case. And it helped keep her mind off the custody trial, which was set for the following month.

And there was Booth. Even the idea of working with him excited her. The daily contact would be stimulating. The professional competition and cooperation would keep her sharp. The preproduction stages had shown her that Booth would be as intimately involved with the film as any member of the cast and crew—and that he had unquestioned authority.

Throughout the sometimes hysterical meetings, he'd remained calm and had said little. But when he spoke, he was rarely questioned. It wasn't a matter of arrogance or overbearing, as Ariel saw it. Booth DeWitt simply didn't comment unless he knew he was right.

Perhaps, if it was meant to be, they'd move closer to each other as the film progressed. Emotion. It was what she wanted to give him, and what she needed from him. Time. She knew it was a major factor in whatever happened between them. Trust. This above all was needed—and this, above all, was missing.

There were times during the preproduction stages of the filming that Ariel felt Booth watching her too objectively, and distancing himself from her too successfully.

Ariel found herself at an impasse. The more skillfully she played Rae, the more firmly Booth stepped back from her. She understood it, and was helpless to change it.

The set was elegant, the lighting low and seductive. Across a small rococo table, Rae and Phil shared lobster bisque and champagne. Ariel's costume was clinging midnight silk. Diamonds and sapphires winked at her ears and throat. An armed guard in the studio attested to the fact that paste wasn't used on a Marshell production.

The intimate late-night supper was actually taking place at 8:00 a.m. in the presence of a full crew. Sipping lukewarm ginger ale from a tulip glass, Ariel gave a husky laugh and leaned closer to Jack.

She knew what was needed here—sex, raw and primitive under a thin sheen of sophistication. It would have to leap onto the screen with a gesture, a look, a smile, rather than through dialogue. She was playing a role within a role. Rae was her character, and Rae was never without a mask. Tonight, she would project a warmth, a soft femininity that was no more than a facade. It was Ariel's job to show both this, and the skill with which Rae played the part. If the actress Ariel portrayed wasn't clever, the impact on the character of Phil would waver. The connection between the two was vital. They fed each other, and by doing so, the entire story.

Rae wanted Phil, and the viewer had to know that she wanted him physically nearly as much as she wanted the connections he could bring her professionally. To win him, she had to be what he wanted. Ambition and skill were a deadly combination when added to beauty. Rae had all three and the capacity to use them. It was Ariel's job to show the duality of her nature, but to show it subtly.

The scene would end in the bedroom; that portion of the film would be shot at a different time. Now, the tension and the sexuality had to be heightened to a point where both Phil and the audience were completely seduced.

"Cut!"

Chuck ran a hand over the back of his neck and lapsed into silence. Both the actors and crew recognized the gesture from their director and remained silent and alert. The scene wasn't pleasing him, and he was working out why. Keyed up, Ariel didn't allow the tension to drain out of her. She needed the nerves to maintain the image of Rae. The sight of the ginger ale and the scent of the food in front of her made her stomach roll uneasily. They were already on the fourth take. Objectively, she watched her glass being refilled, her plate replaced. When this was over, she thought, she'd never even look at a glass of ginger ale again.

"Disgusting, isn't it?"

Glancing over, Ariel saw Jack Rohrer grimace at her. She locked Rae in a compartment of her brain before she grinned at him. "I've never wanted a cup of coffee and a bagel so much in my life."

"Please." He leaned back from the table. "Don't mention real food."

"More feline," Chuck said abruptly and focused on Ariel. "That's how I see Rae—a sleek black cat with manicured claws."

Ariel smiled at the image. Yes, that was Rae.

"When you say the line, 'One night won't be enough, you make me greedy,' you should practically purr it."

Ariel nodded while she flexed her hands. Yes, Rae would purr that line, while she calculated every angle.

Ariel had a mental image of a cat—glossy, seductive and just this side of evil.

Just before the clapper was struck for the next take, Ariel caught Booth's eye. He was frowning at her while he stood off camera. Though his hands were casually in his pockets and his expression was still and calm, she sensed the wall of tension around him. Unable to break it down, she used it and the eye contact to pull herself back into character.

As the scene unfolded, she forgot the flat, warm taste of the ginger ale, forgot the intrusion of cameras and crew. Her attention was completely focused on the man across from her, who was no longer a fellow actor but an intended victim. She smiled at something he said, a smile Booth recognized too well. Seductive as black lace, cold as ice. There wasn't a man alive who'd be immune to it.

When she reached the line Chuck had focused on, Ariel paused a beat, dipping her fingertip into Jack's glass, then slowly touched the dampened skin to her mouth, then his. The seductive ad lib had the temperature on the set soaring. Even while he mentally approved the gesture and Ariel's intuition, Booth felt his stomach muscles tighten.

She knew her character, he mused, almost as well as he did himself. So well, it was always an effort to separate them in his mind. This attraction that plagued him—at whom was it directed? That surge of jealousy he felt unexpectedly when the woman on set melted into another man's arms—for whom did he really feel it? He'd entwined reality and fiction so tightly in this script, then had chosen an actress skilled enough to blur those lines. Now, he found himself trapped between fiction and fact. Was the woman he wanted the shadow or the light?

"Cut! Cut and print! Fantastic." Grinning from ear to ear, Chuck walked over and kissed both Ariel and Jack. "We're lucky the camera didn't overload on that scene."

Jack flashed a white-toothed smile. "You're lucky I didn't. You're damn good." Jack laid a hand on Ariel's shoulder. "So damn good I'm going to have a cup of coffee and call my wife."

"Ten minutes," Chuck announced. "Set up for reaction shots. Booth, what'd you think?"

"Excellent." With his eyes on Ariel, Booth walked toward them. There was nothing of the cat about her now. If anything, she looked a bit weary. He found that while the knot in his stomach had loosened, he had to fight the urge to stroke her cheek. Booth was more accustomed to the first sensation. "You look like you could use some coffee yourself."

"Yeah." Again, Ariel forced herself to lock Rae's personality away. She wanted nothing more than to relax completely, but knew she could only allow herself a few degrees. "You buying?"

Nodding, he led her off set where a catering table was already set up with coffee, doughnuts and Danishes. Ariel's stomach revolted at the thought of food, but she took the steaming Styrofoam cup in both hands.

"This schedule's difficult," Booth commented.

"Mmm." She shrugged that off and let the coffee wash away the aftertaste of ginger ale. "No, the schedule's no tighter than the soap's—lighter in some ways. The scene was difficult."

He lifted a brow. "Why?"

The scent of the coffee was real and solid. Ariel

could almost forget the spongy food she'd had to nibble on for the past two hours. "Because Phil's smart and cautious—not an easy man to seduce or to fool. Rae has to do both, and she's in a hurry." She glanced over the rim of her cup. "But then, you know that."

"Yes." He took her wrist before she could drink again. "You look tired."

"Only between takes." She smiled, touched by the reluctant concern. "Don't worry about me, Booth. Frantic's my natural pace."

"There's something else."

She thought of Scott. It's not supposed to show, she reminded herself. The minute you walk into the studio, it's not supposed to show. "You're perceptive," she murmured. "A writer's first tool."

"You're stalling."

Ariel shook her head. If she thought about it now, too deeply, her control would begin to slip. "It's something I have to deal with. It won't interfere with my work."

He took her chin firmly into his hand. "Does anything?"

For the first time, Ariel felt a threat of pure anger run through her. "Don't confuse me with a role, Booth—or another woman." She pushed his hand away, then turning her back on him, walked back onto the set.

The temper pleased him, perhaps because it was easier to trust negative emotions. Leaning back against the wall, Booth made a decision. He was going to have her—tonight. It would ease a portion of the tension in him and alleviate the wondering. Then both of them, in their own way, would have to deal with the consequences.

Ariel found the anger was an advantage. Rae, she

mused, was a woman who had anger simmering just below the surface at all times. It added to the discontent, and the ambition. Instead of trying to rid herself of it—something she wasn't certain she could do in any case—Ariel used it to add more depth to an already complicated character. As long as she clung to Rae's mercurial, demanding personality, she didn't feel her own weariness or frustrations.

True, her senses were keen enough so that she knew exactly where Booth was and where his attention was focused even when she was in the middle of a scene. That was something to be dealt with later. The more he pushed at her—mentally, emotionally—the more she was determined to give a stellar performance.

By six and wrap time, Ariel discovered that Rae had drained her. Her body ached from the hours of standing under the lights. Her mind reeled from the repetition of lines, the drawing and releasing of emotions. It was only the first week of filming, and already she felt the strain of the marathon.

Nobody said it'd be easy, Ariel reminded herself as she slipped into her dressing room to change into her street clothes. And it wouldn't be nearly so important if it were. The trouble was, she was beginning to equate her success in the part with her success in her relationship with Booth. If she could pull one off, she could do the same with the other.

Shaking her head, Ariel stripped out of her costume, shedding Rae as eagerly as she did the silk. An idea like that, she reminded herself, had a very large trapdoor. Rae was a part to be acted, no matter how entangled it was with reality. Booth was real life—her life. No matter how willing she was to take risks or accept a challenge, that was something she couldn't afford to forget.

Gratefully, Ariel creamed off her stage makeup and let her skin breathe. She sat, propping her feet on her dressing table so that the short kimono she wore skimmed her thighs. Taking her time, letting herself come down, she undid the sleek knot the hairdresser had arranged and let her hair fall free. With a contented sigh, Ariel tipped her head back, shut her eyes and fell into a half doze.

That was how Booth found her.

The room was cluttered in her usual fashion so that she seemed to be a single island of calm. The air was assaulted with scents—powder, face cream, the same potpourri just hinting of lilac that she kept at home. The lights around her mirror were glaring. Her breathing was soft and even.

As he shut the door behind him, Booth let his gaze run up the long slender length of her legs, exposed from toe to thigh. The kimono was loosely, almost carelessly knotted, so that it gaped intriguingly down the center of her body nearly to the waist. Her hair fell behind the chair, mussed from her own hands so that the curve of neck and shoulder made an elegant contrast.

Her face seemed a bit pale without the color needed for the camera…fragile. Without it, the faintest of shadows could be seen under her eyes.

Booth wanted almost painfully to possess her, just as she was at that moment. With hardly a thought as to what he was doing, he turned the lock on the door. He sat on the arm of a chair, lit a cigarette and waited.

Ariel woke slowly. She tended to sleep quickly and wake gradually. Even before she'd drifted from that twilight world to consciousness, she knew she was re-freshed. The nap had been no more than ten minutes. Any longer and she'd have been groggy, any shorter, tense. With a sigh, she started to stretch. Then she sensed she wasn't alone. Curious, she turned her head and looked at Booth.

"Hello."

He saw no remnants of the anger in her eyes, nor was there any coolness, that sign of resentment, in her voice. Even the weariness he'd sensed in her briefly had vanished. "You didn't sleep long." His cigarette had burned down nearly to the filter without his notic-ing. He crushed it out. "Though I don't know anyone who could've slept at all in that position."

"For a ten-minute session, I can sleep anywhere." She pointed her toes, tensing all her muscles, then re-leased them. "I had to recharge."

"A decent meal would help."

Ariel put a hand to her stomach. "It wouldn't hurt."

"You barely touched anything at lunch."

It didn't surprise her that he'd noticed, only that he'd commented on it. "Normally I'd have gorged myself. Eating lobster bisque at dawn threw my whole system out of whack. A bagel's more my style. Or a bowl of Krispie Krinkies."

"Of what?"

"Eight essential vitamins," she said with a half grin. Reluctantly, she slid her feet to the floor. The gap in her robe shifted, and absently she tugged at the lapels. "We are wrapped for the day, aren't we? There isn't a problem?"

"We wrapped," he agreed. "And there's a problem."

The brush she'd lifted paused halfway to her hair. "What kind?"

"Personal." He rose and took the brush from her hand. "Every day this week I've watched you, listened to you, smelled you. And every day this week, I've wanted you." He took the brush through her hair in one long, smooth stroke while in the lighted mirror, his eyes met hers. When she didn't move, he drew the brush down again, cupping the curve of her shoulder with his free hand. "You asked me to think of you. I have."

Too close to the surface, Ariel warned herself. Her emotions were always too close to the surface. There was nothing she could do about it. "Every day this week," she began in a voice that was already husky, "you've watched me and listened to me be someone else. You might be wanting someone else."

His eyes remained on hers as he lowered his mouth to her ear. "I'm not watching anyone else now."

Her heart lurched. Ariel would have sworn she felt the jerk of movement inside her breast. "Tomorrow—"

"The hell with tomorrow." Booth let the brush drop as he drew her to her feet. "And yesterday." His gaze was intense, a hot, hot green that had her throat going dry. She'd wondered what it would be like if he allowed any emotion freedom. This was his passion, and it was going to sweep her away.

If she hadn't loved him... But, of course, she did. All caution whipped away as her mouth met his. There was a time for thinking, and a time for feeling. There was a time for withholding, and a time for giving freely. There was a time for reason, and a time for romance.

All that Ariel had, all that she felt, thought, wished, went into the touch of mouth to mouth. And as her body followed her heart, she wrapped herself around him and offered unconditionally. She felt the floor tilt and the air freeze before she became lost in her own longings. Her lips parted, inviting; her tongue touched, arousing. Her breath fluttered, answering.

She was firm, as he was, yet softer. Feeling the hard length of man against her, she became completely, utterly feminine. The pleasure was liquid, passing through her as warmed wine. As his grip tightened, she melted further until she was as pliant as any man's fantasy. But she was very real.

He'd never known another woman like her, so utterly free with emotions that flowed and crested until he was drowning in them. Passion had been expected and was there, but… More, infinitely more, was a range of feeling so intense, so sweet, it was irresistible.

As he'd watched her on the set, he'd wanted her. When he'd come into the room to see her sleeping, desire had assaulted him. Now, with her yielding, vibrating with emotions he could hardly name, Booth needed her as he'd never needed anyone. And had never wanted to.

Too late. The thought ran through his mind that it was too late for her—too late for him. Then his hands were buried in her hair, his thoughts a kaleidoscope of sensations.

She smelled faintly of lemon from the cream she'd used on her face, while her hair carried the familiar fragrance of light sexuality. The thin material of her kimono swished as his hands parted it to find her. And she was softer than a dream, but so small he had a moment's fear that he would hurt her. Then her body arched, pressing against his hand so that it was her strength that aroused him. With a sound that was more of surrender than triumph, he buried his face against her throat.

Even while her mind was floating, Ariel knew she had to feel the texture of his flesh against hers. Slowly, her hands ran up his sides, drawing up his sweater. She followed the movement, over his shoulders, until there was nothing barring her exploration—and nothing to stop her sensitized skin from meeting his.

When he drew her down she went willingly. As her back rested against the littered sofa, she cupped her hands behind his head and brought his mouth back to hers. The taste of his passion rippled through her and lit the next spark.

Not so passive now, not so pliant, she moved under him, sending off twinges of excitement to pulse through both of them. The sudden aggression of her lips was welcome. The kiss went on and on, deeper, moister, while two pairs of hands began to test and appreciate.

He could feel the frantic beat of her heart under his palm. When he pressed his lips against her breast, he felt her shudder. The outrageous desire to absorb her ran through him as he began to draw in her variety of tastes, now with his lips, now with the tip of his tongue. Sometimes, some places, it was hot, others sweet, but always it was Ariel.

The lights glared into the room, reflecting from the mirror as he began a thorough, intense journey over her. The curve of her shoulder held fascinations he'd never known before. The skin at the inside of her wrist was so delicate he almost thought he could hear the blood run through the veins. Everywhere he touched, he felt her pulse. She was so giving. That alone was enough to make his head swim.

And as he touched, tasted, took, so did she. If he became more demanding, she responded in kind, keeping pace with him. Or perhaps it was he who kept pace with her. She stroked with those long, elegant fingers so that he knew what it was to be on the verge of madness, and within sight of heaven.

She wanted nothing more than what she could find in him. Touches of tenderness that moved her. Flares of fires that tormented her. His hair brushed over her skin and that alone excited her. Flesh grew damp with passion and the struggle to control—the struggle to prolong. Ariel learned that pleasure alone was a shallow thing; but pleasure, when combined with love, was all.

Together, they understood that there could be no more waiting. The final barriers of clothing were tugged impatiently away. She opened for him. Madness and heaven became one.

Ariel felt as though she could run for miles. Her body was alive with so many sensations. Her mind leaped with them. She lay beneath Booth, tingling with an awareness that radiated down to her toes and fingertips. With her eyes closed, her body still aligned with his, she counted his heartbeats as they thudded against her. In that private, liquid world they'd gone to, Booth hadn't been calm, he hadn't been detached. Letting her lashes flutter up, she smiled. His hand was laced with hers. She wondered if he were aware of it. He'd wanted her. Just her.

Contentment. Was that what he was feeling? Booth lay sated, drained, aware only of Ariel's warm, slim form beneath him. As far as he could remember, he'd never experienced anything remotely like this. Total relaxation…a complete lack of tension. He didn't even have the energy to dissect the feeling, and instead enjoyed it. With a sound of pure pleasure, he turned his face in to her throat. He felt as well as heard her gurgle of laughter.

"Funny?" he murmured.

Ariel ran her hands up the length of his back, then down again to his waist. "I feel good. So good." Her fingertips skimmed over his hips. "So do you."

Shifting slightly, Booth raised himself on one elbow so that he could look at her. Her eyes were laughing. With a fingertip he traced the spot just below her jaw where he'd discovered delectable, sensitive skin. "I still don't know what I'm doing with you."

She brushed the hair from his forehead and watched it fall back again. "Do you always have to have an intellectual reason?"

He frowned, but his fingers spread over her face as if he were blind and memorizing it. "I always have."

She wanted to sigh but smiled instead. Taking his face in her hands, Ariel brought him down for a hard kiss. "I defy the intellect."

That made him laugh, and because he was off balance, she was able to roll him over. With her body slanted across his, she stretched and nuzzled into his shoulder. Booth felt the crinkle of paper and the rumple of cloth beneath him. "What am I lying on?"

"Mmm. This and that."

Arching, he pulled a crumpled pamphlet from under his left hip. "Anyone ever mention that you're sloppy?"

"From time to time."

Absently, Booth glanced at the pamphlet about the plight of baby seals before he dropped it to the floor. He tugged at another paper stuck to his right shoulder. A halfway house for battered wives. Curiosity piqued, he twisted a bit and found another. ASPCA literature.

"Ariel, what is all this?"

She gave his shoulder a last nibble before she rested her cheek on it. He held several wrinkled leaflets. "I suppose you might call it my hobby."

"Hobby?" He put his free hand under her chin to lift it. "Which one?"

"All of them."

"All?" Booth looked at the leaflets in his hand again and wondered how many others were squashed beneath him. "You mean you're actively involved in all these organizations?"

"Yeah. More or less."

"Ariel, no one person would have the time."

"Oh, no." She shifted, folding her arms across his chest for support. "That's a cop-out. You make time." She tilted her head toward the papers he held. "Those baby seals, do you know what's done to them, how it's done?"

"Yes, but—"

"And those abused women. Most of them come into that shelter without any self-esteem, without any emotional or financial support. Then there's—"

"Wait a minute." He let the papers slide to the floor so he could take her shoulders. How slim they were, he realized abruptly. And how easily she could make him forget just how delicately she was formed. "I understand all that, but how can you be involved in all these causes, run your life and pursue your career?"

She smiled. "There're twenty-four hours in every day. I don't like to waste any of them."

Seeing that she was perfectly serious, Booth shook his head. "You're a remarkable woman."

"No." Ariel bent her head and kissed his chin. It dipped slightly in the center—not quite a cleft. "I just have a lot of energy. I need to put it somewhere."

"You could put all of it into furthering your career," he pointed out. "You'd be top box office within six months. There'd be no question of your success."

"Maybe. But I wouldn't be happy with it."

"Why?"

It was back; she felt it. The doubts, the distrust. With a sigh, Ariel sat up. In silence, she picked up her kimono and pulled it on. How quickly warmth could turn to chill. "Because I need more."

Dissatisfied, Booth took her arm. "More what?"

"More everything!" she said with a sudden passion that stunned him. "I need to know I've done my best, and not just in one area of my life. Do you really think I'm so limited?"

The fire in her eyes intrigued him. "I believe what I said indicated your lack of limitations."

"Professionally," she snapped. "I'm a person first. I need to know I touched someone, helped somehow." She dragged both hands through her hair in frustration. "I need to know I cared. Success isn't just a little gold statue for my trophy case, Booth." Whirling, she yanked open the door of her closet and pulled out her street clothes.

As Booth sat up, the papers beneath him rustled. "You're angry."

"Yes, yes, yes!" With her back to him, Ariel wriggled into her briefs. In the mirror, Booth could see the reflected temper on her face.

"Why?"

"Your favorite question." Ariel flung the kimono to the floor, then dragged a short-sleeved sweatshirt over her head. "Well, I'll give you the answer, and you're not going to like it. You still equate me with her." She flung the words at him; as they hit, he too began to dress. "Still," she continued, "even after what just happened between us, you still measure me by her."

"Maybe." He rose and drew his sweater over his head. "Maybe I do."

Ariel stared at him a moment, then stepped into her jeans. "It hurts."

Booth stood very still as the two words sliced into him. He hadn't expected them—their simplicity, their honesty. He hadn't expected his own reaction to them. "I'm sorry," he murmured.

Stepping closer, he touched her arm and waited for her to look up at him. The hurt was in her eyes, and he knew it was the second time he'd put it there. "I've never been a particularly fair man, Ariel."

"No," she agreed. "But it's hard for me to believe that someone so intelligent could be so narrow-minded."

He waited for his own anger to rise, and when it didn't, shook his head. "Maybe it's simplest to say you weren't in my plans."

"I think that's clear." Turning away, she began to brush her hair methodically. Hurt pulsed from her still, laced with anger. It never occurred to her to rely on pride and conceal them both. "I told you before that I tend to rush into things. I also understand that not everyone keeps the same pace. But I'd think by this time you'd see that I'm not the character you created—or the woman who inspired her."

"Ariel." She stiffened when he took her shoulders. He could see her fingers flex on the brush handle. "Ariel," he said again and lowered his brow to the top of her head. Why did he want so much what he'd cut himself off from? "I'll hurt you again," he said quietly. "I'm bound to hurt you if I continue to see you."

Her body relaxed on a sigh. Why was she fighting the inevitable? "Yes, I know."

"And knowing that, knowing what you could do to my own life, I don't want to stop seeing you."

She reached up to cover the hand on her shoulder with her own. "But you don't know why."

"No, I don't know why."

Ariel turned in his arms and held him. For a moment they stood close, her head on his shoulder, his hands at her waist. "Buy me dinner," she requested, then tipped back her head and smiled at him. "I'm starving. I want to be with you. Those are two definite facts. We'll just take the rest as it comes."

He'd been right to call her remarkable, Booth thought. He pressed his lips to her brow. "All right. What would you like to eat?"

"Pizza with mushrooms," she answered immediately. "And a cheap bottle of Chianti."

"Pizza."

"A huge one—with mushrooms."

With a half laugh he tightened his hold. He was no longer sure he could let go. "It sounds like a good start."

Chapter 8

At 7:00 a.m., Ariel sat in a makeup chair, with a huge white drop cloth covering her costume, going over her lines while a short, fussy-handed man with thinning hair slanted blusher over her cheekbones. She could hear, but paid no attention to, the buzz of activity around her. Someone shouted for gel for the lights. A coil of cable was dropped to the floor with a thud. Ariel continued to read.

The upcoming scene was a difficult one, with something perilously close to a soliloquy in the middle. If she didn't get the rhythm just right, the pitch perfect, the entire mood would be spoiled.

And her own mood wasn't helping her concentration.

She'd had another lovely Sunday with Scott, which had ended with a tense and tearful departure. Though she'd long ago resigned herself to the fact that she was a creature of emotional highs and lows, Ariel couldn't rid herself of the despondency or the nagging sense of guilt.

Scott had clung to her, with great, silent tears running down his cheeks, when she'd returned him to the Andersons' home in Larchmont. It was the first time in all the months since his parents' death that he'd created a scene at the end of their weekly visit. The Andersons had met his tears with grim, tight-lipped impatience while both had cast accusing glares at Ariel.

After she'd soothed him, Ariel had wondered all during the lengthy train ride home if she'd unconsciously brought on the scene. By wanting him so badly, was she encouraging him to want her? Did she spoil him? Was she overcompensating because of her love for his father and her pain in the loss?

She'd spent a sleepless night over it, and the questions had built and pressed on her. But there'd been no firm answers in the morning. Within a few weeks, she'd have to live with the decision of a judge who would see Scott as a minor rather than as a little boy who liked to play pretend games. Could a judge, however experienced, however fair, see the heart of a child? It was one more question that kept her awake at night.

Now, Ariel knew she had to put her personal business aside. Her part in the film was more than a job; it was a responsibility. Both the cast and the crew depended on her to do her best. Her name on the contract guaranteed she would give all her skill. And, she reminded herself as she rubbed an aching temple, worrying wasn't going to help Scott.

"My dear, if you continue to fidget, you'll spoil what I've already done."

Bringing herself back, Ariel smiled at the makeup man. "Sorry, Harry. Am I beautiful?"

"Almost exquisite." He pursed his lips as he touched up her brows. The natural arch, he thought with professional admiration, needed very little assistance from him. "For this scene, you should look like Dresden. Just a little more here…" Ariel sat obediently while he smoothed more color into her lips. "And I'll have to insist that there be no more frowning. You'll spoil my work."

Surprised, Ariel met his eyes. She'd been sure she'd had her expression, if not her thoughts, under control. Foolish, she decided, then reminded herself that problems were to be left on the other side of the studio door. That was the first rule of showmanship.

"No more frowns," she promised. "I can't be responsible for spoiling a masterpiece."

"Well, nothing changes. Still cramming before zero hour."

"Stella!" Ariel glanced up and broke into the first true smile of the day. "What're you doing here?"

"Taking a busman's holiday." Stella dropped into the chair beside Ariel, pulling up her legs, then folding them under her. "I used your name—and some charm," she added with a sweep of her lashes, "to get in. You don't mind if I watch the morning's shooting, do you?"

"Of course not. How're things at Trader's Bend?"

"Heating up, love, heating up." With a wicked smile, Stella tossed her thick mane of hair behind her shoulder. "Now that Cameron's trying to blackmail Vikki over her gambling debts, and the Ripper's claimed his third victim, *and* Amanda and Griff are starting to simmer, they can't keep up with the mail or the phone calls.

Rumor is *Tube* wants to do a two-part spread on the cast. That's big time."

Ariel's brow quirked. "Cover story?"

"That's what I hear through the grapevine. Hey, I got stopped in the market the other day. A woman named Ethel Bitterman gave me a lecture on moral standing and family loyalty over the cucumbers."

Laughing, Ariel drew off her protective drape to reveal a frothy, raspberry-colored sundress. This was what she'd needed, she realized. That sense of camaraderie and family. "I've missed you, Stella."

"Me, too. But tell me…" Stella's gaze skimmed up the dress that, while demure and feminine, reeked of sex. "How does it feel to be playing the bad girl for a change?"

Ariel's eyes lit up. "It's wonderful, but it's tough. It's the toughest part I've ever played."

Stella smiled and buffed her nails on her sleeve. "You always claimed I had all the fun."

"I might've been right," Ariel countered. "And I may've oversimplified. But I don't remember ever working harder than this."

Stella rested her chin on her hand. "Why?"

"I guess because Rae's always playing a part. It's like trying to get inside a half dozen personalities and make them one person."

"And you're eating it up," Stella observed.

"I guess I am." With a quick laugh she settled back. "Yeah, I am. One day I'll feel absolutely drained, and the next so wired…" She shrugged and set her script aside. If she didn't know her lines by now, she never would. "In any case, I know if I have a choice, when this is over, I'd like to do a comedy. A Judy Holliday type. Something full of fun and wackiness."

"What about Jack Rohrer?" Stella dug in her purse and found a dietary lemon drop. "What's he like to work with?"

"I like him." Ariel smiled ruefully. "But he doesn't make it a picnic. He's a perfectionist—like everyone else on this film."

"And the illustrious Booth DeWitt?"

"Watches everything," Ariel murmured.

"Including you." Moving only her eyes, Stella changed the focus of her attention. "At least he has been for the past ten minutes."

Ariel didn't have to turn her head. She already knew. In her mind's eye she could see him, standing a bit apart from the grips and gaffers as they checked the lighting and the set. He'd remove himself from the activity so as not to interfere with the flow, but his presence would be felt by everyone. And that presence alone would make everyone just tense enough to be sharp.

She knew he'd be watching her, half-wary, half-accepting. More than anything else, she wanted to merge the two into trust. And trust into love.

Booth watched her laugh at something Stella said. He watched the animated hand movements, the slight tilt of her head that meant she was avidly interested. Then again, Ariel rarely did anything that wasn't done avidly. Whatever had been clouding her mood when she'd come in earlier had been smoothed over. As he remembered the trouble in her eyes, Booth wondered what problem plagued her and why, when she seemed so willing to share everything, she was unwilling to share that.

Lighting a cigarette, Booth told himself he should be

grateful she kept it to herself. Why should he want to be involved? He knew very well that one of the quickest ways to become vulnerable to someone else was to become concerned with their problems.

Beside him a stagehand thoroughly sprayed an elegant arrangement of fresh flowers. The lighting director called for a final check on the candlepower. A mike boom was lowered into place. Booth wondered what Ariel had done over the weekend.

He'd wanted to spend it with her, but she'd put him off and he hadn't insisted. He wouldn't box her in, because by doing so he set limits on himself. That was a trap he wouldn't fall into. But he remembered the utter peace he'd felt lying with her in her dressing room after passion was spent.

He couldn't say she was a calming influence—too much energy crackled from her. Yet she had a talent for soothing the tension from his mind.

He wanted to talk to her again. He wanted to touch her again. He wanted to make love with her again. And he wanted to escape from his own needs.

"Places!" The assistant director called out as he paced the set, rechecking the blocking.

Booth leaned back against the wall, his thumbs hooked absently in his pockets. It never occurred to him, as it often had to Ariel, how seldom he sat.

They would shoot a section of an extensive scene that morning. The other parts would be filmed later on the lawns of a Long Island estate. The elegant lawn party they'd shoot on location was to be Rae's first full-scale attempt at entertaining since marrying Phil. And afterward, indoors and in private, would come their first full-scale argument.

She looked like something made of spun-sugar icing. Her words were as vicious as snake venom. And all the while, with the fury and the poison oozing from her, she hadn't a hair out of place. The fragile color in her cheeks never fluctuated. It was Ariel's job to keep the character cold-blooded, and the words smoldering.

She knew it was all in the eyes. Rae's gestures were a facade. Her smile was a lie. Both the ice and the fire had to come from the eyes. The scene had to be underplayed, understated from her end. It was a constant strain to keep her own emotions from bubbling out. If *she* were to fight with words, she'd shout them, hurl them—and fling off the ones tossed back at her. Rae drawled them, almost lazily. And Ariel ached.

This was Booth's life, she thought. Or a mirror image of what had been his life. This was his pain, his mistakes, his misery. She was caught up in it. If she hurt, how did he feel watching?

Rae gave Phil a bored look as he grabbed both her arms.

"I won't have it," he raged at her, eyes blazing while hers remained cool as a lake.

"Won't have it?" Rae repeated, transmitting utter disdain with the tone, with the movement of an eyebrow. "What is it you won't have?"

"I will not have you raying the pole." Jack closed his eyes and made a gargling sound.

"Raying the pole?" Ariel repeated. "Having a little trouble with your tongue?"

She felt the tension snap as the scene was cut, but wasn't certain if she was grateful or not. She wanted this one over.

"Playing the role," Jack enunciated carefully. "I will

not have you *playing* the role. I got it." He held up both hands, mocking himself and his flubbed line.

"Fine, as long as you understand that I can and will ray the pole whenever I choose."

He grinned at Ariel. "Smart mouth."

She patted his cheek. "Aw, yours'll wise up, Jack. Give yourself a chance."

"Places. Take it from the entrance."

For the third time that morning, Ariel swung through the French doors with her skirts billowing behind her.

They moved through the scene again, immersing themselves in the characters even with the starts and stops and changes of camera angles.

To end the scene, Rae was to laugh, take the glass of Scotch from Phil's hand, sip, then toss the contents into his face. Caught up in character, Ariel took the glass, tasted the warm, weak tea, then with an icy smile, poured the contents over the elegant floral arrangement. Without missing a beat in the change of staging, Jack ripped the glass out of her hand and hurled it across the room.

"Cut!"

Snapping back, Ariel stared at her director. "Oh, God, Chuck, I don't know where that came from. I'm sorry." With a hand pressed to her brow, she looked down at the now drenched mixture of fragile hothouse blooms.

"No, no. Damn!" Laughing, he gave her a bear hug. "That was perfect. Better than perfect. I wish I'd thought of it myself." He laughed again and squeezed Ariel until she thought her bones might crack. "She'd have done that. She *would* have done just that." With his arm slung around Ariel's shoulder, Chuck turned to Booth. "Booth?"

"Yes." Without moving, Booth indicated a nod. "Leave it as it stands." He pinned Ariel with cool, green eyes. He should have written it that way, he realized. Throwing a drink in Phil's face was too obvious for Rae. Even too human. "You seem to know her better than I do now."

She let out an uneven breath, giving Chuck's hand a squeeze before she walked toward Booth. "Is that a compliment?"

"An observation. They're setting up for the close-ups," he murmured, then brought his attention back to her. "I won't give you carte blanche, Ariel, but I'm willing to feed you quite a bit of rope in your characterization. And obviously so is Chuck. You understand Rae."

She could have been amused or annoyed. As always when she had a choice, Ariel chose amusement. "Booth, if I were playing a mushroom, I'd understand that mushroom. It's my job."

He smiled because she made it easy. "I believe you would."

"Didn't you catch the commercial where I played the ripe, juicy plum?"

"Must've been out of town."

"It was a classic. Over and above my shower scene for Fresh Wave shampoo—though, of course, sensuality was the basis in both spots."

"I want to come home with you tonight," he said quietly. "I want to stay with you tonight."

"Oh." When would she get used to the simple ways he had of saying monumental things?

"And when we're alone," Booth murmured as he

watched the pulse in her throat begin to flutter, "I want to take off your clothes, little by little, so that I can touch every inch of you. Then I want to watch your face while we make love."

"Ariel, let's get these close-ups!"

"What?" A bit dazed, she mumbled the word while she continued to stare at Booth. Already she could feel his hands on her, taste his breath as it mixed with her own.

"They can have your face—for now," Booth told her, more aroused by her reaction to his words than he would have thought possible. "Tonight, it's mine."

"Ariel!"

Flung back to the present, she turned to go back to the set. With a look that was amused and puzzled, she glanced back over her shoulder. "You're not predictable, Booth."

"Is that a compliment?" he countered.

She grinned. "My very best one."

Hour after hour, line after line, scene after scene, the morning progressed. Though the film was naturally shot out of sequence, Ariel could feel it beginning to jell. Because it was television, the pace was fast. Her pace. Because it was DeWitt and Marshell, the expectations were high. As were hers.

You sweltered under the lights; changed moods, costumes; were powdered, dusted and glossed. Again and again. You sat and waited during scene changes or equipment malfunctions. And somewhere between the tension and the tedium was your vocation.

Ariel understood all that, and she wanted all of that. She never lost the basic pleasure in performing, even after ten retakes of a scene where Rae rode an exercise bike while discussing a new script with her agent.

Muscles aching, she eased herself off the bike and dabbed at the sweat, which didn't have to be simulated, on her face.

"Poor baby." Stella grinned as a stagehand offered Ariel a towel. "Just remember, Ariel, we never work you this hard on *Our Lives.*"

"Rae *would* have to be a fitness fanatic," she muttered, stretching her shoulders. "Body conscious. I'm conscious now." With a little moan, Ariel bent to ease a cramp in her leg. "Conscious of every muscle in my body that hasn't been used in five years."

"It's a wrap." Chuck gave her a companionable slap on the flank as he passed. "Go soak in a hot tub."

Ariel barely suppressed a less kind suggestion. She slung the towel over her shoulder, gripped both damp ends and stuck out her tongue.

"You never did have any respect for directors," Stella commented. "Come on, kid, I'll keep you company while you change. Then I've got a hot date."

"Oh, really?"

"Yeah. My new dentist. I went in for a checkup and ended up having a discussion on dental hygiene over linguine."

"Good God." Not bothering to hide a grin, Ariel pushed open her dressing-room door. "He works fast."

"Uh-uh, I do." With a laugh that held both pleasure and nerves, Stella walked into the room. "Oh, Ariel, he's so sweet—so serious about his work. And…" Stella broke off and dropped onto Ariel's cluttered sofa. "I remember something you said a few weeks ago about love—it being a definite emotion or something." She lifted her hands as if to wave away the exact phrase and grip the essence. "Anyway, I haven't come down to earth since I sat in that tilt-back chair and looked up into those baby-blue eyes of his."

"That's nice." For the moment Ariel forgot her sore muscles and the line of sweat dripping down her back. "That's really nice, Stella."

Stella searched for another lemon drop and found her supply depleted. Knowing Ariel, she walked to the dressing table, pulled open a drawer and succumbed to the stash of candy-coated chocolate. "I heard somewhere that people in love can spot other people in love." She slanted her friend a look as Ariel stripped out of her leotard. "To test a theory, my guess is that you've fallen for Booth DeWitt."

"Right the first time." Ariel pulled on the baggy sweatpants and shirt she'd worn to the studio.

With a frown, Stella crunched candy between her teeth. "You always liked the tough roles."

"I seem to lean toward them."

"How's he feel about you?"

"I don't know." Gratefully, Ariel creamed off the last of her makeup. With a flourish, she dumped one more part of Rae into the waste can. "I don't think he does, either."

"Ariel…" Reluctance to give advice warred with affection and loyalty. "Do you know what you're doing?"

"No," she answered immediately, both brows lifting. "Why would I want to?"

Stella laughed as she headed for the door. "Stupid question. By the way—" she stopped with her hand on the knob "—I just thought I'd mention that you were brilliant today. I've worked with you week after week for five years, and today you blew me away. When this thing hits the screen, you're going to take off so fast even you won't be able to keep up."

Astonished, pleased and, perhaps for the first time, a bit frightened, Ariel sat on the edge of her dressing table. "Thanks—I think."

"Don't mention it." Slipping into the character of Vikki, Stella blew Ariel a cool kiss. "See you in a couple of weeks, big sister."

For several moments after the door shut, Ariel sat in silence. Did she, when push came to shove, want to take off and take off fast? She remembered that P. B. Marshell had said something similiar to her after her second reading for the part, but Ariel had seen that more as an overall view of the project itself. She knew Stella, and understood that the praise from her had been directed personally and individually. For the first time the ripple effect of the role of Rae struck her fully. However much a cliché it sounded, it could make her a star.

Wearing her baggy sweats, one hip leaning on her jumbled dressing table, Ariel explored the idea.

Money—she shrugged that away. Her upbringing had taught her to view money for what it was, a means to an end. In any case, her financial status for the past three years had been more than adequate for both her needs and her taste.

Fame. She grinned at that. No, she couldn't claim she was immune to fame. It still brought her a thrill to sign her name in an autograph book or talk to a fan. That was something she hoped would never change. But fame had degrees, and with each rise in height, the payment for it became greater. The more fans, the less privacy. That was something she'd have to think about carefully.

Artistic freedom. It was that, Ariel admitted on a deep breath, that was the clincher. To be able to *choose* a part rather than be chosen. Glory and a big bank account were nothing in comparison. If Rae could bring her that…

With a shake of her head, she rose. Daydreaming about the future couldn't change anything. For now, her career, and her life, would simply have to go a day at a time. Still, she was a woman who liked to expect everything. Ariel would much rather be disappointed than pessimistic. She was grinning when she opened the door and nearly collided with Booth.

"You look happy," he commented as he took her arms to balance her.

"I am happy." Ariel kissed him hard and firm on the mouth. "It's been a good day."

The kiss, casual as it was, shot straight through him. "You should be exhausted."

"No, you should be exhausted after running the New York Marathon. How do you feel about a giant hamburger and a glutton's portion of fries?"

He'd had a quiet restaurant in mind—something French and dimly lit. After a glance at her sweat suit and glowing face, Booth shook his head. "Sounds perfect. It's your turn to buy."

Ariel tucked her arm through his. "You got it. Do you like banana milk shakes?"

His expression stated his opinion clearly. "I don't believe I've ever had one."

"You're going to love it," Ariel promised.

It wasn't as bad as he'd imagined—and the hamburger had been hefty and satisfying. Dusk was settling over the city when they returned to Ariel's apartment.

The moment she opened the door, the kittens dashed for her feet.

"Good grief, you'd think they hadn't been fed in a week." Bending, she scooped up both of them and nuzzled. "Did you miss me, you little pigs, or just your evening meal?"

Before Booth realized what she was up to, Ariel had thrust both kittens into his arms. "Hang on to them for me, will you?" she said easily. "I have to feed Butch, too." She sauntered toward the kitchen, with the three-legged Butch waddling behind. Booth was left with two mewing kittens and no choice but to follow. One—Keats or Shelley—climbed onto his shoulder as he went after Ariel.

"I'm surprised you don't have a litter of puppies, as well." He lifted a brow as the kitten sniffed at his ear.

Ariel laughed as the kitten batted playfully at Booth's hair. "I would if the landlord wasn't so strict. But I'm working on him. Meanwhile—" she set out three generous bowls of food "—it's chow time."

Chuckling, she took the kitten from Booth's shoulder while the other leaped to the floor. Within seconds all three cats were thoroughly involved. "See?" She brushed a few traces of cat hair from his shirt. "They're no trouble at all, hardly any expense and wonderful companions, especially for someone who works most often at home."

Booth gave her a steady look, cupped her face in his hands, then grinned despite himself. "No."

"No what?"

"No, I don't want a cat."

"Well, you can't have one of mine," she said amiably. "Besides, you look more like the dog type."

"Oh, really?" He slipped his arms around her waist.

"Mmm. A nice cocker spaniel that would sleep by your fire at night."

"I don't have a fireplace."

"You should have. But until you take care of that, the puppy could curl right up on a little braided rug by the window."

He caught her bottom lip between his teeth and nipped lightly. "No."

"No one should live alone, Booth. It's depressing."

He could feel her response in the quickening of her heartbeat, the quiet shudder of breath. "I'm used to living alone. I like it that way."

She liked the feel of his roughened cheek against hers. "You must've had a pet when you were a child," Ariel murmured.

Booth remembered the golden Labrador with the lolling tongue that he'd adored—and that he hadn't thought of in years. Oh, no, he thought as he felt himself begin to weaken. She wasn't going to get to him on this. "As a child, I had the time and the temperament for a pet." Slowly, he slipped his hands under her sweatshirt and up her back. "Now I prefer other ways of spending my free time."

But she'd laid the groundwork, Ariel thought with a small smile. Advance and retreat was the secret of a successful campaign. "I have to shower," she told him, drawing back far enough to smile again. "I'm still sticky from that last scene."

"I enjoyed watching it. You've fascinating thigh muscles, Ariel."

Amused, she lifted both brows. "I have *aching* thigh muscles. And I'll tell you something, if I were to ride a

bike for the three or four miles I did today, it wouldn't
be anchored to the floor."

"No." He gathered her hair in his hand to draw her
head back. "You wouldn't be content to stay in the same
place." He touched his mouth teasingly to hers, retreat-
ing when she would have deepened the touch to a kiss.
"I'll wash your back."

Thrills raced up her spine as if he already were.
"Hmm, what a nice idea. I suppose I should warn you,"
she continued as they walked out of the kitchen, "I like
the water in my shower hot—very hot."

When they stepped into the bathroom, he slipped his
hands under the baggy sweatshirt. She was slim and
warm beneath. "Don't you think I can take it?"

"I figure you're pretty tough." Eyes laughing up at
him, Ariel began to unbutton his shirt. "For a screenwriter."

In one surprising move, Booth whipped the sweatshirt over her head and bit down on her shoulder. "I'd
say you're pretty soft." He ran his hands down her rib
cage, then banded her waist. "For an actress."

"Touché," Ariel murmured breathlessly as he tugged
loose the drawstring of her pants.

"I like to feel you," he said, stroking his hands over
her as she continued to undress him. "Though there
isn't much of you. An elegant little body. Long boned,
hipless." His hands journeyed down her back, and farther. "Very smooth."

By the time they were both naked, Ariel was shiver-
ing. But not from cold. Drawing away, she turned the
taps. Water rushed from the showerhead, striking porcelain and steaming toward the ceiling. Stepping in,

Ariel closed her eyes to let her body soak up the heat and the sensuality.

That was one of the things that continued to fascinate him about her—her capacity for experiencing. Nothing was ever ordinary to her, Booth decided as he stepped behind her and drew the curtain closed. She wouldn't know the meaning of boredom. Everything she did or thought was unique, and being unique, exciting.

As the water coursed over them both, he wrapped his arms around her and drew her back against his chest. This was affection, he realized, the sort he'd felt very rarely in his life. Yet he felt it for her.

Ariel lifted her face to the spray. So many sensations buffeted her at that moment, she couldn't keep up. So she stopped trying. It was enough to be close, to be held. And to love. Perhaps some people needed more—security, words, promises. Perhaps one day, she would, too. But now, just for now, she had all she wanted. Turning, she caught Booth close and fastened her mouth to his.

Passion flared in her quickly this time, as if it had been waiting for hours, days. Maybe years. It built so fast that the kiss alone had her gasping for air and fretting for more. Without being aware of it, she stood on her toes so that the curve of their bodies would be aligned. With desperate fingers, she combed through his hair and gripped, as if he might try to break away. But his arms were tight around her, and his mouth was as seeking as hers.

Reeling toward the crest, Ariel clung, and Ariel offered.

God, he'd never known anyone so giving. As he drank in all the flavors of her mouth, Booth wondered if it were possible for a woman to be so confident, so comfortable with herself that she could be this generous. Without any hesitation, her body was there for him. Her mind was tuned to him. Instinctively, Booth knew she thought more of his needs, his pleasures, than her own. And by doing so, she touched off a long dormant tenderness.

"Ariel…" Murmuring her name, he ran kisses over her face, which the water made incredibly soft, incredibly sweet. "You make me want things I'd forgotten— and almost believe in them again."

"Don't think." She rubbed her lips over his to soothe, to entice. "This time don't think at all."

But he would, Booth told himself. Or he'd take her too quickly, and perhaps too roughly. This time, he'd give her back a portion of what she'd already given him. Cupping the soap in his hand, he ran it over her back. He thought he heard her purr like one of her cats. It made him smile.

Her senses began to sharpen. She could hear the hiss of the spray as it struck tile, and feel the steam as it billowed in puffy clouds. Soapy hands slid over her—slick, soft, sensitive. His flesh was wet and warm where her mouth pressed. Through half-closed eyes she could see the lather cling to her, then him, before it was sluiced away.

His hand moved once between their slippery bodies to find her—stunningly—so that she cried out in surprise and rippling pleasure. Then it journeyed elsewhere while his lips traced hot and damp over her shoulder. The tang of citrus from the soap made her head reel.

"Do they still ache?" Booth asked her as his fingers kneaded the backs of her thighs.

"What?" Floating, Ariel leaned against him, her

arms curved over his back, her hands firm on his shoulders. Water struck her back in soft, hissing spurts, then seemed to slither away. "No, no, nothing aches now."

With a laugh, Booth dipped his tongue into her ear and felt her shiver. "Your hair goes to gold when it's wet."

She smelled the shampoo, felt its cool touch on her scalp before he began to massage. Nothing, Ariel thought, had ever aroused her more.

Slowly, lingeringly, he washed her hair while the frothy bubbles of shampoo ran down his arms. The scent was familiar to him now, that fresh, inviting fragrance that caught at him every time he was near her. He enjoyed the intimacy of having the scent spill over him and cling—to her skin, to his. Shifting his weight, he moved them both under the gush of the shower so that water and lather raced down their bodies and away.

And while they stood, hot and wet and entangled, he slipped into her. It seemed natural, as if he'd been her lover for years. It was thrilling, as though he'd never touched her before.

He felt Ariel's nails dig into his shoulders, heard her moan of surrender and demand. He took her there, with more care than he'd ever shown a woman. And he felt a rush of freedom.

Chapter 9

Ariel rode a roller coaster for two weeks. Her time with Booth seemed like a ride with dips and curves and speed and surprises. Of course, she'd always loved them—the faster and wilder the better.

She'd been right when she'd told Booth he was unpredictable. Neither was he a simple man to deal with. Ariel decided she wanted it no other way.

There were times he was incredibly tender, showing her flashes of romance and affection that she'd never expected from him. A box of wildflowers delivered before an early studio call. A rainy-day picnic in his apartment with champagne in paper cups while thunder raged.

Then there were the times he pulled away, drew into himself so intensely that she couldn't reach him. And when she knew, instinctively, not to try.

The anger and impatience in him were ingrained.

Perhaps it was that, contrasting with the glimpses of humor and gentleness, that had caused her to lose her heart. It was the whole man she loved, no matter how difficult. And it was the whole man she wanted to belong to. This man—brooding, angry, reluctantly sweet—was the man she'd been waiting for.

As the film progressed, their relationship grew closer, despite Booth's occasional stretches of isolation. Closer, yes, but without the simplicity she looked for. For love, in Ariel's mind, was a simple thing.

If he was resisting love, so much the better, Ariel told herself. When he accepted it—she wouldn't allow herself to doubt he would—it would be that much stronger. For she needed absolute love, the unconditional giving of heart and mind. She could wait a little longer to have it all.

If she had one regret, it was that she wasn't free to confide in him about Scott. The closer the trial came, the more she felt the need to talk to Booth about it, seek comfort, gain reassurance. Though it was tempting, Ariel never even considered it. This problem was hers, and hers alone. As Scott was hers to protect and defend.

When she thought of the future, it was still in sections. Booth, Scott, her career. She needed her own brand of absolute faith to believe that they'd all come together in the end.

After a long, hectic morning, Ariel considered the lengthy delay anticipated because of equipment breakdown a reward. It was the first time in weeks she'd be able to watch *Our Lives, Our Loves,* and catch up on Amanda's life with the people of Trader's Bend.

"You're not really going to watch television for the

next hour," Booth protested as Ariel pulled him down the corridor.

"Yes, I am. It's like visiting home." She shook the bag of pretzels in her hand. "And I've got provisions."

"When they get the sound board fixed, you're going to have a hell of an afternoon ahead of you." He kneaded her shoulder as they walked. Though it didn't often show, he'd seen brief glimpses of strain in her eyes, isolated moments when she looked a bit lost. "You'd be better off putting your feet up and catching a nap."

"I never nap." When she pushed open her dressing room door, she upended a stack of magazines. Hardly sparing them a glance, she walked over to the small portable television set in the corner.

"I seem to recall coming in here one day and finding you with your feet up on the table and your eyes closed."

"That's different." She fiddled with a dial until she was satisfied with the color. "That was recharging. I'm not ready for recharging, Booth." Eyes wide and excited, she whirled around. "It's really going well, isn't it? I can feel it. Even after all these weeks, the edge is still on. That's a sure sign we're doing something special."

"I was a bit leery about doing a film for television." He took a few pamphlets from the sofa and dropped them onto a table. "Not anymore. Yes, it's going to be very special." He held out a hand to her. "You're very special."

As always, the subtle unexpected statement went straight to her heart. Ariel took the offered hand and brought it to her lips. "I'm going to enjoy watching you accept that Emmy."

He lifted a brow. "And what about yours?"

"Maybe," she said and laughed. "Just maybe." The

lead-in music for the soap distracted her. "Ah, here we go. Back to Trader's Bend." Dropping onto the sofa, she pulled Booth with her. After ripping open the bag of pretzels, Ariel became totally absorbed.

She didn't watch as an actress or as a critic, but as a viewer. Relaxing her mind, she let herself become caught up in the connecting plot lines and problems. Even when she saw herself on the screen, she didn't look for flaws or perfection. She didn't consider she was looking at Ariel, but at Amanda.

"Don't tell me what I want," Amanda told Griff in a low, vibrating voice. "You have no business offering me unsolicited advice on my life, much less coming into my house uninvited."

"Now, you look." Griff took her arm when she would have turned away. "You're pushing yourself right to the edge. I can see it."

"I'm doing my job," she corrected coolly. "Why don't you concentrate on yours and leave me alone?"

"Leaving you alone's the last thing I'm going to do." As the camera zoomed in, the viewer was witness to his struggle for control. When Griff continued, his voice was calmer but edged with his familiar passion. "Damn it, Mandy, you're almost as close to this Ripper thing as the cops. You know better than to stay in this house by yourself. If you won't let me help you, at least go stay with your parents for a while."

"With my parents." Her composure began to crack as she dragged a hand through her hair. "Stay with my parents, while Vikki's there? Just how much do you think I can take?"

"All right, all right." Frustrated, he tried to draw her

against him, only to have her jerk away. "Mandy, please, I'm worried about you."

"Don't be. And if you really want to help, leave me alone. I need to go over the psychiatric profile before I meet with Lieutenant Reiffler in the morning."

Fisted hands were shoved in his pockets. "Okay, look, I'll sleep down here on the couch. I swear I won't touch you. I just can't leave you out here alone."

"I don't want you here!" she shouted, losing her tenuous grip on control. "I don't want anyone, can't you understand that? Can't you understand that I need to be alone?"

He stared at her while she fought back tears, shoulders heaving. "I love you, Mandy," he said so quietly it could barely be heard. But his eyes had already said it.

As the camera zoomed in on her, a single tear spilled out and rolled down Amanda's cheek. "No," she whispered, turning away. But Griff's arms came around her, drawing her back against him.

"Yes, you know I do. There's never been anyone for me but you. It killed me when you left me, Mandy. I need you in my life. I need what we'd planned to have together. We've got a second chance. All we have to do is take it."

Staring into nowhere, Amanda pressed a hand to her stomach where she knew Cameron's baby was sleeping—a baby Griff would never accept, and one she had to. "No, there aren't any second chances, Griff. Please leave me alone."

"We belong together," he murmured, burying his face in her hair. "Oh, God, Mandy, we've always belonged together."

For his sake, for her own, she had to make him leave.

Pain flashed into her eyes before she controlled her expression. "You're wrong," she said flatly. "That was yesterday. Today I don't want you to touch me."

"I can't crawl anymore." Ripping himself away from her, Griff headed for the door. "I won't crawl anymore."

As the door slammed behind him, Amanda slumped down on the couch. Curling on her side, she buried her face in a pillow and wept. The camera panned slowly to the window to show a shadowy silhouette behind the closed curtains.

"Well, well," Booth murmured at the commercial break. "The lady has her problems."

"And then some." Ariel stretched and leaned back against the cushions. "That's the thing about soaps— one problem gets resolved and three more crop up."

"So, is she going to give Griff a break and take him back?"

Ariel grinned at the casualness of the question. He really wants to know, she mused, pleased. "Tune in tomorrow."

His eyes narrowed. "You know the story line."

"My lips are sealed," she said primly.

"Really?" Booth caught her chin in his hand. "Let's see." He pressed his to them firmly, and though hers curved, they remained shut. Challenged, he shifted closer and his fingers spread over her jawline, lightly stroking. With the barest of touches, he traced the shape of her mouth, wetting her lips, using no pressure. When he nibbled at one corner, then the other, he felt the telltale melting of her bones, heard the quiet sigh. Effortlessly, his tongue slipped between her lips to tease hers.

"Cheat," Ariel managed.

"Yeah." God, she made him feel so good. He'd almost stopped wondering how long it would last. The end, what he considered the inevitable end to what they brought each other, was becoming more blurred every day. "I've never believed in playing fair."

"No?" Her sudden aggression caught him off balance. Before he knew it, Booth was on his back, with her body pressed into his. "In that case, no holds barred."

The greedy kiss left him stunned, so that by the time he'd gripped some control again, she'd unbuttoned his shirt for her seeking hands. "Ariel…" Half-amused, half-protesting, he took her wrist, but her free hand skimmed down the center of his body to spread over his stomach.

Amusement, protests, reason, slipped away.

"I never get enough of you." He gripped her hair, destroying the sleek knot the hairdresser had tended so carefully hours before.

"I plan to see that you don't." With quick, open mouthed kisses she moved over his shoulder, drawing away the shirt as she went.

She took him over hills and into valleys with such speed and fury he could only follow. For as long as he could remember, Booth had led in every aspect of his life—not trusting enough to let another guide. But now he could barely keep pace with her. The energy, the verve he'd so long admired in her was in complete control. As he was swept along, Booth wondered why it was suddenly so easy to break yet another rule. Then, as she had once requested, he didn't think at all.

Feelings. Ariel drew them in as they radiated from him. This was what she'd been so patiently, so desperately waiting for. Emotions were finally overtaking him.

As they merged with her own, she felt the bond, the link, and nearly wept with the wonder of it.

He loves me, she thought. Maybe he doesn't know it yet, maybe he won't for days and weeks to come. But it's there. The urge to weep altered to an urge to laugh. And it was with laughter and with joy that she took him into her.

Winded, Booth lay still while Ariel curled like a cat on his chest. "Was all that just to keep me from learning the story line?"

Her chuckle was muffled against his skin. "There're no lengths I won't go to to protect security." She snuggled against him. "No sacrifice too great."

"With that in mind, I think I'll ask about the identity of the Ripper—tonight." Drawing her up, he examined her. The silk blouse she'd been wearing was unbuttoned and trailing over one shoulder. The thin slacks lay in a heap on the floor. Her hair was a provocative tangle. "You're going to catch hell from wardrobe and makeup."

"It was worth it." Straightening her blouse, Ariel began to do up the buttons. "I'll tell them I took a nap."

With a laugh, he sat up and tugged on her tumbled hair. "There's no mistaking what you've been up to. Your eyes always give you away."

"Do they?" Carefully, she stepped into her slacks. "I wonder." Absently smoothing out the creases, she turned to him. "You haven't seen it in all these weeks." As she watched, his brows drew together. "You're a perceptive man, and I've never had a strong talent or a strong desire to hide my feelings." She smiled as he continued to frown at her. "I love you."

His face, his body—Ariel thought even his mind—went very still. He said nothing. "Booth, you don't have to look as though I've just pulled a gun on you." Stepping closer, she touched the back of her hand to his cheek. "Taking love's easy—giving it's a bit harder, for some people anyway. Please, take it as it's offered. It's free."

He wasn't at all certain what he was feeling—only that he'd never felt anything like it before. The very novelty made him wary. "It's not wise to give things away, Ariel, especially to someone who isn't ready for them."

"And holding on to something when it needs to be given's even more foolish. Booth, can't you trust me even now, just enough to accept my feelings?"

"I don't know," he murmured. As he rose, conflicting emotions, conflicting desires tore at him. He wanted to distance himself as quickly and as completely as possible. He wanted to hold her and never let go. Panic, he felt the stab of it. Pleasure, the sweetness of it.

"They're there whether you can or can't. I've never been good at controlling my emotions, Booth. I'm not sorry for it."

Before he could speak there was a brisk knock on the door. "Ariel, you're needed on the set in fifteen minutes."

"Thank you."

He had to think, Booth told himself. Be logical… Be careful. "I'll send the hairdresser in."

"Okay." She smiled, and it almost reached her eyes. When he'd gone, Ariel stared at her reflection in the mirror. The lights around it were dull and dark. "So who expected it'd be easy?" she asked herself.

In just under fifteen minutes, Ariel walked back toward the set. She looked every bit as cool and as sleek as she had when she'd walked off over an hour before.

Despite Booth's reaction, which she'd half expected, she felt lighter, easier, after telling Booth of her feelings. It was, after all, merely stating aloud what was, sharing what couldn't be changed. As a general rule, Ariel considered concealments a waste of time, and consequences a by-product of living. Her gait was free and easy as she crossed the studio.

She knew something was happening before she saw the thicket of people or heard the excited voices. Tension in the air. She felt it and thought instantly of Booth. But it wasn't Booth she saw when she passed the false wall of the living-room set.

Elizabeth Hunter.

Elegance. Ice. Smooth, smooth femininity. Outrageous beauty. Ariel saw her laugh lightly and lift a slender cigarette to her lips. She posed effortlessly, as if the cameras were on and focused on her. Her hair shimmered, pale, frosty. Her skin was so exquisite it might have been carved from marble.

On the screen, she was larger than life, desirable, unattainable. Ariel saw little difference in the flesh. There couldn't be a man alive who wouldn't dream of peeling off that layer of frost and finding something molten and wild inside. If she were truly like Rae, Ariel thought, that man—any man—would be disappointed. Curious, she walked closer.

"Pat, how could I stay away?" Liz lifted one graceful hand and touched Marshell's check. A fantasy of diamonds and sapphires winked on her ring finger. "After all, one might say I have a...vested interest in this film." The provocative pout—a Hunter trademark—touched her mouth. "Don't tell me you're going to chase me away."

"Of course not, Liz." Marshell looked uncomfortable and resigned. "None of us knew you were in town."

"I just wrapped the Simmeon film in Greece." She drew on the slender cigarette again and carelessly flicked ashes on the floor. "I flew right in." She shot a look over Marshell's shoulder. Not hostile, not grim, but simply predatory. It was then Ariel saw Booth.

He stood slightly apart from the circle of people around Liz, as if he again sought distance without wholly removing himself. He met the look his ex-wife sent him without a flicker of expression. Even if Ariel had chosen to intrude, she doubted if she could have gauged his thoughts.

"I wasn't allowed to read the screenplay." Liz continued to talk to Marshell though her eyes remained on Booth. "But little dribbles leaked through to me. I must say, I'm fascinated. And a bit miffed that you didn't ask me to do the film."

Marshell's eyes hardened, but he stuck with diplomacy. "You were unavailable, Liz."

"And inappropriate," Booth added mildly.

"Ah, Booth, always the clever last word." Liz blew smoke in his direction and smiled.

It was a smile Ariel recognized. She'd seen it on the screen in countless Hunter movies. She'd mimicked it herself as Rae. It was the smile a witch wore before she cut the wings off a bat. Without realizing it, Ariel moved forward in direct defense of Booth. Liz's gaze shifted and locked.

It wasn't a pleasant survey. Again, not hostile but simply and essentially cold. Ariel studied Liz in turn and absorbed impressions. She was left with a sensation of emptiness. And what she felt was pity.

"Well…" Liz held out her cigarette for disposal. A small woman with a wrinkled face plucked it from her fingers. "It's easy to deduce that this is Rae."

"No." Unconsciously, Ariel smiled with the same cold glitter as Liz. "I'm Ariel Kirkwood. Rae's a character."

"Indeed." The haughty lift of brow had been used in a dozen scenes. "I always try to absorb the character I portray."

"And it works brilliantly for you," Ariel acknowledged with complete sincerity. "I limit that to when the lights are on, Miss Hunter."

Only the barest flicker in her eyes betrayed annoyance. "Would I have seen you do anything else, dear?"

There was no mistaking the patronizing tone. Again, Ariel felt a flash of sympathy. "Possibly."

He didn't like seeing them together. No, Booth thought violently, by God, he didn't. It had given him a wave of sheer pleasure to see Liz again and feel nothing. Absolutely nothing. No anger, no frustration. Not even disgust. The lack of feeling had been like a balm. Until Ariel had come on set.

Face-to-face, they could have been sisters. The resemblance was heightened by the fact that Ariel's hair, makeup and wardrobe were styled to Liz's taste. He saw too many similarities. And as he looked closer, too many contrasts. Booth wasn't sure which annoyed him more.

No matter how she was dressed, warmth flowed from Ariel. The inner softness edged through. He could feel the emotion from her even three feet away. And he saw…pity? Yes, it was pity in her eyes. Directed at Liz. Booth lit a cigarette with a jerk of his wrist. God, he'd

rid himself of one and was being reeled in by another.
Standing there, he could feel the quicksand sucking at
his legs. Was there any closer analogy for love?

"Let's get started," he ordered briefly. Liz shot him
another look.

"Don't let me hold things up. I'll stay out of the way."
She glided to the edge of the set, sat in a director's chair
and crossed her legs. A burly man, the small woman
and what was hardly more than a boy settled behind her.

The audience had Ariel's adrenaline pumping. The
scene they were to shoot was the same one she'd auditioned with. More than any other, Ariel felt it encapsu-
lated Rae's personality, her motives, her essence. She
didn't think Liz Hunter would enjoy it, but… Ariel felt
she'd be able to gauge just how successful her performance was by Liz's reaction to it.

With a faintly bored expression on her face, Liz sat
back and watched the scene unfold. The dialogue was
not precisely a verbatim account of what had occurred
between her and Booth years before, but she recognized
the tenor. Damn him, she thought with a flicker of anger
that showed nowhere on her sculpted face. Damn him
for his memory and his talent. So this was his revenge.

While she hoped the film fell flat, she was too
shrewd to believe it would. She could shrug that off.
Liz was clever enough, experienced enough to make
the film work for her rather than against her. With the
right angle, she could get miles and miles of publicity
from Booth's work. That balanced things…to a point.

She was a woman of few emotions, but the most
finely tuned of these was jealousy. It was this that ate
at her as she sat, silent, watching. Ariel Kirkwood, she
thought as one rose-tipped nail began to tap on the arm

of the chair. Liz was vain enough to consider herself more beautiful, but there was no denying the difference in age. Years were something that haunted her.

And talent. Her teeth scraped against each other because she wanted to scream. Her own skill, the accolades and awards she'd received for it were never enough. Especially when she was faced with a beautiful, younger woman of equal ability. Damn them both. Her finger began to tap harder, staccato. The young man put a soothing hand on her shoulder and was shrugged away.

Liz could taste the envy that edged toward fury. The part should have been hers, she thought as her lips tightened. If she had played Rae, she'd have added a dozen dimensions to the part—such as it was. She had more talent in the palm of her hand than this Ariel Kirkwood had in her whole body. More beauty, more fame, more sexuality. Her head began to pound as she watched Ariel skillfully weave sex and ice into the scene.

Then her eyes met Booth's, and she nearly choked on an oath. He was laughing at her, Liz realized. Laughing, though his mouth was sober and his expression calm. He'd pay for that, she told herself as her lids lowered fractionally. For that and for everything else. She'd see that he and this no-talent actress from nowhere both paid.

Booth knew his ex-wife well enough to know what was going on in her mind. It should have pleased him; perhaps it would have only a few weeks before. Now, it did little more than slightly disgust him.

Shifting his gaze from her, he focused his attention on Ariel. Of all the scenes in the screenplay, this was the hardest for him. He'd crystallized himself too well as Phil in these few sharp, hard lines. And his Rae was too real here. Ariel made her too real, he thought as he wished for a cigarette. In this short, seven-minute scene, which would take much, much longer to complete, it was almost impossible to separate Ariel from Rae—and Rae from Liz.

Ariel had said she loved him. Fighting discomfort that was laced with panic, Booth watched her. Was it possible? Once before he'd believed a woman who'd whispered those words to him. But Ariel…there was no one and nothing quite like Ariel.

Did he love her? Once before he'd believed himself in love. But whatever emotion it had been, it hadn't been love. And it had been smeared with a fascination for great beauty, great talent, cool, cool sex. No, he didn't understand love—if it existed in the way he believed Ariel thought of it. No, he didn't understand it, and he told himself he didn't want it. What he wanted was his privacy, his peace.

And while he stood there, watching his own scene being painstakingly reproduced on film, he had neither.

"Cut. Cut and print." Chuck ran a hand along the back of his neck to ease the tension. "Hell of a job." Letting out a long breath, he walked toward Ariel and Jack. "Hell of a job, both of you. We'll wrap for today. Nothing's going to top that."

Relieved, Ariel let her stomach relax, muscle by muscle. She glanced over idly at the sound of quiet applause.

Liz rose gracefully from her chair. "Marvelous job." She gave Jack her dazzling, practiced smile before she turned to Ariel. "You have potential, dear," Liz told her. "I'm sure this part will open a few doors for you."

Ariel recognized the swipe and took it on the chin.

"Thank you, Liz." Deliberately, she drew the pins from her hair and let it fall free. She wanted badly to shed Rae. "It's a challenging part."

"You did your best with it." Smiling, Liz touched her lightly on the shoulder.

I must've been on the money, Ariel thought and grinned. *I must've been right on the money.*

Liz wanted to rip the thick, tumbled hair out by the roots. She turned to Marshell. "Pat, I'd love to have dinner. We've a lot to catch up on." She slipped her arm through his and patted his hand. "My treat, darling."

Mentally swearing, Marshell acquiesced. The best way to get her out without a scene was simply to get her out. "My pleasure, Liz. Chuck, I'll want a look at the dailies first thing in the morning."

"Oh, by the way." Liz paused beside Booth. "I really don't think this little film will do much harm to your career, darling." With an icy laugh she skimmed a finger down his shirt. "And I must say, I'm rather flattered, all in all. No hard feelings, Booth."

He looked down at the beautiful, heartless smile. "No feelings, Liz. No feelings at all."

Her fingers tightened briefly on Marshell's arm before she swept away. "Oh, Pat, I must tell you about this marvelous young actor I met in Athens…"

"Exit stage left," Jack murmured, then shrugged when Ariel raised a brow at him. "Must still be functioning as Phil. But let me tell you, that's one lady I wouldn't turn my back on."

"She's rather sad," Ariel said half to herself.

Jack gave a snort of laughter. "She's a tarantula." With another snort he cupped a hand on Ariel's shoulder. "Let me tell you something, kid. I've been in the business a lot of years, worked with lots of actresses. You're first class. And that just gripped her cookies."

"And that's sad," Ariel repeated.

"Better put a layer of something over that compassion, babe," he warned. "You'll get burned." Giving her shoulder a last squeeze, he walked off the set.

Gratefully, Ariel dropped into a chair. The lights were off now, the temperature cooling. Most of the stagehands were gone, except for three who huddled in a corner discussing a poker game. Tipping her head back, she waited as Booth approached.

"That was a tough one," she commented. "How do you feel?"

"I'm fine. You?"

"A little drained. I've only a few scenes left, none of them on this scale. Next week, I'll be back to Amanda."

"How do you feel about that?"

"The people on the soap are like family. I miss them."

"Children leave home," he reminded her.

"I know. So will I when the time's right."

"We both know you won't be signing another contract with the soap." He drew out a cigarette, lighting it automatically, drawing in smoke without tasting it. "Whether you're ready to admit it or not."

Feeling his tension, she tensed in turn. "You're mixing us again," she said quietly. "Just how much longer is it going to take you to see me for who I am, without the shadows?"

"I know who you are," Booth corrected. "I'm not sure what to do about it."

She rose. Maybe it was the lingering strain from the scene, or perhaps her sadness from watching Liz Hunter suffer in her own way. "I'll tell you what you don't want," she said with an edge to her voice he hadn't heard before. "You don't want me to love you. You don't want the responsibility of my emotions or of your own."

He could deal with this, Booth thought as he took another drag. A fight was something he could handle effortlessly. "Maybe I don't. I told you what I thought right up front."

"So you did." With a half laugh, she turned away. "Funny that you're the one who's always preaching change at me, and you're the one so unable to do so yourself. Let me tell you something, Booth." She whirled back, vibrantly glowing Ariel. "My feelings are mine. You can't dictate them to me. The only thing it's possible for you to do is dictate to yourself."

"It isn't a matter of dictating." He found he didn't want the cigarette after all. It tasted foul. Booth left it smoldering, half-crushed, in an ashtray. "It's a matter of not being able to give you what you want."

"I haven't asked you for anything."

"You don't have to ask." He was angry, really angry, without being aware when he'd crossed the line. "You've pulled at me from the start—pulled at things I want left alone. I made a commitment once, I'll be damned if I'll do it again. I don't want to change my lifestyle. I don't want—"

"To risk failure again," Ariel finished.

His eyes blazed at her, but his voice was very, very calm. "You're going to have to learn to watch your step, Ariel. Fragile bones are easily broken."

"And they mend." Abruptly, she was too weary to argue, too weary to think. "You'll have to work out your own solution, Booth. The same as I'll work out mine.

I'm not sorry I love you, or that I've told you. But I am sorry that you can't accept a gift."

When he'd watched her walk away, Booth slipped his hands in his pockets and stared at the darkened set. No, he couldn't accept it. Yet he felt as though he'd just tossed away something he'd searched for all of his life.

Chapter 10

The water was a bit choppy. Small whitecaps bounced up, were swallowed, then bounced back again. Directly overhead the sky was a hard diamond blue, but to the east, dark clouds were boiling and building. There was the threat of rain in the wind that blew in from the Atlantic. Booth estimated he had two hours before the storm caught up with him—an hour before he'd be forced to tack to shore to avoid it.

And on shore the heat would be staggering, the humidity thick enough to slice. On the water, the breeze smelled of summer and salt and storms. He could taste it as it whipped by him and billowed his sail. Exhilaration—he knew it for the sensation that could clear the mind and chill the skin. Holding lightly to the rigging, he let the wind take him.

Booth wore nothing but cutoffs and deck shoes. He

hadn't bothered to shave for two days. His eyes had grown accustomed to squinting against the sun reflecting off the water, and his hands to the feel of rough rope against the palm. Both were harsh, both were challenging.

Exhilaration? This time it hadn't come with the force he'd expected. For days he'd sailed as long as the sun and the weather allowed. He'd worked at night until his mind was drained.

Escape? Was that a better word for what he'd come for? Perhaps, Booth mused as he sailed over the choppy water. Lifting a beer to his lips he let the taste race over his tongue. Perhaps he was escaping, but he was no longer needed on the set, and he had finally had to admit that he couldn't work in the city. He needed a few days away from the filming, from the pressure to produce, from his own standards of perfection.

That was all a lie.

None of those things had driven him out of Manhattan and onto Long Island. He'd needed to get away from Ariel—from what Ariel was doing to him. And perhaps most of all from his feelings for her. Yet the miles didn't erase her from his thoughts. It took no effort to think of her, and every effort not to. Though she haunted him, Booth was certain he'd been right to come away. If thinking of her ate at him, seeing her, touching her would have driven him mad.

He didn't want her love, he told himself savagely. He couldn't—wouldn't—be responsible for the range of emotions Ariel was capable of. Booth took another long pull from the beer can, then scowled at the water. He wasn't capable of loving her in return. He didn't possess those kinds of feelings. Whatever emotions he had were directed exclusively toward his work. He'd promised himself that. Inside, in the compartment that held the brighter feelings one person had for another, he was empty. He was void.

He ached for her—body, mind, soul.

Damn her, he thought as he jerked at the rigging. Damn her for pulling at him, for crowding him…for asking nothing of him. If she'd asked, demanded, pleaded, he could have refused. It was so simple to say no to an obligation. All she did was give until he was so full of her, he was losing himself.

He'd work, Booth told himself as he began to tack methodically back toward shore. The boat bucked beneath him as the wind kicked up. Adjusting the sails, he concentrated on the pure physicality of the task. Use your muscles, your back, not your brain. Don't think, he warned himself, until it's time to write again.

He'd bury himself in work for the rest of the afternoon. He'd pour himself into his writing through the evening, late into the night, until his mind was too jumbled to think of anything—anyone. He'd stay away from her physically until he could stay away from her mentally. Then he'd go back to New York and pick up his life as he'd left it. Before Ariel.

Thunder rumbled ominously as he docked the boat.

Ariel watched the lightning snake across the sky and burst. The night sky was like a dark mirror abruptly cracked then made whole again. Still no rain. The heat storm had been threatening all evening, building up in the east and traveling toward Manhattan. She'd looked forward to it. Wearing a long shirt and nothing else, she stood at the window to watch it come.

Earlier, her neighbors had been sitting on their stoops, fanning and sweating and complaining of the heat. She didn't mind it. Before the night was over the rain would wash away the stickiness. But at the moment, though her thin shirt was clinging damply to her back and thighs, she enjoyed the enervating quality of the heat, and the violence in the sky.

The storm was coming from the east, she thought again. Perhaps Booth was already watching the rain she still anticipated. She wondered if he was working, oblivious to the booming thunder. Or if, like her, he stood and watched the fury in the sky. She wondered when he'd come back—to her.

He would, Ariel affirmed staunchly. She only hoped he'd come back with an easy mind. She'd thrown him a curve. With a half smile, Ariel felt the first rippling breeze pass through the screen and over her skin. She wasn't sorry, though his reaction had hurt, then angered her. That was over. Perhaps, for a moment, she'd forgotten that to Booth love wasn't the open-ended gift it was to her. He'd see the restrictions, the risks, the pains.

The pains, she thought, resting her palms on the windowsill. Why was she always so surprised to find out she could hurt just as intensely as she could be happy? She wanted him, physically, but he was miles from her reach, emotionally, but he'd distanced himself from her feelings.

She hadn't been surprised when Booth had absented himself from the last few days of shooting. All the key scenes had been done. Nor was she surprised when Marshell had mentioned idly that Booth had gone to his secluded Long Island home to write and to sail. She missed him, she felt the emptiness; but Ariel was too independent to mourn the loss of him for a few days. He needed his solitude. A part of her understood that, enough to keep her from misery.

Hadn't she herself painted almost through the night after Liz Hunter had visited the set?

Ariel glanced around at the frantic canvas slashed with cobalt and scarlets. It wasn't a painting she'd keep in the living room for long. Too angry, too disturbing. As soon as she'd fully coped with those feelings, she'd stick the canvas in a closet.

Everyone had his or her own means of dealing with the darker emotions. Booth's was to draw into himself; hers was to let them lash out. Either way, any way, the resolution would come. She had only to hang on a little while longer.

And so she told herself when she thought of Scott. The hearing would begin at the end of the week. That, too, would be resolved, but Ariel refused to look at any more than one solution. Scott had to come to her. The doubts she'd once harbored about her right to claim him, his need to be with her, were gone. As time went on, he became more and more unhappy with the Andersons. His visits were punctuated by desperate hugs, and more and more by pleas that he be allowed to stay with her.

It wasn't a matter of abuse or neglect. It was a simple matter of love, unconditional love that came naturally from her, and didn't come at all from his grandparents. Whatever hardships she and Scott were facing now would be a thing of the past before long. It was a time to concentrate on whens instead of nows. That was how she got through the slowly moving days between the filming and the hearing. Without Booth.

Ariel closed her eyes as the rain began to gush out of the sky. Oh God, if only the night were over.

The rain was just tapering off as Booth pushed away from his computer. He'd gotten more accomplished than he'd anticipated, but the juices were drying up. He knew better than to push himself when he got to this point. In another hour he'd try again perhaps, or maybe not for a day or two. But it would come back, and the story would flow again.

No, he couldn't write anything now, but it was still this side of midnight and he was restless. The storm had cleared the air, making him wish he were on the water again, under the burgeoning moonlight. He should eat. As he rubbed the stiffness from his neck, he remembered he hadn't bothered with dinner. A meal and an early night.

As he walked through the house into the kitchen, silence drummed around him. Strange, he'd never noticed just how thick silence could be, just how empty a house could be when it had only one occupant. And stranger still, how only a few months before he'd have appreciated both, even expected both. Again, before Ariel. His life seemed to have come down to two stages. Before Ariel and after Ariel. It wasn't an easy admission for a man to make.

Booth pulled a tray of cold cuts out of the refrigerator without any real interest. Mechanically, he fixed a sandwich, found a ripe peach and poured a glass of milk. The solitary meal had never seemed less appealing—so much so he considered tipping the entire mess down the sink.

Shaking off the feeling, he carried it into his bedroom and set the plate on the dresser. What he needed was some noise, he decided. Something to occupy his mind without straining the brain. Booth switched on the television, then flipped the channel selector without any particular goal in mind.

Normally he would have bypassed the late-night talk show in favor of an old movie. When Liz's laughter flowed out at him, he paused. He might still have passed it by, but his curiosity was piqued. Thinking it might be an interesting diversion, Booth picked up his plate, set it on the bedside table and stretched out.

He'd been on the show himself a number of times. Though he wasn't overly fond of the format or the exposure, he knew the game well enough to understand the need to reach the public through the form. The show was popular, slickly run, and the host knew his trade. With boyish charm he could draw the unexpected out of celebrities and keep the audience from turning the channel or just flicking off the switch.

"Of course I was terribly excited to film on location in Greece, Bob." Liz leaned just a bit closer to her host while her ice-blue gown glistened coolly in the lights. "And working with Ross Simmeon was a tremendous experience."

"Didn't I hear you and Simmeon had a feud going?" Robert MacAllister tossed off the question with a grin. It said, come on, relax, you can tell me. It was a well-practiced weapon.

"A feud?" Liz fluttered her lashes ingenuously. She was much too sharp to be caught in that trap. She crossed her legs so that the gown shimmered over her body. "Why, no. I can't imagine where anyone would get that idea."

"It must have something to do with the three days you refused to come on set." With a little deprecating shrug, MacAllister leaned back in his chair. "A disagreement over the number of lines in a key scene."

"That's nonsense." *Damn Simmeon and all the rumormongers.* "I'd had too much sun. My physician put me on medication for a couple of days and recommended a rest." She glittered a smile right back at him. "Of course there were a few tense moments, as there will be on any major film, but I'd work with Ross tomorrow…" or the devil himself, her tone seemed to say. "If the right script came along."

"So, what're you up to now, Liz? You've had an unbroken string of successes. It must be getting tough to find just the right property."

"It's always hard to put together the right touch of magic." She gestured gracefully so that the ring on her hand caught the light and glittered. "The right script, the right director, the right leading man. I've been so lucky—particularly since *To Meet at Midnight*."

Booth set his half-eaten sandwich aside and nearly laughed. *He'd* written it for her and had made her a major star. Top box office. Luck had had nothing to do with it.

"Your Oscar-winning performance," Bob acknowledged. "And of course a brilliant screenplay." He sent her an off-center smile. "You'd agree with that?"

It was the opening she'd been waiting for. And maneuvering toward. "Oh, yes. Booth DeWitt is possibly— no, assuredly the finest screenwriter of the eighties. Regardless of our, well, personal problems, we've always respected each other professionally."

"I know all about personal problems," Bob said ruefully and got the laugh. His three marriages had been well publicized. And so had his alimony figures. "How do you feel about his latest work?"

"Oh." Liz smiled and let one hand flutter to her throat before it fell into her lap. "I don't suppose the content's much of a secret, is it?"

Again the expected laugh, a bit more restrained.

"I'm sure Booth's script is wonderful, they all are. If it's, ah, one-sided," she said carefully, "it's only natural. From what I'm told it's common for a writer to reflect some parts of his personal life…and in his own way," she added. "As a matter of fact, I visited the set just last week. Pat Marshell's producing, you know, and Chuck Tyler's directing."

"But…" Bob prompted, noting her obvious reluctance.

"As I said, it's so difficult to find that right brand of magic." She tossed out the first seeds with a smile. "And Booth's never done anything for the small screen before. A difficult transition for anyone."

"Jack Rohrer's starring." Obligingly, Bob fed her the next line.

"Yes, excellent casting there. I thought Jack was absolutely brilliant in *Of Two Minds*. That was a script he could really sink his teeth into."

"But this one…"

"Well, I happen to be a big Jack Rohrer fan," Liz said, apparently sidestepping the question. "I doubt there's any part he can't find some meat on."

"And his costar?" Bob folded his hands on his desk. Liz was out for the jugular, he decided. It wouldn't hurt his ratings.

"The female lead's a lovely girl. I can't quite think of

her name, but I believe she has a part on a soap opera. Booth often likes to experiment rather than to go with experienced actors."

"As he did with you."

Her eyes narrowed fractionally. She didn't quite like that tone, or that direction. "You could put it that way." The haughtiness in her voice indicated otherwise. "But really, when one has the production rate this project has, one should shoot for the best talent available. Naturally, that's a personal opinion. I've always thought actors should pay their dues—God knows, I paid mine—rather than be cast in a major production because of a…shall we say personal whim?"

"Do you think Booth DeWitt has a personal whim going with Ariel Kirkwood? That's her name, isn't it?"

"Why, yes, I think it is. As to the other, I could hardly say." She smiled again, charmingly. "Especially on the air, Bob."

"Her physical resemblance to you is striking."

"Really?" Liz's eyes frosted. "I much prefer being one of a kind, though of course it's flattering to have someone attempt to emulate me. Naturally, I wish the girl the best of luck."

"That's gracious of you, Liz, particularly since the plot line's rumored to be less than kind to the character that some say mirrors you."

"Those that know me will pay little attention to a slanted view, Bob. All in all, I'll be fascinated to see the finished product." The statement was laced with bore-dom, almost as if she'd yawned. "That is, of course, if it's ever actually aired."

"Ever aired? You see some problem there?"

"Nothing I can talk about," she said with obvious

reluctance. "But you and I know how many things can happen between filming and airing, Bob."

"No plans to sue, huh, Liz?"

She laughed, but it came off hollow. "That would give the film entirely too much importance."

Bob mugged at the camera. "Well, with that we'll take a little break here. When we come back, James R. Lemont will be joining us to tell us about his new book, *Hollywood Secrets*. We know about those, too, don't we, Liz?" After his wink, the screen switched to the first commercial.

Leaning back against the pillows, his meal forgotten, Booth drew on his cigarette and sent the smoke to the ceiling. He was angry. He could feel it in the hard knot in his stomach. The swipes she'd taken at the film hadn't even been subtle, he reflected. Oh, perhaps she'd fool a certain percentage of people, but no one remotely connected with the business, and no one with any perception. She'd done her best to toss a few poison darts and had ended up, in Booth's opinion, by making a fool of herself.

But he was angry. And the anger, he discovered, came from the slices she'd taken at Ariel. Quite deliberate, quite calculated, and unfortunately for Liz, quite obvious. She was a cat, and normally a clever one. Jealousy was essentially the only thing that could make her lose that edge.

Naturally she'd be jealous of Ariel, Booth mused. Of anyone young, beautiful and talented. Add that to the bile she'd have to swallow over the film itself, and Liz would be as close to rage as her limited range of emotions would allow. And this was her way of paying back.

Rising, Booth slammed off the set before he paced

the room. She'd bring up the film—and Ariel—in every interview she gave, at every party she attended, in the hope to sabotage both. Of course, she wouldn't do any appreciable damage, but knowing that didn't ease his temper. No one had the right to take potshots at Ariel, and the fact that they were being taken through him, because of him, made it worse.

He could, if he chose, book himself on the circuit to promote the film and to counter Liz's campaign. That would only add fuel to the fire. He knew the best way to make the storm Liz was trying to brew fizzle was to keep silent. Frustrated, he walked to the window. He could hear the water from there. Just barely. He wondered if Ariel had watched the late-night talk show. And how she was dealing with it.

Stretched out in the hammock, plumped by pillows, with a bowl of fresh popcorn resting on her stomach, Ariel listened to Liz Hunter. Her brow lifted once as a reference was made to herself. Ariel crunched on popcorn and smiled as Robert MacAllister reminded Liz that *the girl's* name was Ariel Kirkwood.

Poor Liz, she thought. She was only making it worse for herself. Perhaps because Ariel had been inside Rae's skin for so long, she noticed small things. The tapping of a fingertip on the arm of the chair, the brief tightening of the lips, the flash in the eyes that was a bit of anger, a bit of desperation. The more Liz talked, the shakier her support became.

She'd have been much better off if she'd said nothing, Ariel mused. A no-comment, a shrug of that haughty shoulder. Miscalculation, Ariel thought with a sigh. A foolish one.

I can't hurt her. Ariel shifted her gaze from the screen to the ceiling. No one can take her talent away from her. A pity she doesn't realize that. It's Booth she really wants to hurt, Ariel decided. She'd want to make him pay for using Rae to strip off a few masks. Yet didn't Liz realize he was just as bitterly honest with his own character?

Ariel glanced back at the television screen as Liz's face dominated the screen. There was a line of dissatisfaction between her brows, very faint. Ariel wondered if she were the only one who noticed it, because she was so intimately involved. I know you, Ariel told the image on the screen, I know you inside and out. And that made her swallow hard. It was just a little scary.

Ariel lay back, tuning out the sound of the set and tuning back into the rain. It was nearly over, only a patter now against the windowpane. Booth had probably seen it, she decided. And if he hadn't caught the show, he'd know of the content very soon. He'd be angry. Ariel could almost see his hard-eyed, grim-mouthed reaction. She herself had been fighting an edge of temper that threatened to dominate her other feelings.

Anger was useless; she wished she could tell him. He had to know that he'd opened the door for this when he'd written the script. She'd opened it a bit further when she'd taken the part. She hoped, when he'd calmed, that he'd see Liz Hunter had done the film more good than harm.

When the phone rang, Ariel leaned over. Years of experience kept her balanced rather than tumbling out of the hammock and onto the floor. Swinging a bit dangerously, she gripped the phone and hauled it up to her. "Hello."

"That witch."

With a half laugh, Ariel lay back on the pillows. "Hi, Stella."

"Did you catch the MacAllister show?"

"Yeah, I've got it on."

"Listen, Ariel, she's making a joke out of herself. Anyone with two brain cells will see that."

"Then why're you angry?"

She could hear Stella take a deep breath. "I've been sitting here listening to that woman talk, wishing you the *best* of luck." Stella muttered something under her breath, then began to talk so fast the words tumbled into each other. "The best of luck my foot. She'd like to see you drop off the face of the earth. She'd like to stick a knife in you."

"A nail file, maybe."

"How can you joke about it?" Stella demanded.

Because if I don't I might just start screaming. "How can you take it so seriously?" Ariel said instead.

"Listen, Ariel…" Stella's voice was barely controlled. "I know that kind of woman. I've been playing the type for the past five years. There's nothing she wouldn't do, nothing, if she thought she could get to you. Damn it, you trust everyone."

"Some less than others." Though the concern and the loyalty touched her, she laughed. "Stella, I'm not a complete fool."

"You're not a fool at all," Stella shot back, outraged. "But you're naive. You actually believe the kid who stops you on the street asking for a donation is really collecting for a foundling home."

"He might be," Ariel mumbled. "Besides, what does that have to do with—"

"Everything!" Stella cut her off with something close to a roar. "I care about you. I worry about you every time I think about you walking blithely down the street without a thought to the crazies in the world."

"Come on, Stella, if I thought about it too much I'd never go out at all."

"Well think about this: Liz Hunter's a powerful, vindictive woman who'd like to ruin you. You watch your back, Ariel."

Who'd know that better than I? Ariel thought with a quick shudder. I've been playing her character for weeks. "If I promise, will you stop worrying?"

"No." Slightly mollified, Stella sighed. "Promise anyway."

"You got it. Are you calm now?"

Stella made a quiet sound in her throat. "I don't understand why you're not angry."

"Why should I be when you're doing it for me— and so well?"

Stella heaved a long breath. "Good night, Ariel."

"Night, Stella… Thanks."

Ariel replaced the receiver and swung gently to and fro in the hammock. As she stared up at the ceiling, she marveled over how fortunate she was. Friendship was a precious thing. To have someone ready to leap to your defense, claws bared, was a comforting sensation. She had friends like that, and a job that paid her well for doing what she would gleefully have done for nothing. She had the unquestioning love of a little boy, and God willing, would have him to care for within a few weeks. She had so much.

As Ariel lay back, struggling to count her blessings, she thought of Booth. And ached for him.

Two days later, Ariel received a surprise visit. It was her first free day since resuming her role of Amanda. She was spending it doing something she rarely started, and more rarely finished. Housecleaning.

In tattered shorts and a halter, she sat on her windowsill two stories up, and leaning out, washed the outside of her windows. The volume on her radio was turned up so that the sinuous violins of *Scheherazade* all but shook the panes. Occasionally someone from the neighborhood would shout up at her. Ariel would stop working—something that took no effort at all—and shout back down.

The important thing was to keep busy, to keep occupied. If she gave herself more than a brief moment of spare time, time to think, she might go mad. The next day marked the beginning of the custody hearing. And a full two weeks since she'd last seen Booth. Ariel polished window glass until it shone.

She felt something like an itch between the shoulder blades, like a fingertip on the back of the neck. Twisting her head, she looked down and saw Booth on the sidewalk below. Relief came in waves. Even if she'd tried, even if she'd thought to try, she couldn't have stopped the smile that illuminated her whole face.

"Hi."

Looking up at her, he felt a need so great it buckled his knees. "What the hell are you doing?"

"Washing the windows."

"You could break your neck."

"No, I'm anchored." One of the kittens brushed against her ankles so that she jolted and braced herself with her knees. "Are you coming up?"

"Yeah." Without another word, he disappeared from view.

As he climbed the stairs Booth reminded himself of his promise. He wasn't going to touch her—not once. He would say what he'd come to say, do what he'd come to do, then leave. He wouldn't touch her and start that endless cycle of longings and desires and dreams all over again. Over the past two weeks he'd purged himself of her.

As he reached the landing he nearly believed it. Then she opened the door.

She still held a damp rag in one hand. She wore no makeup; the flush of color in her cheeks came from pleasure and exertion. Her hair was scooped back and tied with a bit of yarn. The scent of ammonia was strong.

His fingers itched for just one touch, just one. Booth curled them into his palms and stuck them in his pockets.

"It's good to see you." Ariel leaned against the door and studied him. People didn't change in two weeks, she reminded herself as she compared every angle and plane in his face with the memory she'd been carrying with her. He looked the same, a bit browner perhaps from the sun, but the same. Love washed over her.

"You've been sailing."

"Yes, quite a bit."

"It's good for you. I can see it." She stepped back,

knowing from the tense way he was standing that he wouldn't accept her hand if she offered. "Come in."

He stepped into chaos. When Ariel cleaned, it was from the bottom up and nothing was safe. Drawers had been turned out, tables cleared off. Furniture and windows gleamed. There wasn't a clear place to stand, much less sit.

"Sorry," she said as she followed his survey. "I'm a bit behind on my spring cleaning." The pressure in her chest was increasing with every second they stood beside each other, and miles apart. "Want a drink?"

"No, nothing. I'll make this quick because you're busy." He'd make it quick because it hurt, physically, painfully, not to touch what he still wanted…and to still want what he'd convinced himself he couldn't have. "I'm assuming you saw the MacAllister show the other night."

"That's old news," Ariel countered. She sat on the hammock, legs dangling free, fingers locked tightly.

With his hands still in his pockets, Booth rocked back on his heels. "How'd you feel about it?"

With a shrug, Ariel crossed her ankles. "She took a couple stabs at the film, but—"

"She took a couple stabs at you," he corrected. His voice had tightened, his eyes narrowed.

Gauging his mood, Ariel decided to play it light. She smiled. "I'm not bleeding."

Booth frowned at her a moment, then judged she was a great deal less concerned than he. That was something he had to change. "She hasn't stopped there, Ariel." He walked closer, the better to study her face, the better to perhaps catch the drift of her scent. "She had quite a little session with the producer of your show, then with a few network executives."

"With my producer?" Puzzled, she tilted her head and tried to reason it out. "Why?"

"She wants them to fire you—or, ah, to let your contract lapse."

Stunned, she said nothing. But her face went pale. The rag slipped silently from her hand to the floor.

"She'd agree to do a series of guest spots for the show, if you were no longer on it. Your producer politely turned her down. So she went upstairs."

Ariel swallowed the panic. All she could think, all that drummed in her mind was, *not now, not during the hearing.* She needed the stability of that contract for Scott. "And?"

He hadn't expected this white-lipped, wide-eyed reaction. A woman with her temperament should have been angry, angry enough to rage, throw things, explode. He could even have understood amusement, a burst of laughter, a shake of the head and a shrug. She was confident enough for that. He'd thought she was. What he saw in her eyes was basic fear.

"Ariel, just how important do you think you are to the show?"

She found she had to swallow before she could form the first word. "Amanda's a popular character. I get the lion's share of mail, a lot of it addressed to Amanda rather than me. In my last contract, my scale was upgraded with the minimum amount of negotiation." She swallowed again and gripped her hands together. That was all very logical, all very practical. She wanted to scream. "Anyone can be replaced. On a soap, that's the number-one rule. Are they going to let me go?"

"No." Frowning at her, he stepped closer. "I'm surprised you'd think they would. You're already their biggest reason for the ratings lead. And with the film due in the fall, the show's bound to cash in on it. In a strictly practical way of thinking, you—day after day—are worth a great deal more to the network than Liz in a one-shot deal." When Ariel let out a long breath he had to fight the urge to take her into his arms. "Does the show mean that much to you?"

"Yes, it means that much to me."

"Why?"

"It's my show," she said simply. "My character." As the panic faded, the anger seeped in. "If I leave it, it'll be because it's what I want, or because I'm not good enough anymore." Giving in to rage she plucked up a little yellow vase from the table beside her and flung it and the baby's breath it held at the wall. Glass shattered, flowers spilled. "I've given five years of my life to that show." As her breathing calmed again, she stared at the shards of vase and broken blooms. "It's important to me," she continued, looking back up at Booth. "At the moment, for a lot of reasons, it's essential." Ariel gripped the side of the hammock and struggled to relax. "How did you hear about this?"

"From Pat. There's been quite a meeting of the minds as concerns you. We decided you should hear about this latest move privately."

"I appreciate it." The anger was fading. Relief made her light-headed. "Well, I'm sorry she feels so pressured that she'd try to do me out of a job, but I imagine she'll back off now."

"You're smarter than that."

"There's nothing she can do to me, not really. And

every time she tries, she only makes it worse for herself." Slowly, deliberately, she relaxed her hands. "Every interview she gives is free publicity for the film."

"If there's any way she can hurt you, she will. I should've thought of that before I cast you as Rae."

Smiling, Ariel lifted her hands to his arms. "Are you worried about me? I'd like you to be…just a little."

He should have backed off right then. But he needed, badly needed to absorb that contact. Just her hands on his arms. If he were careful, very careful, it might be enough. "Whatever trouble she causes you I'm responsible for."

"That's a remarkably ridiculous statement—arrogant, egotistical." She grinned. "And exactly like you. I've missed you, Booth. I've missed everything about you."

She was drawing him closer, but more, she was drawing him in. Even as her hand reached for his face, he was lowering his mouth to hers. And the first taste was enough to make him forget every promise he'd made during this absence.

Ariel moaned as her lips met his. It seemed she'd been waiting for years to feel that melting thrill again. More. The greed flashed through her. She pulled him down so that the hammock swayed under their combined weight.

There was no gentleness in either of them now. Impatience shimmered. Without words they told each other to hurry—hurry and touch me; it's been too long. And as clothes were tugged away and flesh met flesh, they both took hungrily from the other.

The movement of the hammock was like the sea, and he felt the freedom. There was freedom simply in being near her again. And from freedom sprang the madness. He couldn't stop his hands from racing over her. He couldn't prevent his mouth from trying to devour every inch. He was starving for her and no longer cared that he had vowed to abstain. Her skin flowed warm and soft under his hands. Her mouth was hot and silky. The generosity he could never quite measure simply poured from her.

She'd stopped thinking the moment he'd kissed her again. Ariel didn't need the intellect now, only the senses. She could taste the salt on his skin as they clung together in the moist heat of the afternoon; the dark male flavor along his throat enticed her back, again and again. There was a fury of desire in him, more than she'd ever known in him before. It made her skin tremble to be wanted with such savagery.

But with the trembling came a mirroring desire in herself. The top of the hammock scraped against her back as his body pressed against hers. For one isolated moment, she thought she could feel the individual strands, then that sensation faded into another.

His hands were in her hair, holding her head back so that he could plunder her mouth. She heard his breath shudder, and saw, as her lashes fluttered up, that he was watching her. Always watching.

His eyes stayed open and on hers when he plunged into her. He wanted to see her, needed to know that her need for him was as great as his for her. And he could see it—in the trembling mouth. His name came from there in a breathy whisper. In the stunned pleasure in her eyes. He could bring her that. He could bring her that, Booth thought as he buried his face in her hair. He wanted to bring her everything.

"Ariel..." In the last sane corner of his mind he knew they were both near the edge. He took her face in his hands and crushed his mouth to hers so that they crested, swallowing each other's cry of pleasure.

The movement of the hammock eased, soothing now, like a cradle. They were wrapped together, facing, with her head in the curve of his shoulder. Their bodies were damp from the heat in the air, and from the heat within. A length of her hair fell over her and onto his chest.

"I thought of you," Booth murmured. His eyes were closed. His heartbeat was slowing, but the arms around her didn't loosen. "I could never stop thinking about you."

Ariel's eyes were open, and she smiled. She'd needed no other words but those. "Sleep with me awhile." Turning her head she kissed his shoulder before settling again. "Just for a little while."

For days and nights she'd thought only of tomorrows. The time had come again to think only of now. Long after he slept, she lay awake, feeling the hammock move gently.

Chapter 11

Ariel sat on a small wooden bench outside the court-room. It was a busy hallway with people coming and going, but no one paid much attention to a solitary woman in a cream-colored suit who stared straight ahead.

The first day of the hearing was over, and she felt a curious mixture of relief and tension. It had begun; there was no going back. A door opened down the hall, and a flood of people poured out. She'd never felt more alone in her life.

Bigby had outlined it for her. There'd been no sur-prises. Despite the legal jargon, the first day had dealt basically with establishing the groundwork. Still, to Ariel's mind the preliminary questions had been ter-ribly cut-and-dried. But the wheels had begun to turn, and now that they had, maybe the pace would pick up.

Just let it be over with quickly, she thought and closed her eyes briefly. *Just let it be done.* The tension came from the thought of tomorrow. The relief came from the absolute certainty that she was doing the right thing.

Bigby came out of the courtroom with his slim brief-case in his hand. With his other, he reached out to her. "Let me buy you a drink."

Ariel smiled, linking her hand with his as she rose. "Deal. But make it coffee."

"You did well in there today."

"I didn't do much of anything."

He started to speak, then changed his mind. Maybe it was best not to point out how much she'd done by simply being. Her freshness, the concern in her eyes, the tone of her voice—all of that had been a vital contrast to the stiff backs and stone faces of the Andersons. A judge in a custody suit, a good one, was influenced by more than facts and figures.

"Just keep doing it," he advised, then gave her hand a squeeze as they walked down the hall. Neither of them noticed the dark-suited man in horn rims who followed. "Tell me how the rest of your life's going," he requested. In his unobtrusive way, Bigby guided her through the doors as he guided her thoughts. "It isn't every day I represent a rising celebrity."

She laughed even as the first wave of heat rose off the sidewalk and struck her. New York in midsummer was hot and humid and sweaty. "Is that what I am?"

"Your picture was in *Tube*—and your name was brought up on the MacAllister show." He grinned as she arched a brow. "I'm impressed."

"Read *Tube,* do you, Charlie?" He was trying to keep her calm, she realized. And he was doing it expertly.

She slid a companionable arm through his. "I have to admit, the publicity isn't going to hurt the soap, the film or me."

"In that order?"

Ariel smiled and shrugged. "Depends on my mood." No, she wasn't without ambition. The *Tube* spread had given her a great deal of self-satisfaction. "It's been a long time between shampoo commercials, and I won't be sorry if I don't have to stand, lathered up, for three hours again anytime soon."

They entered a coffee shop where the temperature dropped by twenty-five degrees. Ariel gave a quick shiver and a sigh of relief. "So professionally, everything's rolling along?" Charlie asked.

"No complaints." Ariel slipped into the little vinyl booth and pushed off her shoes. "They're casting for *Chapter Two* next week. I haven't done live theater in too long."

Bigby clucked his tongue as he picked up a menu. The man in the dark suit took the booth behind them, settling with his back to Ariel's. "You don't sit still, do you?"

"Not any longer than I can help it. I have good feelings about the custody suit, maybe because I'm on a professional roll. It's all going to work out, Charlie. I'm going to have Scott with me, and Booth's film's going to be a smash."

He eyed her over his glasses, then grinned. "The power of positive thinking."

"If it works." She leaned her elbows on the table, then rested her chin on her fists. "All my life I've been moving toward certain goals, without really understanding that I was setting them for myself. They're almost within reach."

Bigby glanced up at the waitress before he turned back to Ariel. "How about some pie with the coffee?"

"You twisted my arm. Blueberry." She touched the tip of her tongue to her lip because she could almost taste it.

"Two of each," Bigby told the waitress. "Speaking of Booth DeWitt..." he went on.

"Were we?"

He caught the gleam of amusement in Ariel's eye. "I think you mentioned him to me a few weeks ago. A man who didn't think much of relationships or actresses?"

"You've quite a memory—and very sharp deductive skills."

"It was easy enough to put two and two together, particularly after Liz Hunter's performance on the Mac-Allister show the other night."

"Performance?" Ariel repeated with a half smile.

"An actor can usually see through another, I'd think. A lawyer's got a lot of actor in him." He paused and folded his hands on the chipped Formica much as he did on his desk. "She put DeWitt through the wringer a couple of years ago."

"They damaged each other. You know, sometimes I think people can be attracted to the specific persons who are the worst for them."

"Is that from personal experience?"

Her eyes became very sober, her mouth very soft. "Booth is right for me. In a lot of ways he'll make my life difficult, but he's right for me."

"What makes you so sure?"

"I'm in love with him." When the pie was brought

over, Ariel ignored the coffee and concentrated on it. "Bless you, Charlie," she said after the first bite.

He lifted a brow at the sliver of pie she was in raptures over. "You're easily impressed."

"Cynic. Eat it."

He picked up a fork and polished it absently with a paper napkin. "At the risk of putting my foot in it, DeWitt isn't the type of man I'd've matched you with."

Ariel swallowed the next mouthful. "Oh?"

"He's very intense, serious-minded. His scripts have certainly indicated that. And you're…"

"Flaky?" she suggested, breaking off the next piece of pie.

"No." Bigby opened one of the little plastic containers of cream that were heaped in a bowl on the table. "You're anything but that. But you're full of life—the joy of it. It's not that you don't face the hard side when it comes up, but you don't look for it. It seems to me DeWitt does."

"Maybe—maybe he expects it. If you expect it and it happens, you aren't as staggered by it. For some people, it's a defensive move." A small frown creased her brow before she smoothed it away. "I think Booth and I can learn a lot from each other."

"And what does Booth think—or am I out of line?"

"You're not out of line, Charlie," she said absently as she remembered how grim Booth had been when he'd come to her door, how intensely he'd made love to her. He'd relaxed, degree by slow degree. Then he'd slept, with his arms tightly around her, as if he'd just needed to hold on. To her, she'd wondered, or to the peace? Perhaps it didn't matter. "It's hard for Booth," she murmured. "He wanted to be left alone, wanted his life to go on a certain way. I've interfered with that. He needs more time, more space."

"And what do you need?"

She looked over and saw her answer hadn't pleased him. *He's thinking of me,* Ariel realized, touched. Reaching over, she laid a hand on his. "I love him, Charlie. That's enough, for now. I do know it's not enough for always, but people can't put a control switch on emotions. I can't," she corrected.

"Does that mean he can?"

"To a certain extent." Ariel opened her mouth again, then shook her head. "No, I don't want to change him, even in that way. Not change. I need the balance he brings me, and I need to be able to lighten some of those shadows he carries around. It's the same with Scott, in a way. I need the stability he brings to my life—the way Scott, maybe children in general, can center it. Basically, I have an outrageous need to be needed."

"Have you told Booth about Scott? About the custody hearing?"

"No." Ariel stirred sugar into her coffee but didn't drink it. "It doesn't seem fair to saddle him with a problem that was already in full swing when we met. Instinct tells me to handle it myself, then when it's resolved, to tell Booth in my own way."

"He might not like it," Bigby pointed out. "The one thing Ford brought up in our last meeting that I have to agree with is that some men can't or won't be responsible for another man's child."

Ariel shook her head. "I don't believe that of Booth. But if it's true, it's something I'll have to deal with."

"If you did have to make a choice?"

She said nothing at first, as she dealt with the ache

even the possibility brought her. "When you make a choice between two people you love," Ariel said quietly, "you choose the one who needs you the most." She lifted her eyes again. "Scott's only a child, Charlie."

He leaned across to pat her hand. "I just wanted to hear you say it. To be completely unprofessional again," he said with a grin, "there isn't a man in the world who'd turn down either you or Scott."

"That's why I'm crazy about you." She paused a moment, then touched her fork to her tongue. "Charlie, would you think I was really a hedonist if I ordered another piece of this pie?"

"Yes."

"Good." Ariel lifted a hand and gestured for the waitress. "Once in a while I just have to be decadent."

Amanda's life was a pressure cooker. As she went over the pacing of her lines one last time, Ariel decided she was grateful for the tension. It helped her deal with reality just a little better. She'd spent the morning in court, and the following day she was scheduled to take the stand. That was one part she couldn't rehearse for. But the good feeling she'd experienced the first day of the hearing hadn't faded, nor had her optimism. It was poor Amanda, Ariel mused, who'd continue to have problems that would never completely be resolved. That was life in a soap opera.

The rest of the cast had yet to return from the lunch break. Ariel sat alone in the studio—lounged, that is, on the rumpled bed she would rise from when Amanda was awakened by the sound of breaking glass. Alone and defenseless, she'd face the Trader's Bend Ripper.

She'd have only her wits and professional skill to protect her from a psychotic killer.

Already in costume, a plain nightshirt in periwinkle-blue, she continued to murmur her lines out loud while doing a few lazy leg lifts. She'd had some vague twinges of guilt about the second piece of blueberry pie.

"Well, well, so this is the lightning pace of daytime television."

Immersed in the gripping scene between Amanda and a psychopath, Ariel dropped the script and gasped. The pages fluttered back down to her stomach while her hand flew to her throat. "Good God, Booth. I hope you're up on your CPR, because my heart just stopped."

"I'll get it started again." Placing a hand on either side of her head, he leaned down and kissed her—softly, slowly, thoroughly. As surprised by the texture of the kiss as she'd been by his sudden appearance, Ariel lay still and absorbed. She knew only that something was different; but with her mind spinning and her blood pumping she couldn't grab on to it.

He knew. As he eased down to sit on the bed and prolonged the kiss, Booth understood precisely what was different. He loved her. He'd awakened alone in his own bed that morning, reaching for her. He'd read something foolish in the paper and had automatically thought how she'd have laughed. He'd seen a young girl with a balloon giggling as she'd dragged her mother toward the park. And he'd thought of Ariel.

And thinking of her, he'd seen that the sky was beautiful and blue, that the city was frantic and full of surprises, that life was a joy. How foolish he'd been to resist her, and all she offered.

She was his second chance... No, if he were honest,

he'd admit that Ariel was his first chance at real happiness—complete happiness. He was no longer going to allow memories of ugliness to bar him from that, or from her.

"How's your heart rate?" he murmured.

Ariel let out a long breath, let her eyes open slowly. "You can cancel the ambulance."

He glanced at the tumbled bed, then down her very sedate, very appealing costume. "Were you having a nap?"

"I," she countered primly, "was working. The rest of the cast is at lunch, I wasn't due in till one." She pushed at the hair that fell dark and disordered over his brow. No tension, she thought immediately, and smiled. "What're you doing here? You're usually knee-deep in brilliant phrases this time of day."

"I wanted to see you."

"That's nice." Sitting up, she threw her arms around his neck. "That's very nice."

It would take so little, Booth mused as he held her close. What would her reaction be when he told her that he'd stopped resisting, and that nothing had ever made him happier than having her in his life? Tonight, he thought, nuzzling into her neck. Tonight when they were alone, when there was no one to disturb them, he'd tell her. And he'd ask her.

"Can you stay awhile?" Ariel didn't know why she felt so wonderful, nor did she want to explore the reasons.

"I'll stay until you wrap, then I'm going to steal you and take you home with me."

She laughed, and as she shifted her weight, the script crumpled beneath her.

"Your lines," Booth warned.

"I know them. This—" she flung back her head so that her eyes glittered "—is a climactic scene full of danger and drama."

He looked back at the bed. "And sex?"

"No!" Shoving him away she scrambled onto her knees. "Amanda's tossing and turning in bed, her dreams were disturbed. Fade out—soft focus—she's wandering through a mist, lost, alone. She hears foot-steps behind her. Close-up. Fear. And then…" While her voice took on a dramatic pitch, she tossed her hair behind her back. "Up ahead, she sees a figure in the fog." Ariel lifted a hand as if to brush away a curtain of mist. "Should she run toward it—away from it? The footsteps behind her come faster, her breathing quick-ens. A sliver of moonlight—pale, eerie—cuts through. It's Griff up ahead holding out a hand to her, calling her name in an echoing, disembodied voice. He loves her, she wants to go to him. But the footsteps are clos-ing in. And as she begins to run, there's the sharp, cruel glimmer of a knife."

Ariel grabbed both of his shoulders then did a mock faint into his lap. Booth grinned. A quick tug of her hair had her eyes opening. "And then?"

"The man wants more." Scrambling up again, Ariel pushed the script aside. "The scream's caught in her throat, and before she can free it, there's a crash, a splin-ter of glass. Amanda jerks up in bed, her face glistening with sweat, her breath heaving." When she demon-strated, Booth wondered if she knew just how clever she was. "Did she dream it, or did she really hear it? Fright-ened, but impatient with herself, she gets out of bed."

Swinging her feet to the floor, Ariel got out of bed,

frowning at the door as Amanda would do, absently pushing back her hair and reaching for the low light beside the bed. "Perhaps it was the wind," she continued. "Perhaps it was the dream, but she knows she'll never get back to sleep unless she takes a look. Music builds—lots of bass—as she opens the bedroom door. Cut to commercial."

"Come on, Ariel." Exasperated, he grabbed her hand and pulled her back toward the bed.

Obligingly she circled his neck with her arms as she stood in front of him. "Now you'll learn the best way to keep that shine on your no-wax floor."

He pinched her, hard. "It's the Ripper."

"Maybe," she said with a flutter of her lashes. "Maybe not."

"It's the Ripper," he said decisively. "And our intrepid Amanda goes downstairs. How does she get out of being victim number five?"

"Six," Ariel corrected. "The saying goes, that's for me to know and you to find out." With a jerk of his wrist, he'd whipped her around so that she tumbled into his lap, laughing. "Go ahead, torture me, do your worst. I'll never talk." Linking her hands around his neck, she looked up at him and smiled. And she was so beautiful, so full of life at its best that she took his breath away.

"I love you, Ariel."

He felt the fingers at his neck go limp, saw the smile fade, her eyes widen. Inside, Ariel felt as though someone had just cut off the flow of blood from her heart. "That's a tough way to find out a plotline," she managed after a moment. She would have sat up if she'd had the strength to resist the gentle pressure of his hand on her shoulder.

"I love you, Ariel," he repeated, forgetting all his plans for telling her with finesse and with intimacy. "I think I always have. I know I always will." He cupped her face in his hand as her eyes filled. "You're everything I've ever wanted and was afraid to hope for. Stay with me." He touched his lips to hers and felt the tremor. "Marry me."

When he would have drawn back, she clutched at his shirt. Burying her face in his shoulder she took a deep breath. "Be sure," she whispered. "Booth, be absolutely sure because I'll never give you a moment's peace. I'll never let you get away. Before you ask me again, remember that. I don't believe in mutual disagreements or irreconcilable differences. With me, it's forever, Booth. It's for always."

He forced her head back. In his eyes she saw the fire and the passion. And the love. "You're damn right." Her breathless laugh was muffled against his mouth. "I want to get married quickly." He punctuated the words with another kiss. "And quietly. Just how soon can they shoot around Amanda so we can have more than a weekend honeymoon?"

Ariel hadn't known anyone could outpace her. Now, her thoughts jumbled as she struggled to keep up. Marriage—he was already talking of marriage and honeymoons. "Well, I, let's see… After Griff saves Amanda from the Ripper, she loses the baby and goes into a coma. The hospital scenes could be—"

"Aha." With a self-satisfied smile, Booth kissed her nose. "So Griff saves her from the Ripper, which removes him from the list of suspects."

Ariel's eyes narrowed. "You rat."

"Just be glad I'm not a spy for another network. You're a pushover."

"I'll show you a pushover," Ariel claimed, and overbalanced him so that he landed on his back. He loved her. The thought brought on such giddiness, she collapsed against him, laughing. Before he could retaliate, they heard someone rushing up the stairs.

"Ariel! Ariel, you'd better take a look at—" Stella skidded to a halt when she saw Ariel and Booth laughing and half lying on the bed. She whipped the paper she held behind her back and swore under her breath. "Whoops!" With the aid of an embarrassed smile she called on all her skill to keep either of them from noticing that she felt slightly ill inside and desperately worried. "Well, I'd've knocked if you'd bothered to close the door." She gestured with her free hand toward the false wall. "Suppose I go out and come in again?" *Right after I burn this paper,* she thought grimly, and grinning, backed up.

"Don't go." Ariel struggled all the way up, but kept one hand tucked into Booth's. "I'm about to bestow a singularly great honor on you." She squeezed Booth's fingers. "My sister, however rotten, should be the first to know."

"By all means."

"Stella…" Ariel stopped because she caught a glimpse of something in her friend's eyes. A glimpse was enough. "What is it?"

"Nothing. I remembered I have to talk to Neal about something, that's all. Look, I'd better catch him before he—"

But Ariel was already rising from the bed. "What was it you wanted me to see, Stella?"

"Oh, nothing." There was a warning, a deliberate one, in her eyes. "It can wait."

Unsmiling, Ariel held out her hand, palm up.

Stella's fingers curled tighter around the paper. "Ariel, it's not a good time. I think you'd better—"

"I think I'd better see it now."

"Damn it." With a glance over Ariel's shoulder at Booth, Stella passed her the paper.

Celebrity Explorer, Ariel noted with a slight flicker of annoyance. As tabloids went it was bottom of the barrel. Half-amused, she glanced over the exploitive headlines. "Really, Stella, if this is the best you can do for lunchtime reading, I'm disillusioned." Absently, she turned it over and scanned under the fold. From behind her Booth saw the tension shoot into her body.

SOAP OPERA QUEEN'S DESPERATE BATTLE

FOR LOVE CHILD

Below the bold print headline was a grainy picture of Ariel sitting on the grass in Central Park with Scott's face caught in her hands. In one part of her mind she remembered that frozen moment from their last Sunday afternoon. As she stared at it, appalled, sickened, she didn't hear Booth rise and come to her.

Something slammed into his stomach—not a hammer but a fist that thrust then ground deep. Even the poor quality of the photo didn't disguise the stunning resemblance between Ariel and the child that laughed into her face. There was no mistaking the tie of blood. As the headline shouted out at him, Booth wanted to murder.

"Just what the hell is this?"

Shaken, Ariel looked up. Scott was not to see it, she thought over and over. This was not to touch him.

How? How had it leaked? The Andersons? No, she rejected that thought instantly. They wanted publicity less than she did.

The picture…who'd taken it? Someone had followed her, she decided. Someone had followed her and found out about Scott, the custody hearing. Then they'd twisted it into an ugly headline and an exploitive article. But who…?

Liz Hunter. Ariel's fingers tightened on the newspaper. Of course, it had to be. There were few women who knew better than Ariel what that type of person was capable of. Liz hadn't been able to get to her professionally, so she'd taken the next step.

"Ariel, I asked you what the hell this is."

Ariel focused on Booth abruptly. *Oh God,* she thought, *now I have to work my way through the ugliness before I can explain.* Already, she saw the anger, the distrust. "I'd like to talk to you privately," she said calmly enough. "Down in my dressing room."

As Ariel turned to go, Stella reached out, then dropped her hand helplessly back to her side. "Ariel, I'm sorry."

She only shook her head. "No, it's all right. We'll talk later."

As they wound their way through the studio, down the corridors, she tried to think logically. All she could see was that nasty headline and grainy picture. When she walked into the dressing room she went directly to the coffeepot, needing to do something with her hands. She heard the door close and the lock click.

"This isn't the way I wanted to handle this, Booth." She pulled in a deep breath as she fumbled with the coffee. "I didn't expect any publicity… I've been so careful."

"Yes, careful." He jammed his hands into his pockets.

She pressed her lips together as the tone of his voice pricked along her skin. "I know you must have questions. If I…"

"Yes, I have questions." He snatched the paper from her dressing table. He, too, needed to occupy his hands. "Are you involved in a custody suit?"

"Yes."

He felt the grinding in his stomach again. "So much for trust."

"No, Booth." She whirled around, then stopped as a hundred conflicting emotions, a hundred opposing answers hammered at her. Would this be the time of choice? Would she have to choose after all, when she almost had everything she needed? "Please, let me explain. Let me think how to explain."

"You're involved in a custody suit." He remembered those brief flashes of strain he'd seen in her from time to time. He wanted to tear the paper to shreds. "You have this child, and you didn't tell me. What does that say about trust?"

Confused, she dragged a hand through her hair. "Booth, I was already deeply involved in this before we even met. I couldn't drag you into it."

Bitterness seeped into him. Booth hated to taste it… again. "Oh, I see. You were already involved, so it was none of my business. It appears that you have two separate standards for your trust, Ariel. The one for yourself, and the one for everyone else."

"That's not true," she began, then fumbled to a halt.

Was it? "I don't mean for it to be." Her voice began to shake, then her hands. "Booth, I've been frightened. Part of the fear was that something would leak out. The most important thing to me was that none of this touch Scott."

He waited, trying to be impassive as she brushed away the first tear. "That's the boy's name?"

"Yes. He's only four years old."

He turned away because the grief on her face was destroying him. "And his father?"

"His father's name was Jeremy. He's dead."

Booth didn't ask if she'd loved him. He didn't have to. She'd loved another man, he thought. Had borne another man's child. Could he deal with that, accept it? Resting his palms on her dressing table he let the emotion run through him. Yes, he thought so. It didn't change her, or him. And yet…and yet she hadn't told him. It was that that brought the change.

"Who has the boy now?" he asked stiffly.

"His grandparents. He's not…he's not happy with them. He needs me, Booth, and I need him. I need both of you. Please…" Her voice lowered to a whisper. "Don't ask me to choose. I love you. I love you so much but he's just a little boy."

"Choose?" Booth flicked on his lighter, then tossed it onto her cluttered dressing table as he took the first drag from his cigarette. "Damn it, Ariel, just how insensitive do you think I am?"

She waited until she could control the throb of her heart at the base of her throat. "Would you take both of us?"

Booth blew out smoke. Fury was just below the surface. "You kept it from me. That's the issue now. I could hardly turn away from a child that's part of you."

She reached for him. "Booth—"

"You kept it from me," he repeated, watching her hand drop away. "Why?"

"Please understand, if I kept it from you it was only because I wanted to protect him. He's had a difficult time already, and I was afraid that if I talked about the hearing to anyone, anyone at all, there was a risk of something like that." She gestured to the paper, then turned away.

"There's nothing you don't know about my life, Ariel. I can't help but resent that there was something so vital to yours that you kept from me. All this time, almost from the first minute, you've asked me to trust you. Now that I've given that to you, I find you haven't trusted me."

"I put Scott first. He needed someone to put him first."

"I might be able to understand that, if you could explain to me why you ever gave him up."

"Gave him up?" Ariel stared, but tears blurred her vision. "I don't know what you mean."

"I thought I knew you!" Booth exploded. "I believed that, and believing it fell in love with you when I'd sworn I'd never get emotionally involved again. How could you give up your child? How could you have a child and say nothing to me?"

"Give up my child?" she repeated dumbly. "But no, no! It's nothing like that."

"Damn it, Ariel, you've let someone else raise your child. And now that you want him back, now that you're involved in something as serious as a custody battle, you do it alone. How could you love me, how could you preach trust at me and say nothing?"

"I was afraid to tell you or anyone. You don't understand how it might affect Scott if he knew—"

"Or how it might affect you?" He swung his arm toward the discarded paper.

Ariel sucked in her breath and barely controlled a raging denial. Perhaps she'd deserved that. "My concern was for Scott," she said evenly. "A custody suit would hardly damage my reputation. Any more than an illegitimate child would—though he's not my child. Jeremy was my brother."

It was Booth's turn to stare. Nothing made sense. Underlying his confusion was the thought that tears didn't belong in Ariel's eyes. Her eyes were for laughter. "The boy's your nephew?"

"Jeremy and his wife died late last winter." She couldn't go to him now; she could see he wasn't ready. And neither was she. "His grandparents, the Andersons, were appointed guardians. He's not happy with them."

Not her child, Booth thought again, but her brother's child. He waited to gauge his own reaction and found he was still hurt, still angry. Whether the boy was her son or not hadn't been the issue. She'd blocked that part of her life from him.

"I think," Booth said slowly, "that you'd better start at the beginning."

Ariel opened her mouth, but before she could speak, someone pounded on her door. "Phone for you, Ariel, in Neal's office. Urgent."

Banking back frustration, she left the room, heading for Neal's office. So much to explain, she thought. To

Booth and to herself. She rubbed her temple with two fingers as she picked up the phone. "Hello."

"Ms. Kirkwood."

"Yes, this is Ariel Kirkwood." Her frown deepened. "Mr. Anderson?"

"Scott's missing."

Chapter 12

She said nothing. Only seconds passed, but a hundred thoughts raced through her mind, tumbling over each other one at a time so that none was clear. Every nerve in her stomach froze. Vaguely she felt the ache in her hand where she gripped the receiver.

"Ms. Kirkwood, I said that Scott is missing."

"Missing?" she repeated in a whisper. The word itself brought up too many visions. Terrifying ones. She wanted to panic, but forced herself, by digging her nails into her palm, to talk, and to listen carefully. But even the whisper she forced out shook. "How long?"

"Apparently since around eleven o'clock. My wife thought he was next door, playing with a neighbor's child. When she called him home for lunch, she learned he'd never been there."

Eleven… With a sick kind of dread Ariel looked

at her watch. It was nearly two. Three hours. Where could a small boy go in three hours? Anywhere. It was an eternity. "You've called the police?"

"Of course." His voice was brisk but through it ran a thread of fear Ariel was too dazed to hear. "The neighborhood's been searched, people questioned. Everything possible's being done."

Everything possible? What did that mean? She repeated the phrase over in her mind, but it still didn't make sense. "Yes, of course." She heard her own words come hollowly through the rushing noise in her head. "I'll be there right away."

"No, the police suggest that you go home and stay there, in case Scott contacts you."

Home, she thought. They wanted her to go home and do nothing while Scott was missing. "I want to come. I could be there in thirty minutes." The whisper shattered into a desperate plea. "I could help look for him. I could—"

"Ms. Kirkwood," Anderson cut her off, then breathed deeply before he continued. "Scott's an intelligent boy. He knows where you live, he knows your phone number. At a time like this it's best to admit that it's you he wants to be with. If he— If it's possible for him to contact anyone, it would be you. Please, go home. If he's found here, I'll call you immediately."

The single phrase ran through her mind three times. *If it's possible for him to contact anyone...*

"All right. I'll go home. I'll wait there." Dazed, she stared at the phone, not even aware that she'd replaced the receiver herself. Marveling that she could walk at all, she moved to the door.

Of course she could walk, Ariel told herself as she

pressed a hand to the wall for support. She could function—she had to function. Scott was going to want her
when he was found. He'd be full of stories and adven-
tures—especially if he had the chance to ride in a police car. He'd want to tell her about all of it. The phone
would probably be ringing when she opened her front
door. He'd probably just been daydreaming and wandered a few blocks away, that was all. They'd be calling, so she should get home quickly. Her legs felt like
rubber and would hardly move at all.

Booth was brooding at the picture of Ariel and Scott
when he heard the door open. He turned, the paper still
in his hand, but the questions that had been pressing at
him faded the moment he saw her. Her skin was like
parchment. He'd never seen her eyes look vacant, nor
had he expected to.

"Ariel…" He was crossing to her before he'd finished
speaking her name. "What is it?"

"Booth." She put her hand on his chest. Warm, solid.
She could feel the beat of his heart. No, none of it was
a dream. Or a nightmare. "Scott's missing. They don't
know where he is. He's missing."

He took a firm hold on her shoulders. "How long,
Ariel?"

"Three hours." The first wave of fear rammed
through the shock. "Oh God, no one's seen him in three
hours. Nobody knows where he is!"

He only tightened his hold on her shoulders when
her body began to shake. "The police?"

"Yes, yes, they're looking." Her fingers curled, digging at his shirt. "They don't want me to come, they
want me to go home and wait in case he… Booth."

"I'll take you home." He brushed the hair away from

her face. His touch, his voice, was meant to soothe. "We'll go home and wait for the call. They're going to find him, Ariel. Little boys wander off all the time."

"Yes." She grabbed on to that, and to his hand. Of course that was true. Didn't she have to watch him like a hawk when they went to the park or the zoo? "Scott daydreams a lot. He could've just walked farther than he should. They're going to call me... I should be home."

"I'm going to take you." Booth kept hold of her as she took a disoriented study of the room. "You change, and I'll let them know you can't tape this afternoon."

"Change?" Puzzled she looked down and saw she still wore Amanda's nightshirt. "All right, I'll hurry. They could call any minute."

She tried to hurry, but her fingers kept fumbling with the most basic task. She needed her jeans, but her mind seemed to fade in and out as she pulled them on. Then her fingers slid over the snap. She tried to think logically but the pounding at the side of her head made it impossible. Holding off the nausea helped. It gave her something tangible to concentrate on while she fought with the laces of her shoes.

Booth was back within moments. When she turned to look at him he could feel her panic. "Ready?"

"Yes." She nodded and walked out with him, one foot in front of the other, while images of Scott, lost, frightened, streamed through her head. Or worse, much worse—Scott getting into a car with a stranger, a stranger whose face was only a shadow. She wanted to scream. She climbed into a cab.

Booth took her icy hand in his. "Ariel, it isn't like you to anticipate the worst. Think." He put his other hand over hers and tried to warm it. "There're a hundred harmless reasons for his being out of touch for a few hours. He might've found a dog, or chased a ball. He might've found some fascinating rock and taken it to a secret place to study it."

"Yes." She tried to picture those things. It would be typical of Scott. The image of the car and the stranger kept intruding. He had no basic fear of people, something she'd always admired in him. Now it filled her with fear. Turning her face in to Booth's shoulder she tried to convince herself that the phone would be ringing when she opened the front door.

When the cab stopped, she jerked upright and scrambled for the handle. She was dashing up the steps before Booth had paid the driver.

Silence. It greeted her like an accusation. Ariel stared at the phone and willed it to ring. When she looked at her watch, she saw it had been less than thirty minutes since Anderson's call. Not enough time, she told herself as she began to pace. *Too much time*. Too much time for a little boy to be alone.

Do something! The words ran through her mind as she struggled to find something solid to grip on to. She'd always been able to do something in any situation. There were answers, and if not answers, choices. But to wait. To have no answer, no choice but to wait... She heard the door close and turned. Her hands lifted, then fell helplessly.

"Booth. Oh God, I don't know what to do. There must be something—anything."

Without a word he crossed to her, wrapped his arms around her and let her cling to him. Strange that it would have taken this—something so frightening for her—to make him realize she needed him every bit as much as he needed her. Whatever doubts he'd had, and whatever anger had lingered that she'd kept part of her life from him, dropped away. Love was simpler than he'd ever imagined.

"Sit down, Ariel." As he spoke, he eased her toward a chair. "I'm going to fix you a drink."

"No, I—"

"Sit down," he repeated with a firmness he knew she needed. "I'll make coffee, or I'll see about getting you a sedative."

"I don't need a sedative."

He nodded, rewarded by the sharp, quick answer. If she was angry, just a little angry, she wouldn't fall apart. "Then I'll make coffee."

The moment he went into the kitchen she was up again. Sitting was impossible, calm out of the question. She should never have agreed to come back and wait, Ariel told herself. She should have insisted on going out and looking for Scott herself. It was useless here—she was useless here. But if he called and she wasn't there to answer... Oh, God. She pressed her hands to her face and tried not to crumble. What time was it?

This time when she looked at her watch she felt the first hysterical sob build.

"Ariel." Booth carried two cups of coffee, hot and strong. He watched as she shuddered, swallowing sobs, but the tears ran freely.

"Booth, where could he be? He's hardly more than a baby. He doesn't have any fear of strangers. It's my fault because—"

"Stop." He said the word softly, but it had the effect of cutting off the rapidly tumbling words. He held out the cup, waiting for her to take it in both hands. It shook, nearly spilling the coffee over the rim. As it depleted, she sat again. "Tell me about him."

For a moment she stared at the coffee, as if she had no idea what it was or how she'd come to be holding it. "He's four…almost five. He wants a wagon, a yellow one, for his birthday. He likes to pretend." Lifting the cup, she swallowed coffee, and as it scalded her mouth, she calmed a bit. "Scott has a wonderful imagination. You can give him a cardboard box and he'll see a space-ship, a submarine, an Egyptian tomb. Really see it, do you know what I mean?"

"Yes." He laid a hand on hers as he sat beside her.

"When Jeremy and Barbara died, he was so lost. They were beautiful together, the three of them. So happy."

Her eyes were drawn to the boxing gloves that hung behind the door. Jeremy's gloves. They'd be Scott's one day. Something ripped inside her stomach. Ariel began to talk faster. "He's a lot like his father, the same charm and curiosity. The Andersons, Barbara's parents, never approved of Jeremy. They didn't want Barbara to marry him, and rarely saw her after she did. After… after the accident, they were appointed Scott's guardians. I wanted him, but it seemed natural that he go with them. A house, a yard, a family. But…" Breaking off, she cast a desperate look at the phone.

"But?" Booth prompted.

"They just aren't capable of understanding the kind of person Scott is. He'll pretend he's an archeologist and dig a hole in their yard."

"That might annoy anyone," Booth said and drew a wan smile from her.

"But he wouldn't dig up the yard if he had a sand

dump and someone told him it could be a desert. Instead, he's punished for his imagination rather than having it redirected."

"So you decided to fight for him."

"Yes." Ariel moistened her lips. Had she waited too long? "Even if that were all, I might not have started proceedings. They don't love him." Her eyes shimmered as she looked up again. "They just feel responsible for him. I can't bear thinking he could grow up without all the love he should have."

Where is he, where is he, where is he?

"He won't." Booth drew her against him to kiss the tears at the corners of her eyes. "After you get custody, we'll see that he doesn't."

Cautiously, she pulled back, though her fingers were still tight on his shoulders. "We?"

Booth lifted a brow. "Is Scott part of your life?"

"Yes, he—"

"Then he's part of mine."

Her mouth trembled open twice before she could speak. "No questions?"

"I've wasted a lot of time with questions. Sometimes there's no need for them." He pressed her fingers to his lips. "I love you."

"Booth, I'm so afraid." Her head dropped against him. The dam burst.

He let her weep, those harsh sobs that were edged with grief and fear. He let her hold on and pull out whatever strength she could find in him. He lived by words, but knew when clever phrases were of no use. So in silence, Booth held her.

Crying would help, he thought, smoothing her hair. It would allow her to give in to fear without putting a name on it. While she was vulnerable to tears, it was he who willed the phone to ring. And he was denied.

The passion exhausted her. Ariel lay against Booth, light-headed, disoriented, only aware of that hollow ache inside that meant something vital was wrong. Her mind groped for the reason. *Scott.* He was missing. The phone hadn't rung. He was still missing.

"Time," she murmured, staring over his shoulder at the phone through eyes that were swollen and abused by tears. "What time is it now?"

"It's nearly four," he answered, hating to tell her, hating the convulsive jerk he felt because her body was pressed so close to his. There were a dozen things he could say to offer comfort. All useless. "I'll make more coffee."

At the knock on the door, she looked around listlessly. She wanted no company now. Ignoring the knock, she turned her back to the door. It was the phone that was important. "I'll get the coffee." Forcing herself to move, she rose. "I don't want to see anyone, please."

"I'll send them away." Booth walked to the door, already prepared to position himself in front of it to shield her. When he opened it, he saw a young woman wearing a bandanna and paint-smeared overalls. Then he saw the boy.

"Excuse me. This little boy was wandering a couple blocks from here. He gave this address. I wonder if—"

"Who are you?" Scott demanded of Booth. "This is Ariel's house."

"I'm Booth. Ariel's been waiting for you, Scott."

Scott grinned, showing small white teeth. Baby teeth, Booth realized. *He's hardly more than a baby.* "I would've been here sooner, but I got a little lost. Bobbi was painting her porch and said she'd walk me over."

Booth laid a hand on Scott's head and felt the softness of hair—like Ariel's. "We're very grateful to you, Miss…"

"Freeman, Bobbi Freeman." She grinned and jerked her head toward Scott. "No trouble. He might've lost his way a bit, but he sure knows what he wants. It seems to be Ariel and a peanut butter sandwich. Well, hey, I've got to get back to my porch. See you later, Scott."

"Bye, Bobbi." He yawned hugely. "Is Ariel home now?"

"I'll get her." Leaving Scott to climb onto the hammock, Booth walked toward the kitchen. He stopped Ariel in the doorway then took the two cups from her hands. "There's someone here to see you."

She shut her eyes. "Oh, please, Booth. Not now."

"I don't think he'll take no for an answer."

Something in his tone had her opening her eyes again, had her heart drumming against her ribs. Skirting passed him, she hurried into the living room. A small blond boy swung happily in her hammock with two kittens in his lap. "Oh, God, Scott!"

His arms were already reaching for her as she dashed across the room and yanked him against her. Warmth. She could feel the warmth of his small body and moaned from the joy of it. His rumpled hair brushed against her face. She could smell the faintest memory of soap from his morning wash, mixed with the sweat of the day and the gumdrops he was forever secreting in his pockets. Weeping, laughing, she sank to the floor holding him.

"Scott, oh, Scott. You're not hurt?" The quick fear

struck at her again and she pulled him away to examine his face, his hands, his arms. "Are you hurt anywhere?"

"Uh-uh." A bit miffed at the question, Scott squirmed. "I didn't see Butch yet. Where's Butch?"

"How did you get here?" Ariel grabbed him again and gave in to the need to kiss his face—the rounded cheeks, the straight little nose, the small mouth. "Scott, where've you been?"

"On the train." His whole face lit. "I rode on the train all by myself. For a surprise."

"You…" Incredulous, Ariel stared at him. "You came from your grandparents', all alone?"

"I saved up my money." With no little pride he reached in his pocket and pulled out what he had left— a few pennies, two quarters and some gumdrops. "I walked to the station, but it took lots longer than a cab does. It isn't as far in a cab," he decided with a small boy's logic. "And I paid for the ticket all by myself— just like you showed me. I'm hungry, Ariel."

"In a minute." Appalled at the idea of his traveling alone and defenseless, she took both his arms. "You walked all the way to the train station, then rode the train here?"

"And I only got a little bit lost once, when Bobbi helped me. And I was hardly scared at all." His lip trembled. Screwing up his face, he buried it against her. "I wasn't."

All the things that might have happened to him flashed hideously through her mind. Ariel tightened her hold and thanked God. "Of course you weren't," she murmured, struggling to hold on to her emotions until she'd both schooled and scolded. "You're so brave, and so smart to remember the way. But Scott—" she tilted his face to hers "—it was wrong for you to come here all alone."

"But I wanted to see you."

"I know, and I always want to see you." Again she kissed him, just to feel the warmth of his cheek. "But you left without telling your grandparents, and they're so worried. And I've been worried," she added, brushing the hair from his temple. "You have to promise you won't ever do it again."

"I don't want to do it again." With his mouth trembling again, he rubbed his fists against his eyes. "It took a long time and I got hungry, and then I got lost and my legs were so tired. But I wasn't scared."

"It's all right now, baby." Still holding him, she rose. "We'll fix you something to eat, then you can rest in the hammock. Okay?"

Scott sniffled, snuggling closer. "Can I have peanut butter?"

"Absolutely." Booth came back into the room and watched as both heads turned toward him. He might be her own child, he thought, wonderingly. Surprised, he felt a yearning to hold the boy himself. "I just saw a peanut butter sandwich in the kitchen. I think it's yours."

"Okay!" Scott scrambled out of Ariel's arms and bounced away.

Getting unsteadily to her feet, Ariel pressed the heel of her hand to her brow. "I could skin him alive. Oh, Booth," she whispered as she felt his arms go around her. "Isn't he wonderful?"

By dusk, Scott was asleep, with a tattered stuffed dog that had been his father's gripped in one hand. The three-legged Butch kept guard on the pillow beside him. Ariel sat on the sofa next to Booth and faced

Scott's grandfather. Coffee grew cold on the table between them. As always, Mr. Anderson sat erect; his clothes were impeccable. But there was a weariness in his eyes Ariel had never seen before.

"Anything might've happened to the boy on a jaunt like that."

"I know." Ariel slipped her hand into Booth's, grateful for the support. "I've made him promise he won't ever do anything like it again. You and your wife must've been sick with worry. I'm sorry, Mr. Anderson. I feel partially to blame because I've let Scott buy the train tickets before."

He shook his head, not speaking for a moment. "An intrepid boy," he managed at length. "Sharp enough to know which train to take, when to get off." His eyes focused on Ariel's again. "He wanted badly to be with you."

Normally the statement would have warmed her. Now, it tightened the already sensitive muscles of her stomach. "Yes. Children often don't understand the consequences of their actions, Mr. Anderson. Scott only thought about coming, not about the hours of panic in between or about the dangers. He was tired and frightened when he got here. I hope you won't punish him too severely."

Anderson took a deep breath and rested a hand on either thigh. "I realized something today, Ms. Kirkwood. I resent that boy."

"Oh, no, Mr. Anderson—"

"Please, let me finish. I resent him, and I don't like knowing that about myself." His voice was clipped, unapologetic and, Ariel realized, old. Not so much in years, she thought, but in attitude. "And more, I've realized that his presence in the house is a constant strain on my wife. He's a reminder of something we lost. I'm not going to justify my feelings to you," he added briskly. "The boy is my grandchild, and therefore, I'm responsible for him. However, I'm an old man, and not inclined to change. I don't want the boy, and you do." He rose while Ariel could only stare at him. "I'll notify my attorney of my feelings on the matter."

"Mr. Anderson." Shaken, Ariel rose. "You know I want Scott, but—"

"I don't, Ms. Kirkwood." With his shoulders straight, Anderson gave her a level look. "It's as basic as that."

And as sad. "I'm sorry" was all she could say.

With a nod only, he left.

"How," Ariel began after a stretch of silence, "could anyone feel that way about a child?"

"About the child?" Booth countered. "Or about themselves?"

She turned to him, puzzled only for a moment. "Yes, that's it, isn't it?"

"I'm an expert on the subject. The difference is—" he drew her down to him again, circling her with his arm so that her head rested against his shoulder "—someone pushed her way into my life and made me see it."

"Is that what I did?" She laughed, riding the next curve on the roller coaster the day had been. Scott was sleeping on her bed, with kittens curled at his feet. He could stay there now. No more tearful goodbyes. "Pushed my way into your life?"

"You can be very tenacious." He gave her hair a sharp tug then captured her mouth as she gasped. "Thank God."

"Should I warn you that once I push my way in, I won't ever get out?"

"No." He shifted so that she could sit across his lap, and he could watch her face. "Let me find out for myself."

"It won't be easy for you, you know."

"What?"

"Dealing with me if you decide to marry me."

His brow rose, and unable to resist, she traced it with a fingertip. "If?"

"I'm giving you your last chance for escape." Half-serious, Ariel pressed her palm to his cheek. "I do most things on impulse—eating, spending, sleeping. I much prefer living in chaos to living in order. The fact is I can't function in order at all. I'll get you involved, one way or the other, in any number of organizations."

"That one remains to be seen," Booth muttered.

Ariel only smiled. "I haven't scared you off yet?"

"No." He kissed her, and as the shadows in the room lengthened, neither of them noticed. "And you won't. I can also be tenacious."

"Remember, you'll be taking on a four-year-old child. An active one."

"You've a poor opinion of my stamina."

"Oh, no." This time when she laughed, it held a husky quality. "I'll drive you crazy with my disorganization."

"As long as you stay out of my office," he countered, "you can turn everything else into a building lot."

She tightened her arms around his neck and clung for a moment. He meant it, she told herself, giddy. He meant it all. She had Booth, and Scott. And with them, her life was taking the next turning point. She could hardly wait to find what waited around the corner.

"I'll spoil Scott," she murmured into Booth's neck. "And the rest of our children."

He drew her back slowly, a half smile on his mouth. "How many is implied by *the rest*?"

Her laughter was free and breezy. "Pick a number."

* * * * *

THE BEST MISTAKE

Chapter 1

No one answered the door. Coop glanced at the scrawled note in his hand to make sure he had the right address. It checked out, and since the tidy two-story Tudor in the neat, tree-lined neighborhood was precisely what he was after, he knocked again. Loudly.

There was a car in the drive, an aging station wagon that could use a good wash and a little bodywork. Somebody was in there, he thought, scowling up at the second-floor window, where music pumped out—high-volume rock with a thumping backbeat. He stuffed the note and his hands in his pockets and took a moment to survey the surroundings.

The house was trim, set nicely off the road behind clipped bayberry hedges. The flower garden, in which spring blossoms were beginning to thrive, was both colorful and just wild enough not to look static.

Not that he was a big flower lover, but there *was* something to be said for ambience.

There was a shiny red tricycle beside the driveway, and that made him a little uneasy. He wasn't particularly fond of kids. Not that he disliked them. It was just that they always seemed a kind of foreign entity to him, like aliens from an outlying planet: they spoke a different language, had a different culture. And, well, they were short, and usually sticky.

Still, the ad had talked of quiet, privacy, and a convenient distance from Baltimore. That was exactly what he was looking for.

He knocked again, only to have a thundering wave of music wash out the window over him. The rock didn't bother him. At least he understood it. But he wasn't a man to kick his heels outside a closed door for long, so he tried the knob.

When it turned, he pushed the door open and walked in. In an old habit, he pushed back the dark hair that fell over his forehead and scanned the none-too-neat living room he'd entered.

There was a lot of clutter, and he, a bachelor who'd spent a great deal of his thirty-two years living alone, wondered over it. He wasn't fussy or obsessive, he often told himself. It was simply that everything had a place, and it was easier to find if it had been put there. Obviously his prospective landlord didn't agree.

There were toys that went along with the tricycle outside, piles of magazines and newspapers, a pint-size fielder's cap that declared for the O's.

At least the kid had taste, Coop decided, and moved on.

There was a small powder room done in an amazing

combination of purple and green, and a den that had been converted into a makeshift office. File drawers were open, papers spilling out. In the kitchen dishes waited in the sink to be washed, and lurid drawings, created by a child with a wild imagination, decorated the front of the refrigerator.

Maybe, he thought, it was just as well no one had answered the door.

He considered backtracking and wandering upstairs. As long as he was here, it made sense to check the rest of the place out. Instead, he stepped outside to get the lay of the land. He spotted open wooden steps leading to a short deck. The private entrance the ad had mentioned, he mused, and climbed.

The glass door was open, and the music rolling through it was overwhelming. He caught the smell of fresh paint, one he'd always enjoyed, and stepped inside.

The open area combined kitchen and living space cleverly enough. The appliances weren't new, but they were gleaming. The tile floor had been scrubbed recently enough for him to identify pine cleaner beneath the scent of paint.

Feeling more hopeful, he followed the music, snooping a bit as he went. The bathroom was as scrupulously clean as the kitchen, and, fortunately, a plain glossy white. Beside the sink was a book on home repair, open to the plumbing section. Wary, Coop turned on the tap. When the water flowed out fast and clear, he nodded, satisfied.

A small room with definite office potential and a nice view of the yard was across the hall. The ad had claimed two bedrooms.

The music led him to it, a fair-sized room that fronted

the house, with space enough for his California king. The floor, which seemed to be a random-width oak in good condition, was covered with splattered drop cloths. There were paint cans, trays, brushes, extra rollers. A laborer in baggy overalls and bare feet completed the picture. Despite the hair-concealing cap and oversize denim, Coop recognized a woman when he saw one.

She was tall, and the bare feet on the stepladder were long and narrow and decorated with paint splotches and hot-pink toenails. She sang, badly, along with the music.

Coop rapped on the doorjamb. "Excuse me."

She went on painting, her hips moving rhythmically as she started on the ceiling border. Stepping across the drop cloths, Coop tapped her on the back.

She screamed, jumped and turned all at once. Though he was quick on his feet, he wasn't fast enough to avoid the slap of the paintbrush across his cheek.

He swore and jerked backward, then forward again to catch her before she tumbled off the ladder. He had a quick, and not unpleasant, impression of a slim body, a pale, triangular face dominated by huge, long-lashed brown eyes, and the scent of honeysuckle.

Then he was grunting and stumbling backward, clutching the stomach her elbow had jammed into. She yelled something while he fought to get his breath back.

"Are you crazy?" he managed, then shot up a hand as she hefted a can, slopping paint over the sides as she prepared to use it as a weapon. "Lady, if you throw that at me, I'm going to have to hurt you."

"What?" she shouted.

"I said, don't throw that. I'm here about the ad."

"What?" she shouted again. Her eyes were still wide and full of panic, and she looked capable of anything.

"The ad, damn it." Still rubbing his stomach, Coop marched to the portable stereo and shut it off. "I'm here about the ad," he repeated, his voice loud in the sudden silence.

The big brown eyes narrowed with suspicion. "What ad?"

"The apartment." He swiped a hand over his cheek, studied the smear of white on it, and swore again. "The apartment."

"Really?" She kept her eyes glued to his. He looked tough, she thought. Like a brawler with those broad shoulders, lean athletic build and long legs. His eyes, a light, almost translucent green, looked anything but friendly, and the faded Baltimore Orioles T-shirt and battered jeans didn't contribute any sense of respectability. She figured she could outrun him, and she could certainly outscream him. "The ad doesn't start to run until tomorrow."

"Tomorrow?" Nonplussed, he reached into his pocket for his scribbled note. "This is the right address. The ad was for this place."

She stood her ground. "It doesn't run until tomorrow, so I don't see how you could know about it."

"I work at the paper." Moving cautiously, he held out the note. "Since I've been looking for a place, I asked one of the girls in Classifieds to keep an eye out." He glanced down at his note again. "Two-bedroom apartment on second floor, private entrance, quiet neighborhood convenient for commuters."

She only continued to frown at him. "That's right."

Realizing his inside track wasn't strictly ethical, he winced. "Look, I guess she got a little overenthusiastic. I gave her a couple of tickets to a game, and she must've figured she'd do me a favor and pass the information along a little early."

When he saw that her grip on the can had relaxed, he tried a smile. "I knocked, then I came around back." Probably best not to mention he'd wandered through the house first.

"The ad didn't run the address."

"I work at the paper," he repeated. He was taking a good look at her now. There was something vaguely familiar about her face. And what a face it was. All slashing cheekbones and liquid eyes, that creamy porcelain skin women's face cream ads always raved about. Her mouth was wide, with an alluringly full lower lip. At the moment, the face continued to frown.

"They had the address for billing," he continued. "Since I had a couple of hours, I thought I'd come by and check it out. Look, I can come back tomorrow, if you'd feel more comfortable. But I'm here now." He shrugged. "I can show you my press pass."

He pulled it out for her, and was pleased when she narrowed her eyes to study it. "I do a column. J. Cooper McKinnon on sports. 'All in the Game'?"

"Oh." It meant nothing to her. The sports page wasn't her choice of reading material. But the smile had appeased her. He didn't look so much like a thug when he smiled. And the smear of paint decorating the lean, tanned face added just enough comedy to soothe her. "I guess it's all right, then. I wasn't expecting to show the apartment for a couple of days yet. It's not ready." She held up the can, set it down again. "I'm still painting."

"I noticed."

She laughed at that. It was a full-throated, smoky sound that went with the natural huskiness of her voice.

"Guess you did. I'm Zoe Fleming." She crouched down to dampen a rag with paint remover.

"Thanks." He rubbed the rag over his cheek. "The ad said immediate occupancy."

"Well, I figured I'd be finished in here by tomorrow, when the ad was scheduled to run. Are you from the area?"

"I've got a place downtown. I'm looking for something with a little more space, a little more atmosphere."

"This is a pretty good-sized apartment. It was converted about eight years ago. The guy who owned it had it done for his son, and when he died, the son sold it and moved to California. He wanted to write sitcoms."

Coop walked over to check out the view. He moved fluidly, Zoe thought, like a man who knew how to stay light and ready on his feet. She'd had the impression of wiry strength when her body tumbled into his. And good strong hands. Quick ones, too. She pursed her lips. It might be handy to have a man around.

"Is it just you, Mr. McKinnon?" She thought wistfully how nice it would be if he had a family—another child for Keenan to play with.

"Just me." The place felt right, he decided. It would be good to get out of a box that was just one more box in a building of boxes, to smell grass now and then. Barbecue smoke. "I can move in over the weekend."

She hadn't thought it would be so easy, and she nibbled her lip as she thought it through. She'd never been a landlady before, but she'd been a tenant, and she figured she knew the ropes. "I'll need first and last months' rent."

"Yeah."

"And, ah, references."

"I'll give you the number of the management company that handles my building. You can call Personnel at the paper. Have you got a lease for me to sign?"

She didn't. She'd checked out a book from the library, and she'd meant to type up a scaled-down copy of a lease from it the next morning. "I'll have it tomorrow. Don't you want to look at the rest of the apartment, ask any questions?" She'd been practicing her landlady routine for days.

"I've seen it. It's fine."

"Well." That deflated her a bit. "I guess I can cancel the ad."

There was a sound like a herd of rampaging elephants. Zoe glanced toward the open door and crouched to intercept the missile that hurtled through.

It was a boy, Coop saw when she scooped the child up. He had glossy golden hair, red sneakers, and jeans that were streaked with some unidentifiable substance that looked like it would easily transfer to other surfaces. He carried a plastic lunch box with a picture of some apocalyptic space battle on it, and a sheet of drawing paper that was grimy at the edges.

"I drew the ocean," he announced. "And a million people got ate by sharks."

"Gruesome." Zoe shuddered obligingly before accepting his sloppy kiss. She set him down to admire the drawing. "These are really big sharks," she said, cagily distinguishing the shark blobs from the people blobs.

"They're monster sharks. Mutant monster sharks. They have teeth."

"So I see. Keenan, this is Mr. McKinnon. Our new tenant."

Keenan wrapped one arm around Zoe's leg for security as he eyed the stranger. His eyes were working their way up to Coop's face when they lit on the T-shirt. "That's baseball. I'm gonna learn. Mama's getting a book so's she can teach me."

A book. Coop barely checked a snort. As if you could learn the greatest game invented by Man from a book. What kind of nerd did the kid have for a father?

"Great." It was all Coop intended to say. He'd always thought it wise to avoid entangling himself in a conversation with anyone under sixteen.

Keenan had other ideas. "If you're going to live here, you have to pay rent. Then we can pay the mortgage and stuff and go to Disney World."

What *was* the kid? An accountant?

"Okay, old man." Zoe laughed and ruffled his hair. "I can handle it from here. Go on down and put your stuff away."

"Is Beth coming to play with me tonight?"

"Yes, Beth's coming. Now scoot. I'll be down in a minute."

"'Kay." He made a dash for the door, stopping when his mother called him. It only took one look, the raised brow for him to remember. He looked back at Coop, flashed a quick, sunny grin. "Bye, mister."

The herd of elephants rampaged again, then there was the crash of a door slamming. "He makes an entrance," Zoe said as she turned back to Coop. "The dramatic flair comes from my mother. She's an actress, off-off-Broadway." Tilting her head, Zoe rested one bare foot on the bottom rung of the stepladder. "You look like you're ready to change your mind. You have a problem with children?"

"No." The kid might have thrown him off, but Coop

doubted it would be a problem. The boy would hardly be beating a path to his door. And if he did, Coop thought, he could send him off again quickly enough. "No, he's, ah, cute."

"Yes, he is. I won't claim he's an angel, but he won't make a nuisance of himself. If he gives you any trouble, just let me know."

"Sure. Look, I'll come by tomorrow to sign the lease and give you a check. I'll pick up the keys then."

"That'll be fine."

"Any special time good for you?"

She looked blank for a moment. "What's tomorrow?"

"Friday."

"Friday." She closed her eyes and flipped through her messy internal calendar. "I'm working between ten and two. I think." She opened her eyes again, smiled. "Yeah, I'm pretty sure. Anytime after two-thirty?"

"Fine. Nice meeting you, Mrs. Fleming."

She took his offered hand. "It's Miss," she said easily. "I'm not married. And since we'll be living together, so to speak, you can make it Zoe."

Chapter 2

No one answered the door. Again. Coop checked his watch and saw that it was quarter to three. He didn't like to think he was a man obsessed with time, but as his living centered around deadlines, he did respect it. There was no rusting station wagon in the driveway this time, but he walked around the back of the house, hoping. Before he could start up the stairs to the apartment, he was hailed from across the chain-link fence.

"Young man! Yoo-hoo, young man!" Across the yard next door came a flowered muumuu, topped with a curling thatch of brightly hennaed hair that crowned a wide face. The woman hurried to the fence in a whirl of color. It wasn't just the dress and the improbable hair, Coop noted. The face itself was a rainbow of rich red lipstick, pink cheeks and lavender eye shadow.

When she reached the fence, she pressed a many-ringed hand over the wide shelf of her breasts. "Not as young as I used to be," she said. "I'm Mrs. Finkleman."

"Hi."

"You're the young man who's going to live upstairs." Mrs. Finkleman, a born flirt, patted her curls. "Zoe didn't tell me you were so handsome. Single, are you?"

"Yeah," Coop said cautiously. "Miss Fleming was supposed to meet me. She doesn't seem to be home."

"Well, that's Zoe, flying here, flying there." Mrs. Finkleman beamed and leaned comfortably on the fence, as if she were settling in for a nice cozy gossip. "Got a dozen things on her plate at once, that girl does. Having to raise that sweet little boy all alone. Why, I don't know what I'd have done without my Harry when our young ones were coming up."

Coop was a reporter, after all. That, added to the fact that he was curious about his landlady, put him in interview mode. "The kid's father doesn't help out any?"

Mrs. Finkleman snorted. "Don't see hide nor hair of him. From what I'm told, he lit out the minute he found out Zoe was expecting. Left her high and dry, and her hardly more than a child herself. Far as I know, he's never so much as seen the boy. The little sweetheart."

Coop assumed she was referring to Keenan. "Nice kid. What's he, five, six?"

"Just four. Bright as a button. They grow them smarter these days. Teach them faster, too. The little love's in preschool now. He'll be home any minute."

"His mother went to pick him up, then?"

"Oh, no, not her week for car pool. Alice Miller—that's the white house with blue trim, down the block?—it's her week. She has a boy and a girl. Little darlings. The youngest, Steffie, is Keenan's age. Now her oldest, Brad, there's a pistol for you."

As she began to fill Coop in on the neighborhood rascal, he decided it was time to draw the interview to a close. "Maybe you could tell Miss Fleming I was by? I can leave a number where she can reach me when—"

"Oh, goodness." Mrs. Finkleman waved a hand. "I do run on. Nearly forgot why I came out here in the first place. Zoe called and asked me to look out for you. Got held up at the flower shop. She works there three days a week. That's Floral Bouquet, down in Ellicott City? Nice place, but expensive. Why, it's a crime to charge so much for a daisy."

"She got held up," Coop prompted.

"Her relief had car trouble, so Zoe's going to be a little late. Said you could go right on into the kitchen there, where she left the lease and the keys."

"That's fine. Thanks."

"No problem at all. This is a friendly neighborhood. Always somebody to lend a helping hand. I don't think Zoe mentioned what you did for a living."

"I'm a sportswriter for the *Dispatch*."

"You don't say? Why, my Harry's just wild for sports. Can't budge him from in front of the TV when a game's on."

"That's what makes this country great."

Mrs. Finkleman laughed and gave Coop's arm an affectionate bat that might have felled a lesser man. "You men are all the same. You can come over and talk sports with Harry anytime. Me, if it's not baseball, it isn't worth talking about."

Coop, who'd been about to retreat, brightened. "You like baseball?"

"Son, I'm a Baltimore native." As if that said it all. "Our boys are going to go all the way this year. Mark my word."

"They could do it, if they heat those bats up. The pitching rotation's gold this year, and the infield's tight as a drum. What they need—"

Coop was interrupted by a cheerful toot. He glanced over to see Keenan burst out of a red sedan and rocket across the side yard.

"Hi, mister. Hi, Mrs. Finkleman. Carly Myers fell down, and there was blood." The big brown eyes gleamed wickedly. "Lots and lots of it, and she screamed and cried." He demonstrated, letting go with a piercing yell that had Coop's ears ringing. "Then she got a Band-Aid with stars on it." Keenan thought it would have been worth losing some blood for such a neat badge of honor. "Where's Mama?"

"Little lamb." Mrs. Finkleman leaned over the fence to pinch Keenan's cheek. "She's working a little late. She said you could come stay with me until she gets home."

"Okay." Keenan liked his visits next door, since they always included cookies and a rock on Mrs. Finkleman's wonderfully soft lap. "I gotta put my lunch box away."

"Such a good boy," Mrs. Finkleman cooed. "You come on over when you're done. Why don't you show the nice man inside so he can wait for your mother?"

"Okay."

Before Coop could take evasive action, his hand was clutched by Keenan's. He'd been right, he thought with a wince. It was sticky.

"We've got cookies," Keenan told him, cannily deducing that he could have double his afternoon's treat if he played his cards right.

"Great."

"We baked them ourselves, on our night off." Keenan sent Coop a hopeful look. "They're really good."

"I bet." Coop caught the back door before it could slam shut.

"There." Keenan pointed to a ceramic cookie jar in the shape of a big yellow bird on the counter. "In Big Bird."

"Okay, okay." Since it seemed like the best way to appease the kid, Coop reached in and pulled out a handful of cookies. When he dumped them on the table, Keenan's eyes went as wide as saucers. He could hardly believe his luck.

"You can have one, too." He stuffed an entire chocolate chip deluxe in his mouth and grinned.

"That good, huh?" With a shrug, Coop sampled one himself. The kid, Coop decided after the first bite, knew his cookies. "You'd better get next door."

Keenan devoured another cookie, stalling. "I gotta wash out my thermos, 'cause if you don't, it smells."

"Right." Cooper sat at the table to read through the lease while the boy dragged a stool in front of the sink.

Keenan squirted dishwashing liquid in the thermos, and then, when he noticed Coop wasn't paying any attention, he squirted some more. And more. He turned the water up high and giggled when soap began to bubble and spew. With his tongue caught between his teeth, he jiggled the stopper into the sink and began to play dishwasher.

Coop forgot about him, reading quickly. The lease seemed standard enough, he decided. Zoe had already signed both copies. He dashed his signature across from hers, folded his copy, then set the check he'd already written on the table. He'd picked up the keys and rose to tuck his copy in his pocket when he spotted Keenan.

"Oh, God."

The boy was drenched, head to foot. Soap bubbles dotted his face and hair. A good-sized puddle was forming on the tile at the base of the stool.

"What are you doing?"

Keenan looked over his shoulder, smiled innocently. "Nothing."

"Look, you've got water everywhere." Coop looked around for a towel.

"Everywhere," Keenan agreed, and, testing the opposition, he slapped his hands in the sink. Water and suds geysered.

"Cut it out! Jeez! Aren't you supposed to be somewhere else?" He grabbed a dish towel and advanced, only to be slapped in the face by the next geyser. His eyes narrowed. "Look, kid—"

He heard the front door slam. Like mother, like son, he thought.

"Keenan?" Zoe called out. "I hope you haven't been into those cookies."

Coop looked at the crumbs on the table, on the floor, floating in the soapy water.

"Oh, hell," he muttered.

"Oh, hell," Keenan echoed, beaming at him. He giggled and danced on his stool. "Hi, Mom."

Zoe, her arms full of day-old irises, took in the scene with one glance. Her son was as wet as a drowned dog, her kitchen looked as though a small hurricane had blown through. Hurricane Keenan, she thought. And her new tenant looked damp, frazzled, and charmingly sheepish.

Like a boy caught with his hand in the cookie jar, she noted, glancing at the telltale crumbs.

"Been playing dishwasher again?" With a calm that baffled Coop, she set the flowers down. "I'm just not sure it's the right career choice, Keen-man."

Keenan fluttered his long, wet lashes. "He wanted cookies."

Coop started to defend himself, then simply scowled at the boy.

"I'm sure he did. Go on into the laundry room and get out of those wet clothes."

"Okay." He jumped from the stool, splashing more water before he zoomed away. He stopped only long enough to give his mother a wet kiss before he disappeared into an adjoining room.

"Sorry I'm late," Zoe said easily, yanking the stopper out of the sink then walking to a cupboard to get a vase.

Coop opened his mouth. He started to explain what had gone on in the past ten minutes, but realized he wasn't at all sure. "I signed the lease."

"I see that. Would you mind putting some water in this?" She held out the vase. "I need to get a mop."

"Sure."

She was probably going to wallop the kid with it, Coop thought, and felt a quick tug of regret and guilt. But the sounds from the laundry room where she'd disappeared weren't those he associated with corporal punishment. They were a young boy's giggles, a woman's lusty laugh. Coop stood, a vase of water in his hands, and wondered at it.

"You're standing in a puddle," Zoe commented when she came back with a mop and pail.

"Oh, right." Coop glanced down at his wet hightops, shifted. "Here's your vase."

"Thanks." She tended to her flowers first. "You met Mrs. Finkleman, I hear."

"News travels fast."

"Around here it does." When she handed him a dishcloth to dry his face with, he caught her scent—much more potent, much more colorful, than the flowers. She was wearing jeans and a baggy T-shirt with Floral Bouquet across the chest. Her hair, he noted, was some elusive shade between brown and blond. She wore it tied back in a jaunty ponytail.

When she lifted her brows, he realized he'd been staring. "Sorry. I mean—I'm sorry about the mess."

"Were you playing dishwasher, too?"

"Not exactly." It was impossible not to smile back, to ignore the quick pull of attraction.

It wouldn't be so bad, he mused, having a pretty landlady, sharing the house with her, maybe an occasional meal. Or an occasional—

"Mama!" Keenan stood in the doorway, wearing nothing but skin. "I can't find my pants."

"In the basket by the washing machine," she told him, without taking her eyes from Coop's.

He'd forgotten about the kid, let himself fantasize a little before remembering she didn't come as a single. He took a long mental step backward and jingled the keys to his new apartment.

"I've got some boxes out in the car," he told her. "I'm going to move some things in this afternoon."

"That's fine." It was silly to feel disappointed, Zoe

thought. Foolish to have felt that fast feminine flutter when she recognized interest in his eyes. More foolish to feel let down because the interest had blanked out when her child called her. "Do you need any help?"

"No, I can handle it. I've got a game to cover tonight, so I'm going to move the rest in tomorrow." He backed toward the door. "Thanks."

"Welcome aboard, Mr. McKinnon."

"Coop," he said as he stepped outside. "It's Coop."

Coop, she thought, leaning on the mop handle. It had seemed like such a good idea to make use of the apartment upstairs. The extra income would take some of the pressure off, and maybe add a few bonuses. Like that trip to Disney World that Keenan wanted so badly.

It had been a risk to buy the house, but she'd wanted her son to grow up in a nice neighborhood, with a yard, maybe a dog when he was a little older. The rental income would take away some of the risk.

But she hadn't realized it could add another, more personal risk. She hadn't realized how awkward it might be to have a tenant who was male, single, and absolutely gorgeous.

She laughed at herself. Dream on, Zoe, she thought. J. Cooper McKinnon was just like the rest, who ran like a hound when they heard the patter of little feet.

Something crashed in the laundry room. She just shook her head.

"Come on, sailor," she called to Keenan. "It's time to swab the deck."

Chapter 3

"**P**retty good digs, Coop. Really, pretty good." Ben Robbins, a staff reporter for the *Dispatch,* sipped a cold one while surveying Coop's apartment. "I didn't think much of it when we hauled all your junk up here, but it ain't half-bad."

It was a lot better than not half-bad, and Coop knew it. He had everything exactly where he wanted it. The living room was dominated by his long, low-slung sofa of burgundy leather and his big-screen television, so perfect for viewing games. A couple of brass lamps, a nicely worn coffee table scuffed from the heels of the dozens of shoes that had rested on it and a single generous chair completed the formal section of the room.

There was an indoor basketball hoop, small-scaled, for practice—and because shooting a little round ball helped him think. A used pinball machine called Home

Run, a stand that held two baseball bats, his tennis racket and a hockey stick, a pair of old boxing gloves hanging on the wall and a scarred Fooz Ball table made up the recreation area.

Coop wouldn't have called them toys. They were tools.

He'd chosen blinds, rather than curtains, for the windows. Blinds, he thought, that would close out the light if a man decided to treat himself to an afternoon nap.

The bedroom held little other than his bed, a nightstand and another TV. The room was for sleeping—or, if he got lucky, another type of sport.

But it was his office that pleased him most. He could already imagine himself spending hours there at his computer, a game playing on his desktop TV. He'd outfitted it with a big swivel chair, a desk that had just the right number of scars and burns, a fax, a dual-line phone and a VCR—to play back those controversial calls or heart-stopping plays.

With all the plaques and photos and sports memorabilia scattered about, it was home.

His home.

"Looks like the neighborhood bar," Ben said, and stretched out his short, hairy legs. "Where the jocks hang out."

Coop considered that the highest of compliments. "It suits me."

"To the ground," Ben agreed, and toasted Coop with his bottle of beer. "A place where a man can relax, be himself. You know, since I started living with Sheila, I've got little china things all over, and underwear hanging in the bathroom. The other day she comes home with a new bedspread. It's got *flowers* all over. Pink flowers." He winced as he drank. "It's like sleeping in a meadow."

"Hey." With all the smug righteousness of the unencumbered, Coop propped his feet on the coffee table. "Your choice, pal."

"Yeah, yeah. Too bad I'm nuts about her. And her an Oakland fan, too."

"Takes all kinds. Talk is the A's are trading Remirez."

Ben snorted. "Yeah, yeah, pull the other one, champ."

"That's the buzz." Coop shrugged, took a pull on his own beer. "Sending him to K.C. for Dunbar, and that rookie fielder, Jackson."

"They got to be crazy. Remirez hit .280 last season."

".285," Coop told him. "With twenty-four baggers. Led the team in errors, too."

"Yeah, but with a bat like that… And Dunbar, what's he? Maybe he hit .220?"

"It was .218, but he's like a vacuum cleaner at second. Nothing gets by him. And the kid's got potential. Big, strapping farm boy with an arm like a bullet. They need new blood. Most of the starting lineup's over thirty."

They argued baseball and finished their beers in complete male harmony.

"I've got a game to cover."

"Tonight? I thought the O's were in Chicago until tomorrow."

"They are." Coop pocketed his tape recorder, his pad, a pencil. "I'm covering the college game. There's a hot third baseman who's got the scouts drooling. Thought I'd take a look, cop an interview."

"What a job." Ben hauled himself to his feet. "Going to games, hanging around locker rooms."

"Yeah, it's a rough life." He slung an arm over Ben's

shoulders as they headed out. "So, how's the story on neutering pets going?"

"Stuff it, Coop."

"Hey, some of us hang around the pound, some of us hang around the ballpark."

And a hell of a day it was for it, too, Coop thought. Balmy and clear-skied. He could almost smell roasting peanuts and hot dogs.

"While you're hanging around a bunch of sweaty college boys in jockstraps, I'll be snuggled up with a woman."

"Under a flowered bedspread."

"Yeah, but she says flowers make her feel sexy. And I'm here to tell you— My, oh, my…"

When Ben's small, square face went lax, Coop turned. He felt his own jaw drop. And, if he wasn't mistaken, his tongue landed on his shoes.

She was wearing what had to be the shortest skirt ever devised by man. Beneath it were a pair of endless legs that were molded into black fishnet hose. She swayed when she walked. How could she help it, when she stood in black skyscraper heels?

A tiny white bustier exposed a delicious amount of cleavage. Around her neck was a shiny black bow tie that, for reasons utterly inexplicable to Coop, made every male cell in his body sizzle.

Her hair was down, falling straight as a pin to her shoulders in a melding of tones that made him think of wild deer leaping through a sunlit forest.

She stopped, smiled, said something, but his mind had checked out the moment his eyes landed on her legs.

"…if you've settled in okay."

"Ah…" He blinked like a man coming out of a coma. "What?"

"I said I haven't had a chance to check and see if you've settled in okay."

"Fine." He folded his tongue back in his mouth and got a grip on himself. "Just fine."

"Good. Keenan came down with a cold, so things have been hectic. I caught a glimpse of you hauling things up the steps a couple of days ago."

"Hauling," he repeated. "Yeah. Ben," he said when his friend jabbed him. "This is Ben. He's been giving me a hand moving."

"Hi, Ben. I'm Zoe."

"Hi, Zoe," Ben said stupidly. "I'm Ben."

She just smiled. It was the outfit, she knew. As much as she hated it, she couldn't help but be amused by how it affected certain members of the species. "Do you work at the paper, too?"

"Yeah, I'm, ah, doing a story on neutering pets."

"Really?" She almost felt sorry for him, the way his Adam's apple was bobbing. "I'll be sure to look for it. I'm glad you're settling in okay. I've got to get to work."

"You're going out?" Coop said. "In that?"

Her lips twitched. "Well, this isn't my usual outfit when I'm carpooling, but I thought I'd wear it to work tonight. At Shadows? I'm a waitress. Nice meeting you, Ben."

She walked to her car. No, Coop thought, swayed to it, in those long, lazy strides. They were both still staring when she pulled out of the drive and cruised down the street.

"Your landlady," Ben said in a reverential whisper. "That was your landlady."

"I think it was." She hadn't looked like that when he signed the lease. Beautiful, yes—she'd been beautiful, but in a wholesome, unthreatening sort of way. She hadn't looked so…so… Words failed him. She was a mother, for God's sake, he reminded himself. She wasn't supposed to look like that. "She's got a kid."

"Yeah? What kind?"

"Human, I think."

"Come on."

"A boy," Coop said absently. "This high." He held a hand, palm down, about three feet from the ground.

"She may have a kid, but she's also got legs. This high." Ben waved a hand in front of his own throat. "You got a charmed life, Coop. My landlord's got arms like cinder blocks, and a tattoo of a lizard. You got one who looks like a centerfold."

"She's a mother," Coop said under his breath.

"Well, I wouldn't mind coming home to her for milk and cookies. See you at the sweatshop."

"Sure." Coop stood where he was, frowning at the quiet street. Mothers weren't supposed to look like that, he thought again. They were supposed to look…motherly. Safe. Comfortable. He blew out a breath, willed away the knot in his stomach.

She wasn't *his* mother, he reminded himself.

By midnight, Zoe's feet were screaming. Her back ached, and her arms felt as though she'd been hauling boulders rather than drink trays. She'd deflected six propositions, two of them good-hearted enough to amuse, one of them insulting enough to earn the gentleman in question a bruised instep, courtesy of one of her stiletto heels. The others had been the usual, and easily ignored.

It went with the territory, and it didn't bother her overmuch.

The lounge earned its name from the shadowy effect of neon and all the dim corners. The decor was fifties tacky, and the waitresses were dolled up like old-fashioned mindless floozies to match.

But the tips were excellent, and the clientele, for the most part, harmless.

"Two house wines, white, a Black Russian and a coffee, light." After calling out her order to the bartender, Zoe took a moment to roll her shoulders.

She hoped Beth had gotten Keenan to bed without any fuss. He'd been cranky all day—which meant he was nearly over his sniffles. He'd put up quite a fuss that morning, Zoe remembered, when she'd nixed the idea of him going to school.

Didn't get that from me, she thought. She'd never fussed about not going to school. Now, at twenty-five, she deeply regretted letting her education slide. If she'd applied herself, tried for college, she could have developed a skill, had a career.

Instead, she had a high school diploma she'd barely earned, and was qualified for little more than serving drinks to men whose eyes tried to crawl down her cleavage.

But she wasn't one for regrets. She'd done what she'd done, and she had the greatest prize of all. Keenan. In a couple of years, she figured, she'd have saved enough that she could turn in her bustier and take a night course. Once she had a few business courses under her belt, she could open her own flower shop. And she wouldn't have to leave Keenan with sitters at night.

She served her drinks, took an order from another table and thanked God her break was coming up in five minutes.

When she saw Coop walk in, her first thought was Keenan. But the sick alarm passed almost as quickly as it had come. Coop was relaxed, obviously scoping the place out. When his eyes met hers, he nodded easily and made his way through the scattered tables.

"I thought I'd stop in for a drink."

"This is the place for it. Do you want to sit at the bar, or do you want a table?"

"A table. Got a minute?"

"At quarter after I've got fifteen of them. Why?"

"I'd like to talk to you."

"Okay. What can I get you?"

"Coffee, black."

"Coffee, black. Have a seat."

He watched her head toward the bar and tried not to dwell on how attractive she looked walking away. He hadn't come in because he wanted a drink, but because she seemed like a nice woman in a tight skirt—spot, he corrected. A tight spot.

Get hold of yourself, Coop, he warned himself. He knew better than to let a pair of long legs cloud his judgment. He'd only come in to ask a few questions, get the full story. That was what he did, and he was good at it. Just as he was good at dissecting a game, any game, and finding those small triumphs and small mistakes that influenced the outcome.

"We've been busy tonight." Zoe set two coffees on the table before sliding onto a chair across from Coop.

She let out a long, heartfelt sigh, then smiled. "This is the first time I've been off my feet in four hours."

"I thought you worked in a flower shop."

"I do, three days a week." She slid her cramped feet out of her shoes. "Around Mother's Day, Christmas, Easter—you know, the big flower days, I can squeeze in more." She sipped the coffee she'd loaded with sugar and let it pump into her system. "It's just a small shop, and Fred—that's the owner—only keeps on a couple of part-timers. That way he doesn't have to pay any of the bennies, like hospitalization, sick leave."

"That's lousy."

"Hey, it's a job. I like it. It's just Fred and Martha—she's his wife. They've taught me a lot about flowers and plants."

Someone pumped quarters into the jukebox. The room heated up with music. Coop leaned over the table so that she could hear him. For a moment he lost the thread somewhere in her big brown eyes.

"Have I met you somewhere before?" he asked her.

"In the apartment."

"No, I mean…" He shook his head, let it go. "Uh, why here?"

"Why here what?"

"Why do you work here?"

She blinked, those long lashes fluttering down, then up. "For a paycheck."

"It doesn't seem like you should be working in a bar."

"Excuse me?" Zoe wasn't sure if she should be amused or insulted. She chose the former simply because it was her nature. "Do you have a problem with cocktail waitresses?"

"No, no. It's just that, you're a mother."

"Yes, I am. I have a son to prove it." She laughed and leaned her chin on her fist. "Are you thinking it would be more appropriate for me to be home baking cookies or knitting a scarf?"

"No." Though it embarrassed him that he did. "It's that outfit," he blurted out. "And the way all these men look at you."

"If a woman's going to wear something like this, men are going to look. Looking's all they do," she added. "If it makes you feel better, I don't dress like this for PTA meetings."

He was feeling more ridiculous every second. "Look, it's none of my business. I just have a habit of asking questions. Seems to me you could do better than this. I mean, you've got the flower job, and the rent—"

"And I have a mortgage, a son who seems to outgrow his clothes and shoes every other week, a car payment, grocery bills, doctor bills."

"Doctor? Is the kid sick?"

Zoe rolled her eyes. Just when she was starting to get irritated, he deflated her. "No. Kids Keenan's age are always bringing some germ or other home from school. He needs regular checkups with his pediatrician, with the dentist. Those things aren't free."

"No, but there are programs. Assistance." He stopped, because those big brown eyes had turned fierce.

"I'm perfectly capable of earning a living, and of taking care of my child."

"I didn't mean—"

"Maybe I don't have a college degree or any fancy skills, but I can pay my own way, and my son doesn't lack for anything." She jammed her feet into the backbreaking heels and stood. "We've been doing just fine on our own, and I don't need some nosy jock reporter coming in here and telling me how to be a mother. Coffee's on the house, you jerk."

He winced as she stormed away from the table, then let out a long breath. Handled that one *real* well, Coop.

He wondered if there would be an eviction notice on his door in the morning.

Chapter 4

She didn't kick him out. She had thought of it, but had decided the satisfaction she'd gain didn't quite equal the rental income. Besides, she'd heard it all before.

One of the reasons she'd moved from New York was that she'd grown impossibly weary of friends and family telling her how to run her life. How to raise her son.

Baltimore had been a clean slate.

She'd had enough money put aside to afford a nice two-bedroom apartment and invest the rest. And because she was willing to work at any job, and work hard, she'd rarely been unemployed. It had been difficult for her to put Keenan in day care. But he'd thrived. He had his mother's knack for making friends.

Now, two years after the move, she had a house, and a yard, in the kind of neighborhood she wanted for her son. And she'd paid for every bit of it on her own.

Too many people had told her she was crazy, that she was too young, that she was throwing her life and her chances away. With a grunt, Zoe shoved the lawn mower around and began to cut another strip of grass. *Her* grass, she thought with clenched teeth.

She'd proved them wrong. She'd had her baby, kept her baby, and she was making a decent life for him. She and Keenan weren't statistics. They were a family.

They didn't need anyone to feel sorry for them, or to offer handouts. She was taking care of everything, one step at a time. And she had plans. Good, solid plans.

The tap on her shoulder made her jump. When she whipped her head around and looked at Coop, her hands tightened on the mower. "What?"

"I want to apologize," he shouted. When she only continued to glare at him, he reached down and shut off the engine. "I want to apologize," he repeated. "I was out of line last night."

"Really?"

"I'm sort of addicted to poking into other people's business."

"Maybe you should go cold turkey." She reached down to grab the pull cord. His hand closed over hers. She stared at it a moment. He had big hands, rough-palmed. She remembered the impression she'd gotten of strength and energy. Now the hand was gentle and hard to resist.

She hadn't felt a man's hands—hadn't wanted to feel a man's hands—in a very long time.

"Sometimes I push the wrong buttons," Coop continued. He was staring at their hands, as well, thinking how small hers felt under his. How soft. "It's earned me a fist in the face a time or two." He tried a smile when her gaze slid up to his.

"That doesn't surprise me."

She didn't smile back, but he sensed a softening. The roar of the mower had awakened him. When he'd looked out and seen her marching along behind it in baggy shorts, a T-shirt and a ridiculous straw hat, he'd wanted to go back to bed. But he'd been compelled to seek her out.

It was only a flag of truce, he told himself. After all, he had to live with her. More or less.

"I didn't mean to be critical. I was curious about you. And the kid," he added quickly. "And maybe seeing you in that outfit last night pushed a few of my buttons."

She lifted a brow. That was honest enough, she thought. "All right. No permanent damage."

It had been easier than he'd expected. Coop decided to press his luck. "Listen, I've got to cover the game this afternoon. Maybe you'd like to come along. It's a nice day for baseball."

She supposed it was. It was warm and sunny, with a nice, freshening breeze. There were worse ways to spend the day than in a ballpark with an attractive man who was doing his best to pry his foot out of his mouth.

"It sounds like fun—if I didn't have to work. But Keenan would love it." She watched his jaw drop, and smothered a smile.

"Keenan? You want me to take him?"

"I can't think of anything he'd rather do. Some of the kids play in their yards, and they let him chase the ball. But he's never seen the real thing, except on TV." She smiled now, guilelessly, and held back a hoot of laughter. She could all but see Coop's mind working.

"I don't know too much about kids," he said, back-pedaling cautiously.

"But you know about sports. It'll be great for Keenan to experience his first real game with an expert. When are you leaving?"

"Ah…a couple of hours."

"I'll make sure he's ready. This is awfully nice of you." While he stood staring, she leaned over and kissed his cheek. After one hard tug, she had the mower roaring again.

Coop stood planted like a tree when she strolled away. What the hell was he supposed to do with a kid all afternoon?

He bought popcorn, hot dogs and enormous cups of soft drinks. Coop figured food would keep the kid quiet. Keenan had bounced on the seat of the car throughout the drive to Camden Yards, and since they had arrived he'd goggled at everything.

Coop had heard "What's that?" and "How come?" too many times to count. Nervous as a cat, he settled into the press box with his laptop.

"You can watch through the window here," he instructed Keenan. "And you can't bother anybody, because they're working."

"Okay." Almost bursting with excitement, Keenan clutched his hot dog.

There were lots of people in the press box, some with neat computers, like Coop, others with headphones. A few of them had smiled at him, and all of them had said hello to Coop. Keenan knew Coop was important. As his mother had instructed, he kept close and didn't ask for any presents. Even though there had been really neat stuff at the stands. His mother had given him five whole dollars and told him he could buy a souvenir. But there'd been so many he didn't know which to pick. And Coop had walked so fast he'd hardly been able to look.

But it didn't matter, because he was at a real ball game.

Wide-eyed, he stared down at the field. It was bigger than anything he'd imagined. He knew where the pitcher would stand, and he recognized home plate, but he wasn't sure of anything else.

The big scoreboard exploded with pictures, and words he couldn't read. Circling it all were the stands, filled with more people than he'd ever seen.

When they announced the lineup, he looked down at the players with naked admiration. The national anthem began, and, recognizing it, Keenan stood up, as he'd been taught.

Coop glanced over, saw the boy standing, with a hot dog in one hand and a big, dazzling grin on his face. Suddenly he remembered his first time at a ballpark. His eager hand gripping his father's, his eyes trying to see everything at once, and his heart so full of the excitement, of the game, of just being a boy.

As the players took the field, Coop reached over and tugged on Keenan's bright hair. "Pretty cool, huh?"

"It's the best ever. Those are our guys, right?"

"Those are our guys. They're gonna kick butt."

Keenan giggled and leaned closer to the glass to watch the first pitch. "Kick butt," he said with relish.

He didn't, as Coop had expected, fidget, whine or make a general nuisance of himself. Because he was accustomed to working under noisy and confusing conditions, Keenan's constant questions didn't annoy him overmuch. At least, he thought, the kid had the good sense to ask.

Between innings, Keenan peered over Coop's shoulder and sounded out the words that were popping up on the computer screen, and he did transfer some mustard from his hands onto Coop's sleeve. But it wasn't the disaster Coop had envisioned.

Coop even felt a quick tug of pride when the play-by-play announcer called Keenan over and let the boy sit in his lap for an inning.

Most kids would've been running around the booth begging for more candy. But this one, Coop thought, had come for the game.

"How come he didn't run all the way? How come he didn't?" Keenan shifted from foot to foot. His bladder was past full, but he couldn't bear to miss a minute.

"The throw went to second, so he was forced out," Coop explained. "See, the second baseman caught the ball and stepped on the bag to retire the side."

"Retire the side," Keenan repeated reverently. "But we're still winning?"

"The O's are up by one going into the top of the ninth. Looking at the batting order, I'd say they'll put in a southpaw."

"Southpaw," Keenan repeated, as if it were gospel.

"A left-handed reliever. Probably Scully." He glanced over and noted that Keenan was holding his crotch. "Uh, got a problem?"

"Nuh-uh."

"Let's hit the john—the bathroom." He took Keenan's hand and hoped it wasn't too late. As they passed through the door, Scully was announced as the relief.

"Just like you said." Keenan looked up at Coop with dazzling admiration. "You're smarter than anybody."

Coop felt a grin break out over his face. "Let's just say I know the game."

When they arrived home, Keenan was wearing a new Orioles jersey and carrying an autographed baseball in a pint-size baseball glove. He waved a pennant in his other hand as he scrambled up the steps.

"Look! Look what Coop got me!" He barreled into his mother who'd barely walked in the door herself. "We went into the locker room with the real Orioles, and they signed the baseball for me. To keep."

"Let's see." She took the ball and examined it. "This is really special, Keenan."

"I'm gonna keep it forever. And I got this shirt, too, like they wear. And a glove. It even fits."

Emotion backed up in her throat. "It certainly does. Looks like you're all ready to play ball."

"I'm gonna play third base, 'cause it's the...the..."

"Hot corner," Coop supplied.

"Yeah. Can I go show Mr. Finkleman? Can I show him my baseball?"

"Sure."

"He's gonna be surprised." He turned and threw his arms around Coop's legs. "Thanks, thanks for taking me. I liked it best of anything. Can we go again, and take Mama?"

"Uh, yeah, I guess. Sure." Feeling awkward again, he patted Keenan's head.

"Okay!" Giving Coop one last squeeze, Keenan raced out the door to show off his treasures.

"You didn't have to buy him all that stuff," Zoe began. "Taking him was enough."

"No big deal. He didn't ask for it, or anything." Coop stuck his hands in his pockets. "He got such a charge out of meeting the players, and one thing kind of led to another."

"I know. I hear our team won."

"Yeah. Clipped them by one. I had to stop by the paper and file the story, or we'd have been here sooner."

"I just got in myself." On impulse, she walked over, wrapped her arms around him and hugged. Coop's hands stayed paralyzed in his pockets. "I owe you. You gave him a great day. He won't forget it." She drew back. "Neither will I."

"It's no big deal. He just hung out in the press box."

"It's a very big deal, especially since I trapped you into it." She laughed and tossed back her hair. "You were so transparent this morning, Coop. The idea of having a four-year-old tagging along terrified you. But you did good, real good. Anyway— Sorry," she said when the phone rang. "Hello? Oh, hi, Stan. Tonight? I'm not scheduled." Letting out a breath, she sat on the arm of a chair. "I'll have to let you know. No, Stan, I can't tell you now. I have to see if I can find a sitter. An hour, then. Yes, I understand you're in a jam. I'll call you back."

"Problem?"

"Hmmm… Two of the waitresses called in sick for tonight. They're short-staffed." She was already dialing the phone. "Hi, Mrs. Finkleman. Yeah, I know. He had a great time. Mmm-hmm…" Zoe's gaze flicked up to Coop as Mrs. Finkleman told her how important it was for a boy to have a man in his life. "I'm sure you're right.

I was wondering if you're busy tonight. Oh. That's right, I forgot. No, it's nothing. Have a good time."

Zoe hung up and pursed her lips. "It's their bingo night," she told Coop. "Beth's got a date. Maybe Alice." She reached for the phone again, shook her head. "No, she's having her in-laws over for dinner." Her eyes lit on Coop and narrowed in speculation. "You didn't have any problem with Keenan today."

"No," Coop said slowly, wary of another trap. "He was cool."

"Stan doesn't need me in until nine. Keenan goes to bed at eight, so you wouldn't have to do anything but hang around, watch television or whatever."

"Hang around here, while you work?" He took a step back. "Just me and the kid—like a babysitter? Listen…"

"I'll pay you. Beth gets two an hour, but I can up the ante."

"I don't want your money, Zoe."

"That's so sweet." She smiled, took his hand and squeezed. "Really, so sweet of you. If you could come down about eight-thirty."

"I never said—"

"You can help yourself to anything in the kitchen. I'll make some brownies, if I have time. I'd better call Stan back before he pulls out what's left of his hair." She picked up the phone, beamed at Coop. "Now I owe you two."

"Yeah, right." He hurried out before she could find some way to owe him three.

Chapter 5

For the next couple of hours, Coop immersed himself in "All in the Game," his weekly syndicated column. The kid had given him the hook, he thought. The first visit to a ball game, the passing on of tradition, and the bond that was forged over the cheers, the crack of the bat, the peanut shells.

It was a good piece, Coop decided, and wrote easily. He supposed since he owed the idea to Keenan the least he could do was hang around downstairs and eat brownies while the kid slept.

He wandered back down just as Zoe came through the kitchen door.

She hadn't been sure he'd come. She knew she'd hustled him, and after she'd finished being amused by it, she felt guilty. But here he was, right on time, standing at the foot of the steps.

"I pushed you into a corner…" she began.

"Yeah, you did." She looked so somber, he had to smile. "You've got a real talent for it."

She shrugged her shoulders and smiled back at him. "Sometimes being pushy's the only way to get things done, but I always feel bad about it after. I did bake brownies."

"I could smell them all the way upstairs." When she didn't move, he tilted his head. Funny, though she was wearing that sexy waitress rig again, she didn't seem so outrageous. Except for that bow tie, he thought. Something about that black tie around that slim white throat shot straight to his libido.

"You going to let me in, or do you want me to stand out here?"

"I have this guilt thing," she explained, "whenever I have to ask anyone for a favor. And it was so sweet of you to take Keenan to the game, especially when…"

"When I'd been asking you out?"

She shrugged her shoulders again, let them fall. He was looking at her that way again, and something in her body was reacting helplessly. Better, she thought, to set the rules quickly. "I don't go out with men. I should have told you straight out."

He had to force himself not to lift a hand to that neat little bow and tug. "At all?"

"It's just easier not to. They're not interested in Keenan, or they pretend they are so they can talk me into bed." When he rocked back on his heels and cleared his throat, she laughed. "What they don't know is that they're clear as cellophane. You see, Keenan and I are a team. As a sportswriter, you should know what that means."

"Sure. I get it."

"Anyway, you gave him a really wonderful day, and I feel like I'm twisting your arm about tonight."

He decided, after a moment, that she wasn't doing it on purpose. There was just too much sincerity in that glorious face for a con. And if there was a twinge of guilt because he had given considerable thought to talking her into bed, that was his problem.

"Look, he's asleep, right?"

"Yes. All the excitement wore him out."

"So, I'll eat your brownies and watch your TV. No big deal."

Her smile came easily now, beautifully, and made his mouth water. "I left the number of the club by the phone, just in case. The Finklemans should be home by eleven. She'd come over and relieve you if you want."

"We'll play it by ear."

"Thanks, really." She stepped back into the kitchen to let him in. "My shift ends at two, at closing."

"Long day for you."

"I've got tomorrow off." After grabbing her purse, she took a quick look around. "Make yourself at home, okay?"

"I will. See you."

She hurried out, those incredibly sexy heels clicking across the tile. Coop let out a long breath and told himself to settle down. The lady had just set the ground rules. Fun and games were out.

She had the face of a siren, the body of a goddess, and legs designed to make a strong man whimper—but deep in her heart she was Betty Crocker.

Coop took a deep sniff and decided to content himself with a plate of double fudge brownies.

* * *

The storm rolled in just before midnight. Coop had taken Zoe at her word and made himself at home. He was stretched out on her couch, sunk deep in the cushions, with his feet propped comfortably on her coffee table. He was dozing in front of an old war movie, his only regret being that he hadn't thought to bring a couple of beers down with him.

Zoe's selection ran to milk, juice and some unidentified green liquid.

He'd poked around a little—it was simply in his nature. The clutter ran throughout the house, but he began to see a pattern to it. Obviously she wasn't a detail person, but the general lack of order made the house comfortable, even cozy. Coop wasn't sure if the result was by design or simply because she was a woman who worked two jobs and had a kid to raise.

And from the library books he'd found stacked here and there, it seemed she spent most of her free time reading up on flowers, car repair, tax laws and time management.

He couldn't help but think it was a waste of a perfectly stunning woman, this voluntary burial of self in books and nowhere part-time jobs.

But it wasn't his problem.

The crash of thunder from outside harmonized nicely with the artillery barrage on the TV screen. Coop had just decided that this baby-sitting racket was a snap.

Then he heard the wailing.

Marines didn't wail, he thought fuzzily, especially when they were battling Nazi scum. He yawned, circled his neck until it cracked, then spotted Keenan.

The boy stood at the base of the stairs in Batman pajamas, a battered stuffed dog clutched in one arm and tears pouring down his face.

"Mama!" His voice sharpened like an ice pick, then hitched. "Where's my mama?"

"She's at work." Coop straightened on the sofa and stared helplessly. "Something wrong?"

A flash of lightning lit the room. By the time the thunder rolled in answer, Keenan screamed like a banshee and launched himself into Coop's lap.

"I'm scared. There's monsters outside. They're coming to get me."

"Hey…" Coop gave the head buried in his chest an inadequate pat. "Hey, it's just a thunderstorm."

"Monsters," Keenan sobbed. "I want Mama."

"Well, she's—" He started to swear, caught himself. The poor kid was shaking. With an instinct he didn't recognize, Coop cuddled Keenan in his lap. "You don't like storms, huh?" All Keenan could do was shake his head and burrow deeper. "They're just like fireworks. You know, on the Fourth of July, or after your team wins the pennant? They probably just had a big game up there. They're celebrating."

"Monsters," Keenan repeated, but he'd calmed enough to lift his head and look at Coop. "Big black monsters with sharp teeth." He jolted at the next clap of thunder. Fresh tears started to roll. "They want to eat me."

"Nah." Experimentally, Coop tested Keenan's biceps. "You're too tough."

"I am?"

"You bet. Any monsters who looked in here would see you and run for their lives. They'd never take on Coop and the Keen-man."

Keenan sniffled, rubbed a fist over his eyes. "Really?"

"Absolutely." Coop saw Keenan's lower lip tremble when thunder grumbled. "Home run," he said, and Keenan's trembling mouth curved in a hesitant smile.

"Can I stay out here with you?"

"Sure. I guess."

Keenan, an expert in such matters, settled himself comfortably in Coop's lap, laid his head against Coop's heart and sighed.

Zoe was swaying with fatigue by the time she let herself in. It was nearly 3:00 a.m., and she'd been up and going for twenty hours straight. All she wanted was to fall facedown on her bed and sleep.

She saw them in the gray light of the snowy television screen. They were curled together on the couch, the boy snuggled deep against the man. Something shifted inside her at the sight of them, both sleeping deeply, Keenan's tousled golden hair beneath Coop's broad, tanned hand.

She set her purse and her keys aside without taking her eyes off them.

How small her son looked, and how safe.

She slipped out of her shoes and walked to them on stockinged feet. In a natural gesture, she brushed a hand over Coop's hair before gently lifting her son. Keenan stirred, then settled against her.

"Mama."

"Yes, baby," she murmured. She nuzzled him as she carried him away, caught the scent of man mixed with boy.

"The monsters came, but we scared them away."

"Of course you did."

"Coop said the thunder's just fireworks. I like fireworks."

"I know." She laid him in his bed, smoothing the sheets, his hair, kissing his soft cheeks. "Go back to sleep now."

But he already had. She watched him a moment longer in the faint glow of his night-light, then turned and went back downstairs to Coop.

He was sitting up now, his head in his hands, the heels rubbing against his eyes. She switched off the buzzing television set, then sat on the arm of the couch. Any man who could sleep so comfortably with a child, to her mind, had unlimited potential.

She wondered, just for an instant, what it would feel like to curl up beside him.

"The storm woke him?"

"Yeah." His voice was rusty. He cleared it. "He was pretty spooked."

"He said you chased the monsters away."

"Seemed like the right thing to do." He turned his head to look at her. Those big brown eyes were sleepy and smiling. The quick hitch in his heartbeat warned him to be on his way. But he lingered. "He's okay now?"

"He's fine. You'd make a good daddy."

"Oh, well…" That had him moving. He stood, working out the kinks. "That's not my line. But it was no big deal."

"It was to me." She'd embarrassed him, she noted, and she hadn't meant to. "Why don't I fix you breakfast tomorrow?"

"Huh?"

"Pay you back with pancakes. Mrs. Finkleman tells

me you bring in a lot of pizza and Chinese, so I don't imagine you cook. Do you like pancakes?"

"Who doesn't?"

"Then let me know when you're up and around. I'll flip some for you." She lifted a hand, brushed the hair from his brow. "Thanks for helping me out."

"No problem." He took a step away, swore under his breath and turned back. "Listen, I've just got to do this, okay?"

Before she could respond, he took her face in his hands and closed his mouth over hers.

The kiss was quick, and it was light, and it sent sparks snapping down her nerve ends.

When she didn't move a muscle, he lifted his head, looked at her. She was staring at him, her eyes heavy and dark. He thought he saw the same stunned reaction in them that was curling somewhere in his gut. She opened her mouth as if to speak, but he shook his head and kissed her again. Longer, deeper, until he felt her bones begin to melt. Until he heard the small whimper of pleasure purr in her throat.

Her hands slid up his arms, gripped, then moved up to tangle in his hair. They stood there, locked against each other.

One of them quivered, perhaps both. It didn't seem to matter as the warm taste of her seeped into his mouth, into his blood. It was like a dream that he hadn't yet shaken off, one that tempted him to sink back in, to forget reality.

She'd forgotten it. All she knew for one glorious moment was that she was being held in strong arms, that her mouth was being savored wonderfully, and that needs, so long dormant, were swimming to the surface and breaking into life.

Touch me. She wondered if she said it, or if the words simply whirled hazily in her head. But his hand, hard and sure, ran once down her body, kindling fires.

She remembered what it was to burn, and what it was like when the flames died out and left you alone.

"Coop." Oh, she wanted, so badly, just to let it happen. But she wasn't a young, reckless girl this time. And she had more to think of than herself. "Coop. No."

His mouth clung to hers for another moment, his teeth nipping. But he drew back. He was, he realized, as breathless as a man who'd slid headfirst into home plate.

"Now I'm supposed to say I'm sorry."

She shook her head. "No, you're not. I'm not."

"Good." The hands that were resting on her shoulders kneaded once, then slipped away into his pockets. "Me neither. I've been thinking about doing that since I first saw your feet."

Her brows rose. Surely she'd heard him wrong. "My what?"

"Your feet. You were standing on the ladder, painting. You weren't wearing any shoes. You've got tremendously sexy feet."

"Really?" It amazed her that he could tie her into helpless knots one minute, then make her laugh the next. "Thanks. I think."

"I guess I'd better go."

"Yeah, you'd better."

He nodded, started out. This time, when he stopped, she braced, and she yearned. But he simply turned and looked at her. "I'm not going to try to talk you into bed. But I want you there. I figured I should let you know."

"I appreciate it," she said in a shaky voice.

When the door closed behind him, she let her weak legs fold and sat down on the couch. What, she asked herself, was she supposed to do now?

Chapter 6

When Coop dragged himself out of bed, it was nearly noon. He stumbled into the shower and nearly drowned himself before both of his eyes opened. Wet and out of sorts, he rubbed himself down, gave a moment's thought to shaving, then dismissed the idea.

He tugged on gym shorts and a T-shirt before heading directly to the coffeemaker. While it brewed, he opened his front door and let the full power of the sun shock him the rest of the way awake.

They were in the yard, Zoe and Keenan, laughing as mother tried to help son hit fungoes with a plastic bat. The kid wasn't having much luck, Coop noted. But he was sure having fun. He started to step back inside before either of them spotted him. But the jock in him had him kibitzing.

"He'll never hit anything standing that way," Coop

called out, and had two pairs of big brown eyes looking up in his direction.

"Hi, Coop. Hi. I'm playing baseball." Thrilled to have an audience, Keenan waved his bat and nearly caught his mother on the chin.

"Watch it, champ," she said, and shifted out of range. "Good morning," she called out. "Want your breakfast?"

"Yeah, maybe."

Keenan took another pathetic swing and had Coop muttering under his breath. Swung like a girl. Somebody had to show the kid how to hold a bat, didn't they? he asked himself as he started down.

"You're choking it too much."

Zoe's brows drew together. "The book I got said—"

"Book." He cursed automatically. Keenan echoed him. "Sorry," he muttered when Zoe gave him a narrow-eyed look. "Now listen, you learn how to add and subtract from books. You don't learn baseball. Just like a girl." He crouched down and adjusted Keenan's hands.

Zoe had been ready to concede to the expert, but the last statement stopped her. "Excuse me? Are you implying that females can't play sports?"

"Not what I said. Swing from the shoulders," he told Keenan. Coop might have been grouchy, but he wasn't stupid. "There are plenty of terrific female athletes. Keep your eye on the ball, kid." He kept one hand around Keenan's and lightly tossed the ball up in the air with the other. The bat connected with a hollow thud.

"I hit it! I hit it really, really hard!"

"Major league stuff." Coop slid his eyes back up to Zoe's. "I thought you were making pancakes."

"I was— I am." She blew out a breath. "I guess you're taking over."

"Well, I don't know diddly about pancakes, and you don't know squat about baseball. Why don't we both do what we know?"

"Like it's a big deal to hit a stupid ball with a stupid bat," she muttered as she strode to the back door.

"You can't do it."

She stopped dead in her tracks, eyes narrowed, turned. "I certainly can."

"Yeah, right. Okay, Keenan, let's try it again."

"I believe it's my turn." Challenge in her every movement, Zoe slipped the bat from her son's hands.

"Are you going to hit it, Mama? Are you?"

"You bet I am." She held out a hand for the ball Coop was holding. She tossed it up, swung, and batted the ball to the chain-link fence bordering the side yard. Keenan let out a cheer and raced to retrieve it.

Coop sniffed, smiled. "Not bad, for a girl. But anybody can hit a fungo."

"Keenan's too young for anything but a plastic ball."

"No, a fungo's when you toss it up yourself and hit it."

"Oh."

"I'm gonna throw it, Coop. You catch."

"Sure, zip it in here."

It took Keenan three tries, running in closer each time, to send the ball anywhere near Coop.

"I suppose you don't think I could hit it if you threw it at me…" Zoe began.

"Pitch it to you," Coop said patiently. "I would pitch it to you."

"All right, pitch it to me, then." She raised the bat.

"Fine, but you might want to turn a little more to the side. That's it," he said, backing away. "Zoe, you're holding the bat like you're going to use it to hammer a nail. Okay, here it comes."

He tossed the ball soft and underhand, but she still had to grit her teeth to keep herself from jerking away. Because her pride and her son's respect for women were at stake, she swung hard. No one was more stunned than Zoe when she connected. Coop snatched the ball an instant before it could smash his nose.

"Well." Zoe handed the bat back to a wide-eyed Keenan, dusted her hands. "I'll go see about those pancakes."

"She hit it really hard," Keenan said admiringly.

"Yeah." Coop watched the back door swing shut behind her. "Your mother's really…something, kid."

"Will you pitch to me, Coop? Will you?"

"Sure. But let's work on that stance, huh? You gotta look like a ballplayer."

When Zoe finished flipping the last pancake on the stack, she looked out the window and saw her son swing the bat. The ball didn't go far, but Coop made a pretense of a diving catch, missing, while Keenan danced gleefully in place.

"Too hot to handle," Coop claimed, and Keenan jumped on top of him. "Hey, there's no tackling in baseball. Football's out of season." He scooped the wriggling boy up and held him upside down. Somewhere along the line, his sour mood had vanished.

It became a habit to spend time with the boy. Nothing planned, just playing a little catch in the yard or showing Keenan how to dunk baskets in the apartment. It wasn't as though he were attached to the kid, Coop assured himself. But when he had some free time and the boy wanted to hang around, what was the harm? Maybe it was sort of nice to see those big eyes all full of hero worship. And maybe it wasn't so much of a hardship to listen to that rollicking belly laugh Keenan burst into when something struck his fancy.

If the boy sometimes came along with the bonus of his mother, it wasn't exactly a hardship.

The fact was, he had seen a great deal more of Keenan than Zoe since the night of the thunderstorm. She was friendly enough, but she'd been careful—or so it seemed to Coop—not to be alone with him.

That was something he was going to fix, he decided as he shut down his computer.

He grabbed a couple of miniature race cars, some of the flotsam and jetsam of boyhood that Keenan had left in his apartment. If Coop knew Zoe as he thought he was beginning to, the toys would be an easier entry than a bouquet of long-stemmed roses.

Jiggling the cars in his hand, he strode down the steps to knock on her kitchen door.

In the laundry room, Zoe slammed down the lid on the washer. "Who is it?"

"It's Coop."

She hesitated, started the machine. "Come on in. I'll be right out." She hefted a basket of clean laundry, as much out of defense as out of necessity, and went into the kitchen.

God, he looked good. She had really, really tried not to dwell on how good the man looked. So damn male, she thought, the rangy, athletic body, the muscles, the dark, untidy hair, and those wonderful pale green eyes.

She wished her heart wouldn't always stutter when he aimed one of his cocky grins in her direction.

"Hi." She plopped the basket on the kitchen table and immediately began busying her hands folding socks.

"Hi." The kitchen was cluttered, as always. She really needed someone to help her organize, he thought. God, she smelled fantastic. "Keenan left these upstairs." Coop set the cars on the table. "I thought he might be looking for them."

"Thanks."

"So where is he?"

"In school."

"Oh, right." Coop knew Keenan's schedule as well as he knew yesterday's box scores. "You just get in from the flower shop?"

"Mmm-hmm... Business is picking up. We've got a couple of weddings. Actually, I could work full-time for the next three weeks, but it just doesn't fit Keenan's schedule."

"What do you mean?" Idly he plucked a shirt from the basket.

"Well, the spring weddings. The arrangements take a lot of extra hands, so Fred asked if I could put in full days for a while."

"So, that's good, right?"

"The school Keenan goes to is really more of a pre-school than day care. It doesn't stay open after three. And I have the car pool next week, anyway. Plus, I promised to take him and some of the other kids swimming at the community center on Friday. He's really looking forward to it."

"Yeah, he mentioned it." About twenty times, Coop recalled.

"I don't want to let him down."

"So, I'll do it."

She looked back up, socks dangling from her hands. "What?"

He couldn't believe he'd said that. He stared at her for another moment, then shrugged. "I said I'd do it. It's no big deal. He can hang with me when he gets home from school."

She tilted her head. "Don't you have a job?"

"That's what I call it, since they pay me." He smiled, finding the idea went down easily. "I do most of my writing here, and he could tag along when I go in to the paper or on an interview. He'd probably get a kick out of it."

"I'm sure he would." She narrowed her eyes. Why couldn't she get a handle on J. Cooper McKinnon? "But why would you?"

He wasn't sure he had the answer to that, so he punted. "Why not? He's not that much of a pest."

With a laugh, she went back to her laundry. "Maybe he's not, but you forgot the car pool."

"I can drive. What's the big deal about hauling a bunch of kids to school and back?"

"I can't begin to tell you," she murmured. It was, perhaps, something every adult should experience for himself. "And the swimming."

"I was captain of the swim team in college. All-state."

She glanced up at that. "I thought you played baseball. Uh, Keenan mentioned it."

"Yeah, I did. Two hundred and twelve RBIs my last season. I played basketball, too, averaged forty-two points a game." He was bragging, Coop realized. Like some gawky teenager trying to impress the head cheerleader. He frowned down at the little cars, began to slide one over the table.

"Keenan says you make great engine noises."

"Yeah, it's a talent."

He'd embarrassed himself, Zoe realized, and she wanted to hug him. "Tell you what. Why don't we take it a day at a time? If you decide you can't handle it—"

His eyes flashed up at that. "I think I can handle one scrawny kid and a few of his pals."

"Okay. If you decide you don't *want* to handle it, no hard feelings."

"Fine. When do you want to start?"

"Tomorrow would be great."

"Okay." That was settled. Now, he thought, it was on to other business. "How about dinner?"

Her eyes widened in surprise. "Um…sure. We're just going to have chicken. I'll probably fry it."

"No." He stepped closer. She stepped back. "I mean, why don't we have dinner? Out. You and me."

"Oh, well…" Good answer, she thought foolishly. Very succinct. She took another step in retreat. "I have to work tonight."

"Tomorrow."

"I don't really go out."

"I've noticed. What are you backing away from, Zoe?"

"You." Annoyed with herself, she held up a hand. And found it pressed against his chest. "I don't want to date anyone. Start anything. I have very good reasons."

"You'll have to tell me about them sometime." He reached up, combed a hand through her hair and loosened the band that held it back.

"You're not going to kiss me again."

"Sure I am." He touched his lips to hers to prove it. His eyes remained open as he drew her lower lip into his mouth, as he used his tongue, his teeth, to tease and seduce. "You've got an incredible mouth."

She couldn't get her breath. Even as she gasped for it, her vision dimmed. It was all she wanted. It seemed her life depended on keeping her lips against his. This wasn't fair, she thought dimly as she began to sink into the glory of sensation. Too long, she told herself. Surely she was reacting this way only because it had been so terribly long since she'd allowed herself to feel only as a woman.

She was melting against him like wax. He hadn't known how painfully erotic it would be to feel that long, lean body go fluid. He'd only meant to kiss her, to test them both, but his hands were already reaching, stroking, exploring.

His touch, those hard, callused hands against her bare skin, all but brought her to her knees.

"I have to think."

"Think later." He pressed his mouth to her throat.

Oh, it was glorious, glorious to ache again. But she knew too well what came from soothing that ache. "Coop, we can't do this."

"Yes, we can. I'll show you."

With a laugh that came out half moan, she turned her head away. "My head's spinning. You have to stop. God, do you have any idea what you're doing to me?"

"I haven't even started. Come upstairs, come upstairs with me, Zoe. I want to feel you under me. I want to feel myself inside you."

"I want to." She trembled, the needs exploding inside her like firebombs. "Coop, I need to think first. I have to think. I haven't been with anyone in five years."

His mouth stopped its desperate journey over her throat. Slowly he drew back to look at her. Her eyes were clouded, and her mouth was swollen and ripe. "No one?"

"No." She swallowed and prayed for her system to level before she gave in to the urge to rip off his clothes and cut loose. "Since before Keenan was born. I feel like all those needs dried up—like old leaves. You've set a match to them, and I don't know how to handle it."

"The kid's father," Coop said carefully. "You're still in love with him."

"No." She might have laughed at that, if she weren't so shaken. "He has nothing to do with it. Well, of course he does, but… I have to sit down." She walked unsteadily to a chair. "I knew this was going to happen. I think I knew it the first time I saw you. There's been no one, because I didn't want anyone. Because Keenan was all that mattered to me. I have plans." That came out as an accusation, and her eyes darkened. "Damn it, I have plans. I want to go back to school. I want to have my own flower shop one day." Her voice began to catch, alarming him.

"Zoe—"

But she barreled right over him. "And everything was going along fine. I got the house. I wanted him to have a house, and a yard, and neighbors. Everyone said I was crazy, that I'd never be able to do it, that I'd be sorry I'd given everything up to raise a child on my own. But I'm not sorry. He's the best thing that ever happened to me. And I've done a good job. Keenan's happy, and he's bright and funny and wonderful. We have a good life, and I know I can make it even better. I haven't needed anyone. And... Oh, God, I'm in love with you."

The hand he'd lifted awkwardly to pat her head froze. "What?"

"Oh, what a mess. What a mess." She plucked a tiny sock out of the laundry basket and wiped her eyes. "Maybe it's just hormones. It could be, you know. But I walked in and you were sleeping with him on the couch. It was so sweet. Then you were kissing me and everything went crazy. Then you're out in the yard looking so smug and male, showing Keenan how to hit that silly ball. And you're eating pancakes and looking at me. I can hardly breathe when you're looking at me."

Somewhere along the line, his mind had gone blank. "I think I missed a step."

"No, you didn't." She sniffled and struggled to get herself under control. "I've just taken too many. It's my fault. You've been nice to Keenan, and you've been honest with me." She sighed, dropped the damp sock in her lap. "Believe me, I know my emotions are my responsibility." Because he was still staring at her, like a man who'd just had the friendly family dog lunge for his throat, she smiled. "I'm sorry, Coop. I shouldn't have dumped all that on you. I didn't even know it was all bottled up."

This time he took a step back. "Zoe, I like the kid. Who wouldn't? And I'm attracted to you. But—"

"There's no need to explain." Steady now, she rose. "Really, there isn't. I don't expect anything from you, and I'm sorry if I made you uncomfortable. But I feel a lot better." And, oddly enough, she did. "When I go to bed with you, we'll understand each other."

"When you—"

"I think we both know that's going to happen," she said calmly. "We both want it to, and it's smarter to face that than to live with all this tension. Keenan's been wanting to spend the night with a friend of his. I'll arrange it." She laughed a little at Coop's expression. "It's a little hard to be spontaneous with a four-year-old around. I hope you don't mind planning out a night together."

"No, I mean, I don't— God, Zoe."

"If you'd rather not, or if you want some time to decide, that's all right."

He studied her face, felt that same greedy tug, and a flare of something entirely different. Entirely new. "No, I want you. Whenever."

"How about Monday night?"

"I've got a twilight doubleheader on Monday." He couldn't believe he was standing here planning out a wild night of love like a dentist's appointment.

"Ah… Wednesday?"

He nodded. "Wednesday's good for me. Do you want to go out somewhere?"

It was sweet, she thought, really sweet of him to ask. "It's not necessary." She laid a hand on his cheek. "I don't need flowers and candlelight. I'll come upstairs after Keenan's settled."

"Good. Fine. I…better get back to work."

"Do you still want to have Keenan tomorrow?"

"Yeah, no problem. Tell him to come on up." Coop backed toward the door as Zoe began folding laundry again. "I guess I'll see you."

She listened to him walk up the steps. He was certainly a mistake, she told herself. But she'd made others. Life got too mundane when you avoided all the wrong turns.

Chapter 7

"He shoots, he scores!" Coop made appropriate crowd noises as Keenan dunked the basket.

"I can do it again! I can, okay?" From his perch on Coop's shoulders, Keenan swung his sneakered feet.

"Okay, you've drawn the foul." Coop scooped the palm-sized ball up and passed it into Keenan's eager hands. "It's game point, kid, ten seconds to play. This free throw is all-or-nothing. Got it?"

"Got it!"

"A hush falls over the crowd as Fleming steps up to the line. He's played the game of his life tonight, but it all comes down to this one shot. He eyes the basket. You eyeing the basket?"

"Eyeing it," Keenan said, with his tongue caught between his teeth.

"He sets…and shoots." Coop winced as the little rubber ball circled the rim, then watched through squinted eyes as it tipped in and dropped through the net.

"And the crowd goes wild!" Coop danced around the sofa while Keenan hooted and clapped on his shoulders. When he dumped the boy on the cushions of the sofa, Keenan let go with one of the rolling belly laughs that always made Coop grin. "You're a natural."

"You shoot it, Coop! You!"

Obliging, Coop executed a quick turnaround jump shot. This wasn't such a bad way to spend a rainy afternoon, he decided. And it helped keep his mind off how he was going to spend the rainy night ahead.

It was Wednesday.

"Okay, time out. I've got to finish up my piece on the track meet."

"Are we going to go to the paper again? It's neat there."

"Not today. I'm going to fax it in when it's done. You watch some tube." Coop hit the remote, then handed it over.

"Can I get a drink?"

"Yeah, there's some of that juice your mom sent up for you. Stay out of trouble, right?"

"Right."

When Coop headed into his office, Keenan scrambled up from the couch. He liked it best when he got to stay with Coop after school. They always got to do something neat, and Coop never asked if he'd washed his hands or said too many cookies would spoil his appetite.

Best of all, he liked when Coop picked him up. It was different than when his mother did. He liked when she held him, nuzzled him after his bath or rocked him when he had a bad dream. But Coop smelled different, and felt different.

He knew why, Keenan thought as he wandered into the kitchen. It was because Coop was a daddy instead of a mom.

He liked to pretend Coop was his daddy, and figured that maybe if he didn't do anything bad, Coop wouldn't go away.

After a couple of tugs, Keenan had the refrigerator open. He was proud that Coop had hung the pictures he had drawn for him on the door. He peered inside, saw the jug of juice his mother had bought for him. And the green bottles Coop liked.

"B-E-E-R," Keenan said to himself. He remembered that he'd asked Coop if he could have a taste from the bottle, and that Coop had told him he couldn't until he was big. After Coop had let him sniff the beer, Keenan had been glad he wasn't big yet.

There was a new bottle in the fridge today, and Keenan knit his brow and tried to recognize the letters. *C-H-A-R-D-O-N*— There were too many letters to read, so he lost interest.

He took out the jug, gripping it manfully and setting it on the floor. Humming to himself, he dragged a chair over to get cups from the cabinet. One day he'd be as tall as Coop and wouldn't need to stand on a chair. He leaned forward on his toes.

The crash and the howl had Coop leaping up, rapping his knee hard against the desk. Papers scattered as he raced out of the office and into the kitchen.

Keenan was still howling. A chair was overturned, juice was glugging cheerfully onto the floor, and the refrigerator was wide open. Coop splashed through the puddle and scooped Keenan up.

"Are you hurt? What'd you do?" When his only answer was another sob, he stood Keenan on the kitchen table and searched for blood. He imagined gaping wounds, broken bones.

"I fell down." Keenan wriggled back into Coop's arms.

"Okay, it's okay. Did you hit your head?"

"Nuh-uh." With a sniffle, Keenan waited for the kisses he expected after a hurt. "I fell on my bottom." Keenan's lip poked out. "Kiss it."

"You want me to kiss your— Come on, kid, you're joking."

The lip trembled, another tear fell. "You gotta kiss where it hurts. You gotta, or it won't get better."

"Oh, man." Flummoxed, Coop dragged a hand through his hair. He was desperately relieved that no blood had been spilled, but if anyone, anyone, found out what he was about to do, he'd never live it down. He turned Keenan around and made a kissing noise in the air. "Does that do it?"

"Uh-huh." Keenan knuckled his eyes, then held out his arms. "Will you pick me up?"

"Yeah." He didn't feel as ridiculous as he'd expected when the boy's arms went around his neck. "Okay now?"

With his head resting on Coop's shoulder, he nodded. "I didn't mean to do it. I spilled all the juice."

"No big deal." Hardly realizing he did so, Coop turned his head to brush his lips over Keenan's hair. Something was shifting inside him, creaking open.

"You aren't mad at me? You won't go away?"

"No." What the hell was going on? Coop wondered as unexplored and unexpected emotions swirled inside him. "No, I'm not going anywhere."

"I love you," Keenan said, with the simple ease of a child.

Coop closed his eyes and wondered how a grown man was supposed to handle falling for a four-year-old boy.

Well, here she was, Zoe thought as she stood at the bottom of the steps leading to Coop's apartment. All she had to do was go upstairs, open the door and start an affair. Her stomach clenched.

Silly to be nervous, she told herself, and climbed the first step. She was a normal woman with normal needs. If her emotions were too close to the surface, she would deal with it. It was much more difficult to be hurt when you had no expectations.

She'd had expectations once, but she knew better now.

This was simply a physical attraction between two single, healthy people. She'd nearly backed down a step before she forced herself to move forward. All the practical details had been seen to. Her son was safely tucked away for the night at his sleepover. She'd arranged for birth control—that wasn't an oversight she would make again.

No regrets, she promised herself as she lifted a hand to knock. She knew how useless they were.

He answered so quickly, she nearly jumped. Then they stood and stared at each other.

She'd worn a dress, one of those thin, breezy sundresses designed to make a man give thanks for the end of winter. Her hair was loose, falling over thin raspberry-colored straps and bare, peach-toned shoulders. There were nerves in her eyes.

"Hi." He glanced down to the cordless phone she held. "Expecting a call?"

"What? Oh." She laughed, miserably self-conscious. "No, I just don't like to be out of touch when Keenan's not home."

"He's all settled at his pal's?"

"Yeah." She stepped inside, set the phone on the counter. "He was so excited, he—" She broke off when her sandal stuck to the floor.

Coop grimaced. "I guess I missed some of it. We had a spill."

"Oh?"

"The kid took a tumble, sheared off ten years of my life. No blood lost, though. Just a half gallon of orange juice." When she only smiled, he stepped to the refrigerator. Why in hell was he babbling? "Want some wine?"

"That would be nice." Why, he's as nervous as I am, she realized, and she loved him for it. "Keenan's having a wonderful time staying with you. I have to study the sports pages now just to keep up with what he's talking about."

"He catches on fast."

"So do I. Go ahead," she said as he handed her a glass of wine, "Ask me about stats. I know all about RBIs and ERAs." She took a sip, then gestured with her glass. "I think the Orioles would have taken the second game of that doubleheader the other night if they'd put in a relief pitcher in the second inning."

His lips twitched. "Do you?"

"Well, the starter had lost his stuff, obviously. The guy who was announcing—"

"The play-by-play man."

"Yes, he said so himself."

"So, you watched the game."

"I watch 'Sesame Street,' too. I like to keep up with Keenan's interests." She trailed off when Coop reached out to twine a lock of her hair around his finger.

"He's got a thing for dinosaurs, too."

"I know, I've checked a half dozen books out of the library. We've—" The fingers trailed over her shoulder. "We've been down to the natural history museum twice."

She set the glass aside and fell into his arms.

He kissed her as though he'd been starved for her taste. The impact was fast, deep, desperate. The little purring sounds that vibrated in her throat had his muscles turning into bundles of taut wire.

"I wasn't sure you'd come."

"Neither was I. I—"

"Can't think of anything but you," he said as he swept her off her feet. "I thought we'd take this slow."

"Let's not," she murmured, pressing her lips to his throat as he carried her into the bedroom.

She had a quick impression of Spartan neatness and simple masculine colors and lines before they tumbled onto the bed.

Neither of them was looking for patience. They rolled together, a tangle of limbs grasping, groping, glorying. The sheer physicality of it, flesh to flesh, mouth to mouth, had Zoe's head reeling. Oh, she wanted to be touched like this, to feel so desperately like a woman, with a man's hand streaking over her, with his lips savoring every thud of her pulse.

So she lost herself. No more nerves, no more fears. And if she loved, it only made the joy of mating more lovely.

She was every man's fantasy. Stunningly responsive, breathlessly aggressive. And so beautiful, he thought. Undraped, the exquisite body was so slim, so perfect, he couldn't believe it had ever carried a child. In the gilded light of dusk, her face was elegant, heart-stopping. Whenever he touched, wherever he touched, he could see the bold echo of her pleasure reflected in her eyes.

He watched those eyes glaze over, felt her body tense, heard her strangled cry of release. Swamped with the power of it, he drove her upward again until they were both panting for air, until she reared up from the bed and wrapped herself around him.

Damp skin slid over damp skin, hungry mouth sought hungry mouth. They rolled over the bed again, moaning, quivering. Then his hands gripped hers, and his mouth crushed her mouth. And he thrust inside her, hard and deep.

She felt the sensation as if it were a lance through her system, painful, glorious. For an instant, neither of them moved, they just stayed tensed and shuddering on the edge.

Then it was all movement, all speed, a wild race that ended with them both plunging deliriously over the finish line.

It wasn't exactly the way he'd imagined, Coop thought. They were sprawled across his bed, Zoe curled against him. The light was nearly gone, and the room was full of shadows.

He'd imagined they would progress to the bedroom by stages. They were both adults and had known that was the ultimate goal, but he'd thought they would move slowly.

Then she'd been standing there smiling, the nerves shining in her eyes... He'd never wanted anything or anyone more in his life.

Still, he thought she deserved more than a quick tussle, however rewarding. But the night was young.

He flexed his arm to bring her head a little closer, brushed his lips over her temple. "Okay?"

"Mmm... At the very least." Her body felt golden. She was surprised her skin didn't glow in the dark.

"I rushed you a little."

"No, perfect timing."

He began to trail a finger up and down her arm. He wanted her again. Good God, his system was already churning to life. A little control, Coop, he ordered himself. "You're going to stay?"

She opened her eyes, looking into his. "Yes."

"I'm going to go get the wine."

"That's good." She sighed as he left the bed. She'd forgotten how to deal with the after, she realized. Or with the before and during, for that matter, she thought with a wry smile. Though she thought she'd done pretty well so far.

She hadn't known how much had been bottled up inside her. Or just how much she'd needed to feel like a woman again. But then, she hadn't known she could love again.

She shifted, slipping under the tangled sheets, automatically lifting them to her breasts when Coop came back with the wine and glasses.

The sight of her in his bed shot to his loins, with a quick detour through the heart. He said nothing, pouring wine, offering her a fresh glass and settling beside her.

"Why haven't you been with anyone?" The moment the question was out, he wished for a rusty knife to hack off his tongue. "Sorry, none of my business."

"It's all right." Because I haven't fallen in love with anyone before you, she thought. But that wasn't what he wanted to hear, she knew. Nor was it really what he'd asked.

"You want to know about Keenan's father."

"None of my business," he repeated. "Sorry, it's the reporter in me."

"It was a long time ago—a lifetime ago. I don't mind telling you. I grew up in New York. I think I mentioned that my mother's an actress. I was the result of a second marriage. She's had five. So far."

"Five?"

Zoe chuckled into her wine, sipped. "Clarice falls in love and changes husbands the way some women change hairstyles. My father lasted about four years before they parted amicably. Clarice always has friendly divorces. I didn't see much of him, because he moved to Hollywood. He does commercials and voice-overs mostly. Anyway, I think she was on husband number four when I was in high school. He had some pull with the Towers Modeling Agency. They're pretty big."

"I've heard of them."

"Well, he got me in. I started doing some shoots. And I caught on."

"That's it," Coop said, interrupting her. "I knew I'd seen your face before."

She moved her shoulders. "Five, six years ago, it was hard to avoid it. I did twenty covers in one month, the year after I graduated school."

"Cover of *In Sports,* swimsuit edition."

She smiled. "You've got a good memory. That was six years ago."

He remembered the long, sand-dusted legs, the lush wet red excuse for a bathing suit, the laughing, seductive face. He gulped down wine. "It was a hell of a shot."

"And a long, grueling shoot. Anyway, I was making a lot of money, getting a lot of press, going to lots of parties. I met Roberto at one of them."

"Roberto." Coop grimaced at the sound of the name.

"Lorenzi. Tennis player. You might have heard of him."

"Lorenzi? Sure—took the French Open three years ago in straight sets, then blew Wimbledon in the semis. He's got a bad attitude and likes to race cars and chase women on the side. Hasn't been seeded above twenty-fifth in the last two years. Got some bad press this spring when he tipped back too many vinos and punched out a photographer." Coop started to drink, stopped. "Lorenzi? He's Keenan's father? But he's—"

"A womanizer?" Zoe supplied. "A creep, a rich, spoiled egotist? I know—now. What I saw then was a gorgeous, charming man who sent me roses and jetted me off to Monte Carlo for intimate dinners. I was dazzled. He told me he loved me, that he adored me, worshiped me, he couldn't live without me. I believed him, and we became lovers. I thought, since he was my first, he'd be my only. Anyway, I didn't realize he was already getting tired of me when I found out I was pregnant. When I told him, he was angry, then he was very calm, very reasonable. He assumed I'd want an abortion and agreed to pay all the expenses, even to make the arrangements."

"A real prince."

"It was a logical assumption," Zoe said calmly. "I had a career on fast forward, in a field that wouldn't wait while I put on weight and suffered from morning sickness. He, of course, had no intention of marrying me, and thought, rightly enough, that I knew the rules of the game. I did know them," she said quietly. "But something had changed when the doctor confirmed the pregnancy. After the disbelief, the panic, even the anger, I felt good. I felt right. I wanted the baby, so I quit my job, moved away from New York and read everything I could get my hands on about parenting."

"Just like that?"

"Well, there were some scenes, some dire predictions, and a lot of anger, but that's how it worked. Roberto and I parted less than amicably, but with the agreement that he would stay out of my life and I would stay out of his."

"What have you told Keenan?"

"It's tough." And it never failed to make her feel guilty. "So far I've just told him his father had to go away, that he wasn't going to come back. He's happy, so he doesn't ask a lot of questions."

"Are you? Happy?"

"Yes." She smiled and touched his cheek. "I am. All my life I wanted a home, a family, something solid and settled. I didn't even know it until Keenan. He changed my life."

"No urge to go back and smile for the camera?"

"Oh, no. Not even a twinge."

He cupped a hand behind her neck, studying her. "It's such a face," he murmured. Right now he liked the idea of having it all to himself.

Chapter 8

The concept of car pools obviously had been devised by someone with a foul and vicious sense of humor. Having lived most of his life in cities where public transportation or a quick jog would get a man from his home to his office, Coop had never experienced the adult version.

But he'd heard rumors.

Arguments, petty feuds, crowded conditions, spilled coffee.

After a week as designated driver, Coop had no doubt the kiddie version was worse. Infinitely worse.

"He's pinching me again, Mr. McKinnon. Brad's pinching me."

"Cut it out, Brad."

"Carly's looking at me. I told her to stop looking at me."

"Carly, don't look at Brad."

"I'm going to be sick. Mr. McKinnon, I'm going to be sick right now."

"No, you're not."

Though Matthew Finney made gagging noises that had the other kids screeching, Coop gritted his teeth and kept driving. Matt threatened to be sick twice a day unless he rode in the front seat. After five miserable days Coop had his number. But that did very little to soothe his nerves.

Keenan, who had waited all week for his turn in the front, swiveled in his seat to make monster faces at Matt. This incited a small riot of elbow jabs, howls, screaming giggles and shoves.

"Keenan, turn around!" Coop snapped. "You guys straighten up back there. Cut it out! If I have to stop this car…" He trailed off, shuddered. He'd sounded like his own mother. Now Coop was afraid *he* would be sick. "Okay, first stop. Matt, scram."

Fifteen minutes later, his backseat thankfully empty, Coop pulled into the drive and rested his throbbing head on the steering wheel. "I need a drink."

"We got lemonade," Keenan told him.

"Great." He reached over to unbuckle Keenan's seat belt. All he needed was a pint of vodka to go with it.

"Can we go swimming again soon?"

The idea of taking a herd of screaming kids back to the community pool anytime within the next century had a stone lodging in Coop's heart. "Ask your mother."

Coop started to look in the backseat and realized he couldn't face it. Earlier in the week he'd made that mistake, and discovered wads of chewing gum on the rug, cookie crumbs everywhere, and a mysterious green substance smeared on the seat.

In his weakened state, even a candy wrapper was likely to tip the balance.

"Yoo-hoo!" Mrs. Finkleman stripped off her flowered garden gloves and headed across the lawn in a flowing tent dress and electric-blue sandals. "How was your swim, little man?"

"We had races, and Brad dunked Carly and made her cry even though Coop told him not to, and I can hold my breath underwater for twelve seconds."

"My goodness." She laughed and ruffled Keenan's hair. "You'll be in the Olympics next." Her shrewd eyes took in Coop's haggard face. "You look a little frazzled, Coop. Keenan, why don't you run in and tell Mr. Finkleman you want a piece of that cherry cobbler he baked today?"

"Okay!" He tugged on Coop's hand. "Do you want some? Do you wanna come?"

"I'll pass. You go ahead."

Mrs. Finkleman chuckled as Keenan darted away and scrambled up the steps. "Little angel. We'll keep him entertained for a couple of hours—or he'll keep us entertained. You look like you could use a few minutes in a quiet room."

"Padded room," Coop muttered. "How does anyone survive kids?"

"It's easier if you go through the stages with them. Once you've walked the floor all night with a colicky baby, nothing much fazes you." She sighed. "Except science projects. Science projects always took me to the edge. And that first driving lesson." She shook her head at the memory. "That can bring you to your knees."

She beamed and patted his arm. "But there's years yet to worry about that. And you've been doing a fine job. Why, Harry and I were just saying how nice it is that Zoe and Keenan have a man in their lives. Not that Zoe hasn't been handling everything. Raising that sweet-natured boy all alone, and working two jobs and tending the house. But it does my heart good to see you and that little angel playing ball in the yard, or the way Zoe lights up when you're around. You make a lovely little family. Now, you go and take a nice nap. We'll keep an eye on your boy."

"I'm not— He's not—" But even as Coop stammered, she was drifting away.

Family? he thought as a ball of ice formed in his stomach. They weren't a family. Oh, no, he promised himself as he walked around the house to his steps. He hadn't taken that on.

He liked the kid, sure. What wasn't to like? And he was damn near nuts about the mother. But that didn't make them a family. That didn't make things permanent. Maybe he'd volunteered to spend time with the kid, taught him a few things about ball, pitched him a few, but that didn't make him Daddy.

He headed straight for the refrigerator, popped the top off a beer and took a long pull.

Sure, maybe he enjoyed having the kid around, and Lord knows he enjoyed being with Zoe. He'd even been sort of pleased when a woman at the pool mistook Keenan for his and commented on what a handsome son he had. But that didn't mean he was going to start thinking about family health insurance or college funds.

He was single. He liked being single. It meant coming and going as he pleased, planning all-night poker games, spending all day with the sports channel blaring.

He liked working in his own space—that was why he did the bulk of his writing at home, rather than at the paper. He didn't like people messing with his things or structuring his time or planning outings.

Family life—as he remembered from his childhood—was lousy with outings.

No way was he changing his nice comfortable existence to accommodate a family.

So he'd made a mistake, Coop decided, and stretched out on the couch with his beer. He'd given Zoe and the kid a little too much of his time, a little too much of his attention. It hadn't been anything he didn't want to give, but he could see now that the gesture could be misconstrued. Particularly since Zoe had once brought up the *L* word. Only once, he reminded himself, and he'd like to think that had just been a woman thing.

Still, if he didn't back off, they might start to depend on him. He shifted uncomfortably as the idea flitted through his mind that he might also come to depend on them.

It was time to reestablish himself as the tenant upstairs.

Keenan raced out of the house next door the minute his mother pulled her car in the drive.

"Hi, Mama, hi! I held my breath for twelve seconds underwater!"

Zoe caught him on the fly and swung him twice. "You must be hiding gills in there," she said, tickling his ribs. "Hi, Mrs. Finkleman."

"Hi yourself. We've had ourselves a fine hour. I sent

Coop up for a nap when they got home. He looked like he'd had a rough day."

"Thanks." She kissed Keenan's waiting lips, then smacked her own. "Mmm… Cherries."

"Mr. Finkleman baked them, and they were good."

"I bet. Did you say thank you?"

"Uh-huh. Matt almost throwed up in Coop's car."

"Threw up," Zoe said as she carried Keenan inside.

"Uh-huh. 'Cause it was my turn to ride in the front. I had the best time, and Coop helped me to swim without my bubbles. He said I was a champ."

"That's just what you are." She collapsed with him on a chair. The idea of fixing dinner, changing into her uniform and serving drinks for six hours loomed heavily. "Give me a hug," she demanded, then soothed herself with some nuzzling. "Definitely a champion hugger. Why don't you come in the kitchen and tell me what else you did today while I fix dinner?"

A half hour later, as Zoe was draining pasta and Keenan was entertaining himself with crayons and paper on the kitchen floor, she heard the sound of Coop's feet on the stairs. Her heart sped up. The normal, healthy reaction made her smile. Imagine, she thought, believing herself immune to men.

She left the pasta draining in the sink and went to the back door just as he came to the foot of the steps.

"Hi."

"How's it going?" Coop jingled the keys in his pocket. Did she look all lit up? he wondered. She was smiling, and despite the shadows of fatigue under them, her eyes did have the prettiest lights in them.

"I was just going to call upstairs. I thought you'd like some dinner after a hard day at the pool." She opened the screen door and leaned out to kiss him. The smile dimmed a bit when he eased back. "It's just chicken and pasta."

It smelled nearly as good as she did. He glanced inside—the homey scene, cluttered counters, fresh flowers, steam rising from a pan on the stove, the child sprawled on the floor, the pretty woman offering him food and kisses.

A definite trap.

"Thanks, but I'm on my way out."

"Oh. I thought you had a couple hours before game time." She laughed at his arched brow. "I guess I've been paying more attention to the sports scene. Baltimore versus Toronto, game one of three."

"Yeah." *When she starts to take an interest in* your *interests, she's really shutting the cage door.* "I've got some stuff to do."

"Can I go with you?" Keenan dashed to the door to tug on Coop's slacks. "Can I go to the game? I like watching them with you best."

Coop could almost hear the locks clicking into place. "I've got too much to do," he said, with an edge to his voice that had Keenan's lips quivering. "Look, it's not just a game, it's my job."

"You said I was good luck."

"Keenan." Zoe put her hand on her son's shoulder to draw him back, but her eyes stayed on Coop's. "Did you forget Beth was coming over to stay with you tonight? She'll be here soon, and you're going to watch a tape of your favorite movie."

"But I wanna—"

"Now go wash your hands for dinner."

"But—"

"Go on now."

The way Keenan's face crumpled would have softened an ogre's heart. Dragging his feet, he headed out of the kitchen.

"I can't take him with me everywhere..." Coop began defensively.

"Of course not. He's just overtired. I couldn't have let him go, in any case." She hesitated, wishing she could ignore her instincts. "Is everything all right?"

"Everything's fine." He didn't know why he shouted it. He didn't know why he felt like something slimy stuck to the bottom of a shoe. "I have a life, you know. I don't need kids climbing up my back or you fixing me dinner. And I don't have to explain myself."

Her eyes turned very cool, her face very composed. "You certainly don't. I appreciate you helping me out the past couple of weeks. Let me know if I can return the favor."

"Look, Zoe—"

"I've got to get dinner on the table, or I'll be late for work." She let the screen door slam between them. "Enjoy the game."

She knew exactly how long he continued to stand there while she worked at the stove. Knew exactly when he turned and walked away.

It wasn't unexpected, she reminded herself. This backing away was typical, even understandable. Perhaps it had taken Coop a few weeks to completely comprehend that she didn't come as a single. She was part of a pair, a ready-made family, with its share of responsibilities and problems and routines.

And he was opting out.

He might not even know it yet, she thought, but he was in the first stages of a full retreat.

Her eyes blurred, her chest heaved. Resolutely she choked the tears back. She would indulge herself with a nice long cry later, she promised. But for now she had a little boy to soothe.

When he came back in, she crouched down until they were eye-to-eye.

"You had a good time with Coop today, didn't you?"

Keenan sniffled, nodded.

"And he's taken you a lot of places. You've had fun, and done a lot of new things."

"I know."

"You should be grateful for that, baby, instead of pouting because you can't have more."

She straightened again and hoped she could take her own advice.

Chapter 9

"You're spending a lot of time around here." Ben edged a hip onto the corner of Coop's desk. All around Coop's cubicle phones rang, keyboards clattered.

"So?" Without taking his eyes from the computer screen, Coop hammered out the draft of his weekly column.

"I just figured you had it made in that apartment of yours. I mean, great location." He thought of Zoe. "Great view. You didn't spend as much time in here when you lived downtown."

"I needed a change of scene."

"Yeah." Ben snorted and picked up a baseball from Coop's desk. "Trouble in paradise?"

"I don't know what you're talking about. And I've got a column to write."

"Pretty obvious the last few weeks that you've been

stuck on the landlady." He tossed the ball from one hand to the other. "I mean, when a man hauls a kid around, buys little baseball jerseys, it follows that he's hooking a line into Mom."

Coop's eyes flashed up. "I like the kid, okay? I don't have to use a four-year-old to get a woman. The kid's cool."

"Hey, I got nothing against rug rats. Might even have a few of my own one day. The thing is, when a woman's got one, a man has to play Daddy if he wants the inside track."

"Who says I have to play at anything to get a woman?"

"Not me. But it was you who couldn't shoot hoop last week because you were taking the family to the aquarium." Ben winked, set the ball down. "Still, I bet you scored better than I did." Ben jerked back as Coop lunged for his throat.

"It's not like that," Coop said between his teeth.

"Hey, hey. Just yanking your chain. I wouldn't have made any cracks if I'd known you were serious about her."

Coop's grip loosened. "I didn't say I was serious. I said it wasn't like that."

"Whatever you say."

Disgusted with himself, Coop dropped back in his chair. He and Ben had been riding each other about women for better than five years. No reason to overreact, he thought. Or to make a fool of himself. "Sorry. I've got a lot on my mind."

"Forget it. What you need's a distraction. You coming to the poker game tonight?"

"Yeah."

"Good. Losing money should put you back on track."

Something had to, Coop thought as he sat back alone in his cubicle to stare at his screen. For the past three days he'd slept little, eaten less, and gone around in a constant state of flux.

Because he was avoiding the issue, he decided. Opting to bunt, when he should be swinging away. The only solution to getting his life back in order was to face the problem head-on.

He flicked off his terminal.

The beautiful thing about an afternoon off, Zoe thought, was the solitude. No customers to talk to, no orders to fill. It meant she didn't have to be salesclerk, or waitress, or Mom, or anything but Zoe.

Sitting on the back stoop, she struggled to understand the assembly instructions for the new barbecue grill she'd bought. She was going to surprise Keenan with hamburgers.

She liked the quiet—her kind of quiet, which meant there was music throbbing from the kitchen radio. She liked the loneliness—her kind of loneliness, which meant Keenan would dash toward her shortly with open arms and chattering voice.

She knew the upstairs apartment was empty, and she tried not to think about that. Tried not to think about the fact that Coop had been away more than he'd been home in the last few days.

Foolish of her to have thought he was different. He'd wanted her, he'd had her, and now he'd lost interest. Well, she had wanted him, so they were even there. If her heart was suffering it would pass. It had passed before. She and Keenan could get along fine on their own. Just like always.

Her screwdriver slipped, scraped her knuckles, had her swearing.

"What the hell are you doing?"

Eyes hot, she looked up at Coop. "Baking a cake. What does it look like I'm doing?"

"You can't put something together if you're going to spread parts all over the damn place." Automatically he bent down to organize. She rapped his hand away with the rubber grip of the screwdriver.

"I don't need you to put things together for me. I'm not some poor helpless female who needs a man to pick up the slack. I managed just fine before you came along."

Stung, he rammed his hands in his pockets. "Fine. Do it yourself."

"I am doing it myself. I like doing it myself."

"Terrific. And when the thing topples over, you won't have anyone else to blame."

"That's right." She blew her hair out of her eyes. "I accept when something's my fault." She picked up a wrench and locked a bolt in place. "Do you plan to hover over me all afternoon?"

"I want to talk to you."

"So talk."

He had it well planned. He was a writer, after all. "I realize the way I've been hanging around with you and the kid—"

"His name is Keenan," Zoe said between her teeth.

"I know what his name is. The way I've been hanging around the last few weeks might give the wrong impression."

"Oh, really?" She looked up again, tapping the wrench against her palm.

"He's a great kid, he kind of grows on you. I've gotten a kick out of spending time with him."

Though she hated herself for it, Zoe softened. She understood that he was genuinely fond of Keenan. That only made it all the more difficult. "He likes spending time with you. It's been good for him."

"Well, yeah, on the one hand. On the other, I started thinking that he—that you—that both of you might get the wrong idea. I mean, tossing a ball around or taking him to a game, that's cool. I just don't want him thinking it's like—permanent."

"I see." She was calm now, frigidly so. It would help keep the hurt in check. "You're afraid he might begin to see you as a father figure."

"Well, yeah. Kind of."

"That's natural enough. But then, he spends a lot of time with Mr. Finkleman, too, and with Billy Bowers down the street."

"Finkleman's old enough to be his grandfather, and the Bowers kid is eighteen." Coop backed off, realizing there was a touch of jealousy in the defense. "And they don't have the same sort of thing going with you."

She arched both brows. "Thing?"

"Relationship," he said tightly. "Whatever the hell you want to call it. Damn it, we only slept together once."

"I'm aware of that." Carefully she set the wrench aside. It would give her only momentary pleasure to heave it at his head.

"That came out wrong," he said, furious with himself. "It sounded like it didn't mean anything. It did, Zoe." A great deal, he was afraid. A very great deal. "It's just that…"

"Now you're terrified that Keenan and I will trap you into a family. That you'll wake up one morning and be Daddy, with a wife and a mortgage and a small boy who needs attention."

"Yes. No. Something like that." He was burying himself, he realized, and he suddenly didn't know why. "I just want to make myself clear."

"Oh, I think you have. Perfectly." She rubbed her hands on her knees as she studied him. "You needn't worry, Coop. I advertised for a tenant, not a father for my child, or a husband for myself. I slept with you because I wanted to, not because I thought I could lure you to the altar."

"I didn't mean it like that." Frustrated, he dragged a hand through his hair. However well he'd planned this little scene, it was going all wrong. "I wanted you. I still do. But I know how badly you were let down before. I don't want to hurt you, Zoe. Or the kid. I just don't want you thinking I'd slide into the gap."

The anger came back, one swift wave of it that reddened her vision. She was on her feet before either of them realized she'd moved. "Keenan and I don't have a gap. We're a family, as real and as complete and as full a family as any could be." She jabbed the wrench at his chest. "Just because Daddy doesn't make three doesn't mean we're less of a unit."

"I didn't mean—"

"I'll tell you what you mean. You see a woman and a small boy and you think they're just pining away for some big strong man to come along and fulfill them. Well, that's bull. If I needed a man, I'd have one. And if I thought Keenan needed a father to make him happy, I'd find him one. And," she continued, advancing and giving him another jab, "if you think you're at the head of some fictional list, you're wrong. Maybe I'm in love with you, but that's not enough. It's not just me, and it's not just you. Keenan comes first. When and if I want a father for Keenan, he'll be someone with compassion and patience, someone willing to adjust his life to make room for my son. So relax, Cooper. You're in the clear."

"I didn't come here to fight with you."

"Good, because I'm finished."

He grabbed her arm before she could turn away. "I haven't. I'm trying to be straight with you, Zoe. I care about you, okay? About both of you. I just don't want it to get out of hand."

"Out of whose hands?" she retorted. "Yours? Then that's no problem, is it? Because you know how to hold on to everything inside, really tight. Just keep holding on to it, Coop. Don't worry about me or about Keenan. We'll be fine." She jerked her arm free and sat again. Picking up the instruction sheet, she gave it her full attention.

Now why, he wondered, did he feel as though he'd just been rejected? Shaking his head, Coop took a step in retreat. "As long as we're clear."

"We are."

"I've, ah, got a little time, if you want me to help you put that grill together."

"No thanks. I can do it." She slanted him a look. "I'm going to grill burgers later. You're welcome to join us. Unless you're afraid it will lead to a commitment."

She shoots, he thought wryly, she scores. "Thanks anyway. I've got plans. Maybe I could take a rain check."

"Fine. You know where to find us."

* * *

He got drunk. Not sloppily, but thoroughly. When Coop poured himself out of the cab and staggered toward the house, he already knew he'd hate himself in the morning. But it was tonight he had to deal with.

He leaned heavily against Zoe's front door and waited for the porch to settle down under his feet. She might think they'd finished, he told himself blearily, but she was wrong. Dead wrong.

He'd thought of a dozen things he had to say to her.

There was no time like the present.

Lifting a fist, he pounded on the door. "Come on, Zoe." He pounded again. "I know you're in there." He saw a light flick on inside and kept on pounding. "Come on, come on. Open up."

"Coop?" From the other side of the door, Zoe belted her hastily donned robe. She'd been home from the lounge for barely twenty minutes, and in bed for less than five. "It's after two o'clock in the morning. What do you want?"

"I want to talk to you. Let me in."

"We'll talk in the morning."

"You just said it was morning."

When he pounded again, she flicked off the locks. "Stop that—you'll wake Keenan." Furious, she yanked open the door and had the surprise of a hundred-and-seventy-pound male tumbling against her. "Are you hurt? What happened?" The alarm signals that had screamed on shifted when she caught the scent of beer. "You're drunk."

"Mostly." He started to straighten, then lost himself in the smell of her. "God, you feel good. What d'you wash this in?" He nuzzled her hair. "Smells like moon-beams."

"Really drunk," she said with a sigh. "Sit down. I'll get you some coffee."

"Don't want coffee. Doesn't sober you up, only wakes you up. And I'm awake, and I have something to say to you." He drew away then, and discovered he wasn't as steady as he'd hoped. "But I'll sit down." He did, heavily. "Hate getting drunk. Haven't done it like this since I played minor league. Did I tell you I played minor league ball? Triple A."

"No." Baffled, she stood her ground and watched him.

"Right out of high school. Two years. Thought I'd make it to the show. The majors. But I didn't, so I went to college, and now I write about people who did."

"I'm sorry."

"No." He waved that away. "I like writing. Always did. Like watching the games and seeing all the little dramas. If I'd've played, I'd be nearly washed up now. I'm almost thirty-three. Old man for the game." He focused on her, smiled. "You're the most beautiful woman I've ever seen in my life. You know, the kid looks just like you. Look at him, see you. It's spooky. I see you all the time. Minding my own business, and pop! There's your face in my head. What d'ya make of that?"

"I don't know." She wanted to be angry with him, really she did. But he was so foolishly drunk. "Why don't I take you upstairs, Coop? Put you to bed."

"I want you in my bed, Zoe. I want to make love with you. I want to touch you again."

She wanted that, too. Very much. But new lines had been drawn. "You said you wanted to talk to me."

"Do you know what your skin feels like? I can't describe it, it's all soft and smooth and warm. I started thinking about your skin when I was playing poker and getting drunk tonight. I won, too. Took a big pot with a pair of sixes. Pulled in over two hundred and fifty dollars."

"Congratulations."

"But I kept thinking about you. You have this little dimple right here." He nearly poked himself in the eye, then dragged a finger down his cheek to the corner of his mouth. "I kept thinking about that little dimple, and your skin, and those big eyes and killer legs. And I kept thinking how I like to watch you with the kid, like I do sometimes from upstairs, when you don't know. Didn't know that, did you?"

"No," she said quietly. "I didn't."

"Well, see…" He gestured wildly. "You've got this way of running your hand over his hair. It gets to me." He shook his head. "It really gets to me. Keenan loves me, you know. He told me he did. So did you."

"I know."

"And I meant everything I said this afternoon."

"I know." Sighing, she walked over to undo his shoelaces.

"Every word, Zoe. I've got my life set, just like I want it."

"Okay." She pried off his shoes, hefted his legs onto the couch.

"So you can stop popping into my head, 'cause it's not changing anything."

"I'll keep that in mind."

He was asleep before she bent over and kissed his cheek.

Chapter 10

As hangovers went, Coop knew, this would be a champ. He didn't have to open his eyes, he didn't have to move, not when his head was already beating like the Army drum corps.

He wasn't sure how he'd managed to get home and into bed, but the blur of the evening wasn't comforting. Still, he thought it best to wait to tax his brain.

Cautious, close to fearful, he opened his eyes. The little face directly above him had him jerking back, then moaning at the pain.

"Good morning," Keenan said cheerfully. "Did you sleep over?"

"I don't know." Coop lifted a hand to his head. "Where's your mother?"

"She's making my lunch. She said I could come in and look at you if I didn't wake you up. I didn't wake you up, did I? I was really quiet."

"No." Coop closed his eyes again and prayed for oblivion.

"Are you sick? Do you have a temperature?" Keenan laid a small, light hand on Coop's aching forehead. "Mama can make it better. She always makes it better." Very gently, Keenan replaced his hand with a kiss. "Does that help?"

Oh, hell, Coop thought. Even a hangover didn't have a chance against this kid. "Yeah, thanks. What time is it?"

"The big hand's on the ten and the little hand's on the eight. You can sleep in my bed until you're better, and play with my toys."

"Thanks." Coop made the supreme effort and sat up. When his head rolled, he did his best to catch it in his hands. "Keenan, be a pal and ask your mom for some aspirin."

"Okay." He raced off, and the sound of his sneakers pounding the floor had Coop shuddering.

"Headache?" Zoe asked a moment later.

Coop lifted his head. She was still in her robe. The robe he remembered from the night before. He was beginning to remember quite a bit from the night before. "If you're going to yell at me, could you do it later?"

In answer, she held out aspirin and a glass filled with reddish liquid.

"What is it?"

"A remedy from Joe the bartender. He guarantees it'll take the edge off."

"Thanks."

There was a blast of a horn from outside that cut through Coop's skull like a dulled knife. While he was dealing with the shock of that, Keenan came racing back.

"Bye, Mama, bye!" He gave her a smacking kiss, then turned to hug Coop. "Bye."

As the door slammed behind him, Coop gulped down Joe's remedy.

"Do you want coffee?" Zoe ran her tongue around her teeth and tried not to smile. "Some breakfast?"

"You're not going to yell at me?"

"For barging in here, drunk, in the middle of the night? And for passing out on my sofa?" She paused just long enough to make her point. "No, I'm not going to yell at you. I figure you're suffering enough."

"I am, I promise you." He got up to follow her into the kitchen. "Not just physically. I feel like a total jerk."

"You *were* a total jerk." She poured a mug of coffee, set it on the table for him. "My mother's third husband had a fondness for bourbon. He swore eggs the morning after were the cure. How do you want them?"

"Scrambled would be good." He sat gingerly at the table. "I'm sorry, Zoe."

She kept her back to him. "For?"

"For being a jackass yesterday afternoon, and a bigger jackass last night."

"Oh, that." With the bacon frying, she chose a small bowl to scramble eggs in. "I don't imagine it's the first or the last time you'll be one."

"You didn't…" He shifted miserably. "Ah, you didn't tell Keenan I was…"

"Drunk and disorderly?" A half smile on her face, she glanced over her shoulder. "I told him you weren't feeling well and went to sleep on the couch. Which was close enough."

"Thanks. I wouldn't want him to think…you know. I don't make a habit out of it."

"So you said last night." She turned the bacon, whipped the eggs.

He watched her, gradually getting past the astonishment that she wasn't going to rub his nose in the mess he'd made of things. Remembering the afternoon before, when she'd stood up to him with all that pride and fury shining in her eyes. And the other night, when he'd fallen asleep on her couch—the way she'd looked when she slipped the boy from his arms into hers and carried him into bed.

A dozen other pictures, captured in so short a time, flitted through his head, until they were whittled down to one. This one. Zoe standing at the stove, with the morning sun streaming over her tousled hair, her robe flowing down, breakfast smells warming the room.

How could he have thought he didn't want this? Just this. And what did he do now that he knew the truth?

"Food should help." She set the plate in front of him. "I've got to get ready for work."

"Can you— Have you got a minute?"

"I suppose." She poured herself another cup of coffee. "I don't have to be in until ten."

He began to eat while thoughts scrambled in his brain. "This is good. Thanks."

"You're welcome." She leaned back against the counter. "Did you want something else?"

"Yeah." He ate more, hoping eggs equaled courage. Then he put his fork down. It was the ninth inning, he thought, and there were already two outs. "You. I want you."

She smiled a little. "Coop, I doubt you're in any shape for that, and I really have to go to work, so—"

"No, I don't mean that. I mean I do, but not—" He broke off, took a long, deep breath. "I want you to marry me."

"I beg your pardon?"

"I think you should marry me. It's a good idea." Somewhere in the back of his mind, he realized, he'd been working on this all along. He had it figured. "You can quit your night job and go back to school if you want. Or open that flower shop. Whatever. I think that's what we should do."

"Really." Because her hand was unsteady, she set her coffee down. "Well that's very generous of you, Coop, but I don't have to get married to do any of those things. So thanks just the same."

He stared. "No? You're saying no? But you love me. You said it. Twice you said it."

"We can make it three," she said evenly. "Yes, I love you. No, I won't marry you. Now I really have to get ready for work."

"Just a damn minute." Hangover forgotten, he pushed back from the table and rose. "What kind of game is this? You love me, your kid's crazy about me, we're terrific in bed, I even know how to drive a damn car pool, but you won't marry me."

"You're such an idiot. You're such a fool. Do you think because I didn't put up a struggle before I fell into your bed that you can have everything your own way? When you want it, how you want it? Well, you're wrong. And you *are* a jackass."

He winced as she stormed from the room. Strike one, he thought. And he hadn't even seen the pitch.

But the game wasn't over, he thought grimly, until the fat lady sang.

Zoe was still steaming when she came home from work. Of all the arrogant, interfering, self-absorbed idiots she'd ever known, J. Cooper McKinnon took the gold medal. Imagine him telling her that marrying him was a good idea, then ticking off all the advantages she'd gain.

Oh, he thought he was a prize.

One day he's telling her to get any ideas of sneaking him into a relationship out of her head. As if she'd been baiting traps for him. The next he's taking pity on her and offering her a big male helping hand.

She should have bitten it off.

Not once, not once had he said what she would bring to him, what he felt for her, what he wanted. Not once had he brought up the fact that he could or would accept another man's child as his own.

She jerked open the front door, slammed it. He could take his half-baked proposal and sit on it.

"Mama! Hey, Mama!" Keenan zipped into the living room and grabbed her hand. "Come on, come on. We've got a surprise."

"What surprise? What are you doing home, Keenan? You're supposed to be at the Finklemans'."

"Coop's here." He tugged manfully on her hand. "We have a surprise. And we have a secret. And you have to come *now!*"

"All right, I'm coming." She braced herself and let Keenan drag her into the kitchen.

There were flowers, banks of them, vases and baskets overflowing on the counters, on the floor, on the windowsills. There was music, some soft, dreamy classical sonata, on the radio. The table was set, crystal she'd never seen before glinting in the sunlight, a bottle of champagne chilling in a silver bucket. And Coop was standing there, in a neatly pressed shirt and slacks.

"It's a surprise," Keenan announced gleefully. "We made everything look nice so you'd like it. And Mrs. Finkleman said we could use the glasses and the plates. And Mr. Finkleman made his special chicken 'cause it's resistible."

"Irresistible," Coop said, his eyes on Zoe. "You, ah, said you didn't need flowers and candlelight, but I've never taken you out on a date. I thought this was the next-best thing."

"Do you like it, Mama? Do you?"

"Yes, it's very nice." She bent down to kiss Keenan. "Thank you."

"I get to go to the Finklemans' so you can have romance."

"Ah, come on, kid." Coop scooped Keenan up. "Let's get you started. You were supposed to keep quiet about it," he muttered when he carried the boy outside.

"What's romance?"

"I'll tell you later."

Satisfied with that, Keenan draped his arm around Coop's neck. "Are you gonna tell Mama the secret about us all getting married?"

"That's the plan."

"And you'll live with us and you can be my daddy and that'll be okay?"

"That'll be great. It'll be perfect." He stopped by

the fence to press a kiss to Keenan's mouth. "I love you, Keenan."

"Okay." He squeezed his arms hard around Coop's neck. "Bye."

"Bye."

"Yoo-hoo!" Mrs. Finkleman stood at the back door. She sent Coop a wink and an exaggerated thumbs-up sign before whisking Keenan inside.

She was standing pretty much where Coop had left her when he came back. He wasn't sure whether or not that was a good sign.

"So, ready for some champagne?"

"Coop, this is very nice of you, but—"

"Like the flowers?" Nervous as a cat, he popped the cork.

"Yes, they're wonderful, but—"

"I couldn't get them where you work, or I'd have spoiled the surprise. Keenan really gave me a hand setting things up." He handed her the glass, and when she was distracted, he leaned in for a slow, warm kiss. "Hi."

"Coop." She had to wait for her heart to finish its lazy somersault. "I know you must have gone to a lot of trouble—"

"I should have gone to it before. I didn't know I wanted to."

"Oh, Lord." She turned away and struggled to get her emotions under control. "I've given you the wrong impression this time. I don't need the trappings. I don't have to have romantic evenings and—" she waved toward the tapers on the table, waiting to be lit "—candlelight."

"Sure you do. So do I, when they're with you."

"You're trying to charm me," she said unsteadily. "That's new."

"You know what I am. The way this house is set up, we've practically been living together for the past month or so. People get to know each other quicker that way than just by socializing. So you know what I am, and you fell for me anyway."

She took a drink. "You're awfully smug about it. I told you my feelings are my responsibility, and that holds true. A romantic dinner doesn't change it."

It looked like strike two, but Coop knew that if he was going to go down, he'd go down swinging. "So I want to give you a nice evening. Is something wrong with that? I want to do better than propose over scrambled eggs when I've got a hangover." His voice had risen, and he bit down on it. "Damn it, this is my first time, have a little tolerance. No, don't say anything, let me finish this. You don't need me." He took another long breath. "Not for taking care of things, for you or the kid, I mean, for mowing the grass or putting stupid barbecue grills together. What about what I need, Zoe?"

She blinked at him. "Well, that's just it. Don't you see? You made it clear that you don't need or want ties. I come with ties, Coop."

"I made it clear," he muttered. "I didn't make anything clear, because I didn't know. Didn't want to know. I was scared. There. You feel better knowing that?" He glared at her. "I was scared, because I need you. Because I need to see your face and hear your voice and smell your hair. I just need you to be there. And I need to help you mow the grass and put the grill together. I need you to need me back."

"Oh." She shut her eyes. "I like hearing that."

"Then tell me you will." He took her arms until she opened her eyes again. "It's my last swing, Zoe. Marry me."

"I—" Yes. She wanted to say yes. "It's not just me, Coop."

"You think I don't want the kid? God, open your eyes. I'm crazy about him. I fell for him before I fell for you. I want to marry both of you, then maybe have another kid or two so I can start out on the ground floor. We already worked that out."

"You— Who did what?"

He swore, stepped back, shrugged. "I kind of ran it by the kid. I figured I should smooth the way a little, and find out where he stood." When she just stared, he jammed his hands in his pockets. "It didn't seem fair not to bring him into it, since he'd be mine."

"Yours," she murmured, staring blindly into her wine.

"Since you two are a team, it would be sort of like an expansion. Anyway, he's for it. So it's two against one."

"I see."

"Maybe I don't know a lot about the daddy stuff, but I love him. That's a good start."

She looked at him again, looked into his eyes. Her heart opened, flooded. "It's a good one, all right."

"I love you." His hands relaxed in his pockets. "That's the first time I've said that to any woman— except my mother. I love you, Zoe. So why don't you marry me and give me and the kid a break?"

"It looks like I'm outvoted." She lifted a hand to his cheek.

"Is that a yes?"

"That's definitely a yes." She laughed as he swung her into his arms. "Daddy."

"I like the sound of that." He crushed his lips down on hers. "I like it a lot."

* * * * *